I0679262

SHERLOCK HOLMES
in
MONTAGUE STREET

Sherlock Holmes's Early Investigations
Originally Published as
Martin Hewitt Adventures

Volume II

by
ARTHUR MORRISON

Edited, Holmes-ed,
and with
Original Material
by
DAVID MARCUM

Paperback ISBN 9781780926681
ePub ISBN 9781780926698
PDF ISBN 9781780926704

Published in the UK by MX Publishing
335 Princess Park Manor, Royal Drive,
London, N11 3GX

www.mxpublishing.co.uk
Cover design by www.staunch.com

CONTENTS

Introduction

I. About the Author

Arthur Morrison was born in 1863 in the East End of London. Growing up in a working-class family, he could not help but be well aware of the terrible poverty which surrounded him. Very little is known about Morrison's early life, and his probable embarrassment concerning his own family's poverty during this time meant that very few details ever became public knowledge. In later years, he would attempt to alter or hide his biography as a denial of his origins, thus making it difficult indeed to determine anything specific about his early life. The abominable conditions in the East End in the late 1800's have become legendary over the years, and Morrison was there during the worst of those times.

When Morrison was about eight years old, his father, a steamfitter at the London Docks, died, leaving him, as well as his mother and two siblings, to make their way as best they could. Despite oppressive conditions, the family persevered, and when Morrison was in his mid-teens, he found employment with the London School Board as an office boy in the Architect Department. Some of these experiences were no doubt useful when he came to write the Martin Hewitt story, "The Dixon Torpedo" (June 1894), set in an engineer's office. In 1880, his first published work, a poem, appeared in a magazine. He continued to publish small pieces over the next few years, although often anonymously, so that an accurate count of what was written during this span will never be known. In 1885, his first major journalistic piece was accepted and published by *The Globe* newspaper.

Morrison was mostly-self taught, and in 1886, he obtained employment as a secretary with a sizable East End charitable foundation, the People's Palace. He remained in this position while continuing to write, and in a few years he became the editor of *The Palace Journal*. He eventually resigned in 1890 to join the editorial staff of *The Globe* on a full-time basis. The amount of Morrison's writing increased dramatically. In 1891, he published a collection of supernatural short fiction, *Shadows Around Us*, now nearly forgotten. At that point, he began to turn his attention toward writing pieces that reflected the conditions in the East End, a type of work that came to be known as *slum fiction*.

Morrison wrote pieces describing various aspects of poverty that he had observed during his childhood and young adult years. His books on the subject are frequently mentioned as leading examples of that type of work, and Morrison portrayed conditions in a realistic way that had not been done before in literature. These books are: *Tales of the Mean Streets* (1894), a collection of short stories, and two novels, *A Child of the Jago* (1896), and *The Hole in the Wall* (1902).

Unlike many of his contemporaries writing on these same subjects, Morrison's works are decidedly pessimistic, implying that improvement of the condition of the poor is almost overwhelmingly difficult and unlikely to be successful, especially through benevolent intervention by wealthier members of society. In addition, Morrison took a pessimistic view of the poor themselves, and there were no sympathetic or admirable characters in his slum fiction.

During the 1890's and early 1900's, Morrison began developing an interest in Japanese art, and as a collector and writer on the subject, he became a recognized expert. As his interest and expertise grew, he would eventually transition away from both journalism and fiction, abandoning both completely by the early 1900's, except for one short fiction collection, *Fiddle o'Dreams and More*, published in 1933. In 1911, he published *The Painters of Japan*, which is still considered an important work in the field, and in 1913, he sold most of his collection of Japanese art, acquired over the previous decade or so, to the British Museum, receiving enough money to retire.

Very little is known about the last thirty years of Morrison's life. He lived quietly until his death in 1945, and as E.F. Bleiler wrote in his introduction to *Best Martin Hewitt Detective Stories* (1976), "When he died . . . the world was more astonished to learn that he had been still living than that he was dead."

II. About Martin Hewitt

Although Morrison was never forthcoming about his past, he was very accurate in using his experiences while growing up in order to vividly portray the conditions faced by London's East End poor during the late nineteenth century. And yet, while he is usually remembered for his slum fiction and his thought-provoking criticisms of London poverty, Morrison had also inexplicably turned his attention to writing detective stories, which were all the rage in the mid-1890's. It was then that he created and wrote the first and largest portion of his twenty-five Martin Hewitt short stories.

Following the publication of the final (at that time) Sherlock Holmes tale, "The Final Problem" in December 1893, *The Strand* Magazine was in desperate need for some type of serialized-character detective fiction in order to fill the void. Morrison's Martin Hewitt somewhat fit the bill for a while, but not in the same spectacularly successful manner that Holmes had done.

Morrison seemed to have constructed Hewitt so that he would instantly be identified as the opposite of Holmes. Hewitt was first described as plump and of medium height, a genial and smiling man. He was a former law clerk who had decided to take his special investigative talents out on his own. He claims no special powers, but simply the good use of common sense. The stories are narrated by a journalist named Brett, who sometimes appears as Hewitt's Watson, and sometimes remains completely off-stage, allowing Hewitt to investigate alone in third-person narrative.

Hewitt's first case had been "fifteen or twenty years back", when he had made a name for himself, as explained in the first story, "The Lenton Croft Robberies" (March 1894). This would thus indicate that he began his career in the mid-to-late-1870's, based on the story's publication date. After this first success, Hewitt had then set himself up with a clerk named Kerrett in an office near Charing Cross, off the Strand. However, after the initial descriptions which serve to note the differences between Hewitt and Holmes are stated, the similarities between the two start to become very obvious. Hewitt makes use of disguises and knows many obscure facts. He solves cases logically, with close observation of clues missed by others, and he hides the process and explanation until the end. He has few friends, keeps extensive scrapbooks, and on occasions is heard to utter Holmes-like things, such as the following: ". . . all the other ways being impossible, this alone remains, difficult as the feat may seem." ("The Case of Mr. Foggatt", May 1894).

And then there is this exchange in "The Ivy Cottage Mystery" (January 1894), when Hewitt is asked about some clues in the form of scraps of wood.

> "That puttied-up hole in the piece of wood seems to have influenced you. Is it an important link?" Brett asks him.
> "Well-yes," Hewitt replies, "it is. But all those other pieces are important, too."
> "But why?"
> "Because there are no holes in them."

That sounds like the same someone who would give a cryptic answer about the dog that did nothing in the nighttime.

The Strand published the first seven Hewitt stories between March and September 1894. These were immediately collected into book form as *Martin Hewitt, Investigator* (1894). After a break of a few months, the next set of six Hewitt tales were published, not in *The Strand* this time, but rather in *The Windsor*

4

Magazine. This collection was advertised as "The Chronicles of Martin Hewitt: Being the Second Series of the Adventures of Martin Hewitt, Investigator." These stories ran from January to June 1895, and were quickly published in book form as *Chronicles of Martin Hewitt* (1895). Another series of six followed in the same magazine the next year, from January to June 1896, and were billed as "The Adventures of Martin Hewitt: Third Series". These, too, were immediately collected and released as a book entitled *Adventures of Martin Hewitt* (1896).

Through the rest of the 1890's and into the early 1900's, Morrison was slowly withdrawing from publishing fiction. In 1903, he completed one further set of six Hewitt stories, first published in *The London Magazine*, and collected in the same year in book form under the title *The Red Triangle*. These stories, like Agatha Christie's *The Big Four* (1927), which features Hercule Poirot, were a series of separate but loosely-connected Hewitt stories, interconnected by a greater, overall plot, a search for a master criminal.

And then Martin Hewitt languished, except as remembered by aficionados of detective fiction. By the 1930's, Hewitt was slowly being forgotten. In *Challenge to the Reader* (1938), Ellery Queen calls Hewitt "[t]he very famous, but today little-read detective . . . ." In 1941, Howard Haycraft published his important work, *Murder For Pleasure*, listing *Martin Hewitt, Investigator* as one of the cornerstones of detective fiction. Later, this book was still included when Haycraft's list was augmented with additional works chosen by Ellery Queen, to become "The Haycraft-Queen Definitive Library of Detective, Crime, and Mystery Fiction 'A Reader's List of Detective Story Cornerstones' "

In *Queen's Quorum* (1951), Ellery Queen wrote: "Of Doyle's contemporary imitators, the most durable (indeed, the only important one to survive over the ages) is the private investigator, a man of awe-inspiring technical and statistical knowledge, in *Martin Hewitt, Investigator*."

Today, however, when Martin Hewitt is recalled at all, he is lumped into the category of one of "The Rivals of Sherlock

Holmes", that group of characters who appeared in the mid-1890's to fill the vacuum when Watson and Doyle decided to cease publication of The Master's adventures. Morrison was just one of many authors of that period, including Grant Allen, Fletcher Robinson, L.T. Meade, Baroness Orczy, and others. In 1971, three of the Hewitt stories were featured as episodes in a British television show, *The Rivals of Sherlock Holmes,* based on the book of the same name. Oddly, in the first of these, "The Case of the Dixon Torpedo" (November 8, 1971), Hewitt's name was changed to *Jonathan Pryde,* who is presented as a friend of Hewitt's. Hewitt doesn't appear at all as himself in that episode, instead leaving the entire mystery to be solved by Pryde. It is in "The Affair of the Tortoise" (November 22, 1971), that Martin Hewitt first appears under his own name. In the third and last of the Hewitt stories to be dramatized for this series, "The Case of Laker, Absconded" (December 9, 1971), Pryde is introduced into the story to work with Hewitt, although the character of Pryde is not in the original published story at all.

The few Martin Hewitt cases that are currently available today are most likely to be the same repeated titles found in anthologies containing stories by a multitude of Morrison's contemporaries from the same period.

III. About Hewitt, Holmes, and *The Game*

At different times over the years, awareness of Martin Hewitt has resurged, often within Sherlockian circles, in connection with a theory first proposed by J. Randolph Cox in his essay, "Mycroft Holmes: Private Detective" (*The Baker Street Journal*, October 1956). Cox, who admitted that he did not have access to the entire Hewitt Canon – he stated in a footnote that he has been unable to locate the *Adventures of Martin Hewitt* in any condition – postulated that Martin Hewitt, the plump investigator with the initials "M.H.", is actually *Mycroft Holmes,* acting for some unknown reason as a detective in the 1870's and

6

1880's before beginning his more well-known career with the British Government.

Cox went on to explain his interpretation of the internal dating within the stories, deciding that Mycroft Holmes had worked as a private detective, and as a competitor of his brother Sherlock, until the late and highly unlikely date of 1885, before finally closing his office in the Strand and finding more rewarding and useful work in nearby Whitehall with the government. Some of his other use of dates seems even less likely.

I personally did not get around to reading the Martin Hewitt stories until I was in my early thirties, in the mid-1990's, a little over one-hundred years after Hewitt's first appearance in *The Strand*. After ignoring the stories for a long while, I approached them with the preconceived belief, based on reading Cox's essay, that Hewitt was Mycroft. After all, whenever I had read anything at all about Martin Hewitt in various reference books, it was always hinted that his activities were really those of a young Mycroft.

Then, after I had completed reading the Hewitt Canon, two-dozen-plus-one narratives, I was amazed to walk away with the feeling that I hadn't been reading about Mycroft at all. Rather, the stories seemed to be more about a younger *Sherlock Holmes*.

After that initial introduction to Hewitt, it has always been my theory that *Hewitt's* adventures were actually *Holmes's* early investigations while Holmes was living in Montague Street, circa 1876. These adventures were narrated by Brett, Holmes's journalist neighbor. Later, from 1891-93, when Watson's stories about Holmes were taking the world by storm in *The Strand,* Brett chose to write up his own experiences with the younger Consulting Detective. However, when he tried to publish them through his literary agent, Arthur Morrison, he was stopped for some reason, and forced to change Holmes's name to Hewitt so that publication could proceed.

After reaching the point where I always think of Hewitt as Holmes, I decided to do something about it.

Therefore, the three volumes in this series change Martin Hewitt's name to Sherlock Holmes.

Alteration of one character into another has been done before, sometimes by authors of their own works. August Derleth wrote a Sherlock Holmes story, ("The Circular Room") and then changed it in a few years to a Solar Pons story. And in the non-Sherlockian world, it has been done as well. Raymond Chandler revised some of his early short stories so that the original characters' names were changed to Philip Marlowe. Ross MacDonald (Kenneth Millar) rewrote some of his old stories as well, making them into Lew Archer cases instead.

Sometimes, of course, people other than the authors have changed a character's name in the original works after that author was gone. Maurice Leblanc's various *Arsene Lupin vs. Herlock Sholmes* stories from the early 1900's have all been edited and re-released with the name "Herlock Sholmes" correctly replaced with "Sherlock Holmes". In 2012, Alan Lance Andersen edited and produced *The Affairs of Sherlock Holmes*, wherein various non-series Sax Rohmer stories from nearly a hundred years ago were reworked as Holmes tales. Sometimes the original timeline (1920's) was retained, which didn't always work so well for a Holmes story, and the editor might have done better to make them Solar Pons stories, except that Pons is – sadly - a lot less familiar to the general public.

Recently, as of the time of this writing, someone has begun republishing the Dr. Thorndyke mysteries as e-books, but whoever the anonymous editor is, he or she is also rewriting the stories as Holmes stories. In these reworked Thorndyke cases, Thorndyke's name is changed to Holmes, Jervis (Thorndyke's Watson), has his name changed to Watson, and so on. Occasionally the editor makes mistakes, forgetting to consistently change a name, or mistakenly leaving references to Inspector Lestrade as "Superintendent". Also, once-and-a-while the geography around Baker Street still suspiciously matches that of Thorndyke's King's Bench Walk.

Those mistakes aren't too jarring. The worst part is that the anonymous editor insists on indicating that these new versions are by *Arthur Conan Doyle* and *John Hamish Watson*, with no mention at all of the fact that *R. Austin Freeman* actually wrote them. Personally, I'm enjoying reading them, even knowing that they used to be Thorndyke stories. Somehow, Thorndyke was always rather personality-less for me, and reading these stories within the context of the greater Holmes pastiche tradition fleshes them out.

Another example of changing one character to another is the British ITV series "Marple", which has taken non-Miss Marple Agatha Christie stories and converted them into episodes featuring that character. And another fellow, (me, actually) took a non-Nero Wolfe Rex Stout story last year and re-wrote it for *The Gazette* (the Nero Wolfe "Wolfe Pack" official journal) as a Nero Wolfe tale – well, actually an Archie Goodwin tale, since Wolfe doesn't appear in it at all. Several other people have made the same conversion with some of Stout's other non-Wolfe works over the years.

By changing Hewitt to Holmes, I don't mean in any way to diminish or take away from Morrison or Martin Hewitt, but I have always read the Hewitt stories as Holmes stories anyway, so I thought that since I enjoy them this way, maybe other people would as well. I was actually in the process of converting the stories for my own use, planning to print and keep them in a binder in my collection, when it occurred to me to see about getting them actually published. It would be a better way to collect them all in one place, in a complete and uniform edition, even the hard-to-find stories, and also to introduce them to a modern audience. And if they like them, they can go and find out more about Morrison and read the originals, although they are somewhat difficult to find.

Not much is altered or missing from the original published Hewitt versions. Hewitt's name is changed, of course, and the word *office* becomes *rooms*. The location of the *office* is changed from near the Strand to Montague Street, and unfortunately Hewitt's clerk, Kerrett, is eliminated because Holmes would not have had a clerk in 1876. (Also, in one story I have excised some chunks of vile racial epithets. I cannot hear or imagine Holmes

9

using them or putting up with them, and if the purists who probably don't like the idea of this book anyway want to read the stories as they were first written, they can go back to the originals.)

Of course, all of this is one way that the book was produced. And then there is the other explanation . . . .

In previous books, I've described the different ways that I have been able to acquire some of Dr. Watson's writings, and subsequently edit them for publication. On another occasion, I may describe in much greater depth about how I managed to obtain the material that came to form *this* book. Suffice it to say that in September 2013, I was finally able to travel to England, where I've wanted to visit for most of my conscious life.

On September 25th, I was in Charing Cross Road, where I was looking for one of the old Cox & Company locations. I was wearing my deerstalker, as usual. I've worn a deerstalker as my fall/winter/spring hat, day-in-and-day-out, since the mid-1980's, when I received my first (of many) deerstalkers as a nineteenth birthday present. It is the only type of hat that I own or wear, and I proudly wear it whenever the weather is cool enough for it.

And so I was very happy to get the chance to wear my deerstalker in England. For a few weeks in September 2013, a man in a deerstalker roamed Baker Street once again. I wore it everywhere while I was over there, including side-trips to Dartmoor and Sussex, and to any other Holmesian sites that I could jam into my trip. If you live there, maybe you saw me. Someone did. Apparently my hat attracted some attention.

On that day, after finding that particular Cox & Company location, I walked to my nearby appointment with the very gracious and wonderful Catherine Cooke, in order to have a look at the Sherlock Holmes Collection held at the Westminster Reference Library. As expected, it was incredible, and I'm quite thankful for the chance to see it.

Upon my departure, I was accosted in the street by a very small and very old man who had seen me in my deerstalker, taking photographs while standing outside of the old Cox & Company. He had followed me, and waited. He was furtive, and he had a parcel that he was supposed to deliver. His story was hard to follow, but he had been told, very long ago, to deliver the package to a man who would arrive at that location wearing a deerstalker. And after he pushed it into my hands, he sighed with great relief and disappeared into the crowd.

Upon closer examination, I saw that I had been given some of Watson's notes. I recognized the writing. I selfishly took them with me, instead of going back into the library to proudly reveal what I had unexpectedly received

There were several separate narratives in the package, each relating an interesting investigation undertaken by Our Heroes, all of which are currently being edited for future publication. And also, the parcel contained the contents of what became this book, (and also what has already been published in Volume I, and will be in the forthcoming Volume III as well): The "corrected" Martin Hewitt stories, revealing their Holmesian origins, along with an explanatory "Foreword" by Watson.

I was pleased to see that the contents of the parcel confirmed my thoughts that Martin Hewitt was, in fact, a younger Sherlock Holmes, during the days when he lived and worked in Montague Street. I hope that they please you as well.

David Marcum
April 2014

From "The Case of the Flitterbat Lancers"
(Illustration by T.S.C. Crowther)

12

Foreword
by Dr. John H. Watson

It was in the spring of 1894 that I was shocked and amazed to discover that my friend, Mr. Sherlock Holmes, had in fact survived his encounter at the terrible Reichenbach Falls with the late Professor Moriarty of evil fame and memory. It was only due to the reticent nature of Holmes himself that London, nay, England itself, did not immediately ring with the news of his return to Baker Street.

Rather than announce that he had resumed his practice with a triumphant fanfare, he allowed word to spread quietly. First, of course, it was the official force that knew of his reappearance. Our old friend, Inspector Lestrade, was very quick to let everyone know the truth regarding the arrest of Colonel Moran, who had attempted to assassinate Holmes from the window of an empty house facing Holmes's Baker Street rooms. Within weeks, the volume of visitors climbing the seventeen steps to Holmes's sitting room met, and then surpassed, the number that had previously journeyed there. Holmes occasionally stated with amusement that times were certainly different than when he and I had initially taken lodgings there, back when visitors had been much fewer and farther between.

Some weeks after Holmes's return to London at the conclusion of his great hiatus, I sold my practice with no great regret and moved back to the Baker Street lodgings. Only much later did I learn the purchase was made by a young doctor named Verner, a distant relation of Holmes's, who paid the highest price that I had ventured to ask. It was Holmes who really found the money.

There were several confusing days when my possessions were moved back into the house. Mrs. Hudson was quite patient, and - I think - glad of my return. The photographs of Beecher and General Gordon returned to their former resting places, books were replaced on shelves, and my desk between the sitting room windows was cleared of Holmes's accumulated detritus for my own to replace it. This was not a new experience for us, as I had already moved back in once before after the death of my dear first wife, Constance, in late 1887. Somehow, now, in spite of the joy at discovering that my friend still lived, I could not escape the realization that I was returning to Baker Street yet again after the death of a spouse, this time my beloved Mary, gone for a year that very day.

I had fallen into a brown study as I unpacked a crate in my room upstairs when I was startled to hear Holmes's voice. "Watson!" he called. "Watson!"

I made my way down the stairs and into the sitting room, where Holmes was standing by my desk, holding a pair of *Strand* magazines in his hand. I dreaded what he was about to say, having already heard some of his comments on the works that Conan Doyle and I had published during his missing years.

"What is this all about?" he asked, his expression confusing me, as it appeared to be more amused than angry. I had been prepared to explain, yet again, my presentation of his cases in a way that would be enjoyable, rather than as some dry treatise on criminal investigation. Yet, as I began to prepare another defense, I realized that he was holding up two newer issues of the periodical, which did not feature any of my work at all.

"Those are the two latest issues," I replied, somewhat puzzled. "I do continue to read it, even if it does not feature anything that I have written."

"And do you then have any knowledge of what these particular stories could be about?"

I noticed that he had a finger slipped between the pages of the top magazine, and as he let the pages fall open, I suddenly understood.

"Ah," I said. "The Hewitt story. Then Mycroft did not tell you?"

"No," he replied. "There have been a great many other things to discuss since my return. No doubt this has slipped his mind. I take it that you can inform me what this is all about?"

"Certainly," I stated, moving toward my chair by the fire. "But how did you notice the stories in the first place? There was nothing immediately obvious on the cover to indicate any connection with events from your own past."

"I simply picked up the top copy to see how the *Strand* has changed, if at all, from the time it started publication, shortly before the events at Reichenbach and my absence from England. As I flipped through it, I noticed several illustrations by your friend Paget. His style is somewhat unique, you will admit.

"Pausing to study them, in a story ostensibly about someone named 'Martin Hewitt', I was amazed to discover that, except for the change of name and a few other added spurious facts, the investigation described was one of my own early cases, when I lived in Montague Street, and written up by my old friend, Brett, the journalist." He turned, stating, "Of course, my curiosity was also piqued by noticing and remembering the familiar and unusual words 'Lenton Croft' in the title of the piece."

I nodded, and Holmes sat down in his chair, with the two magazines lying in his lap. "Late last year," I explained, "during the time that Doyle and I decided to publish the narrative of your supposed 'death' in 'The Final Problem' – ", Holmes winced, and I continued, " - Newnes at the *Strand* was frantic. He wanted more narratives of your investigations. However, I must admit that I did not feel the need to publish any more. After your disappearance, and then with Mary's passing last year, my need to write had become more intense. However, when I had finally reached the point where I could tell of your final struggle with Professor Moriarty, and also answer his brother's scurrilous charges against your memory, I felt that my work was done. Doyle agreed, having tired of being associated in the venture long before that point.

"Soon after that, Newnes was approached by your old friend, Brett, who had the idea that he could write up some of your earlier cases, when he had lived upstairs from you in the same house in Montague Street."

"In 1876," interrupted Holmes. "Brett was only there for about a year, while my time at No.24 Montague Street stretched for several years on either side of that. But I interrupt. My apologies. Please continue."

"Not at all. Newnes was very happy to reach an agreement with Brett, who would provide the raw information for the narratives. Then, an author that Newnes knew, named Arthur Morrison, would take Brett's rough notes and shape them into more cohesive narratives. As I understand it, Brett's career in journalism had ended a few years ago, and he was not capable of revising the notes and presenting them to Newnes's standards on his own."

Holmes nodded. "I have not seen Brett in over three years, but I fear it was drink that eventually caused his decline. All the signs were there. Even when we lodged in the same building, and he occasionally participated in some of my investigations, he did not have the ambition to write them up at the time, or to use those events that literally fell into his lap in order to advance his career with the news organization where he was employed."

He lifted the magazine in his hands and flipped to the first page of the story in question. "'The Lenton Croft Robberies'," he read. "And I suppose this husky smiling lad, this 'Martin Hewitt', drawn by Paget here, is supposed to represent me? How did that arrangement come to pass?"

"You must understand that I heard this second-hand from your brother," I replied. "As you know, I had first received some encouragement from him to start publishing narratives of your cases in *The Strand* to begin with. When Newnes decided to publish some of your earlier cases late last year, he felt that he ought to check with Mycroft to see if the idea was acceptable. No doubt, he thought it a mere formality. However, he was incorrect, and Mycroft, for whatever reasons of his own, quickly threatened legal action if the publication of the stories were to occur.

"I understand that Newnes was not very happy, and Brett was outraged. Somehow, between them and Arthur Morrison, they worked out that they could still publish the stories if they changed your name, and make a few other minor alterations. This fellow Hewitt was formerly some sort of law clerk who went out on his own. He is described as being heavier than you

16

are, and he has offices with a clerk in the Strand near Charing Cross. I personally believe that the heavy-set description, as well as the use of the initials 'M.H.' for the character's name, are an indirect attack on Mycroft, who tried to stop their efforts."

Holmes nodded, and flipped through the second magazine. "The Sammy Crockett affair," he said. "Brett wasn't even involved in these investigations. I must have told him about them at the time, and he remembered and wrote them up. I shall have to read these and see how accurate they are." He set the magazines on his side table, pushing aside an empty tea cup as he did so. "Are these the only two that have been published?"

"As far as I know," I replied. "The first was only a month or so ago. But I understood from my conversation about it with Mycroft that Brett and Morrison have a whole series of them worked up."

Holmes nodded, more to himself than to me, and then he stood abruptly. Walking past me toward his bedroom, and shedding his dressing gown as he went, he stated, "I believe that I shall pay a visit to my old friend Brett, and see just how long he intends for this foolishness to continue."

And in a moment, he was gone. I reached across for the magazines, and flipped through them for several moments before replacing them on Holmes's table and returning to my unpacking chores upstairs.

It was only a couple of hours later when Holmes returned, a paper-wrapped bundle under his arms. I had been writing at my desk, but I turned when he entered. He moved toward the fire, for there was a chill that day in the late April air. I feared for a moment that he would toss the bundle into the flames, but as he passed my chair, he dropped it into the seat.

"This," he said, "is an incomplete record of my work in 1876, should you care to read it."

"Brett's notes?" I asked.

"The original versions, before he changed my name in them to 'Martin Hewitt'. I am curious as to how he came to choose

17

that particular sobriquet. I am quite sure that you are correct about the initials 'M.H.' and their intended dig at Mycroft, no matter how subtle. But there are other things to consider as well. My name has two vowels in the first name, and two in the last name, as do the names 'Martin' and "Hewitt'. The letter 'O' is in my first and last name, while the letter 'I' is in both of the pseudonymous names. 'I' is the ninth letter of the alphabet, while 'O' is the fifteenth. If – "

I interrupted him before his pondering could lead to a monograph. "Does this mean that there will be no more Martin Hewitt stories in *The Strand*?"

"Hmm? No, I found that I didn't have the heart to stop it entirely. Brett's means are rather limited at the present, and likely to stay that way. He has four or five more of these," he said, gesturing toward the tied and wrapped bundle on my chair, "in the hands of Newnes, ready for immediate publication, and probably a dozen-and-a-half more altered by Morrison for future use.

"Our visit was cordial, and we were able to catch up on what has happened in our lives since the old days. He has assured me that he will continue to mask the narratives so that my participation will remain unknown, and that he will not fabricate any new tales from whole cloth once he runs out of the limited material that he has."

"And he simply gave you his original notes?" I asked.

"He seemed to think it fitting that, as they chronicled my early work, they should end up with me." He sat down and reached for one of his pipes. I was thankful to see that it was not the cherry-wood. He looked up as he scraped the bowl. "Do you mind, Watson? After all, you are my biographer and Boswell."

I laid my pen aside and stood from the desk. Moving toward my own chair, I replied, "Not at all. I am fascinated to learn more about your earlier cases, and how you developed your methods." I lifted the package and sat down, holding it in my lap. "And of course, more about your days in Montague Street as well."

"It was an interesting time," Holmes said, between puffs as he lit the pipe. "I seem to recall mentioning something of it to you before, regarding the incident of 'The Musgrave Ritual', for instance." He then proceeded to tell me some of his other adventures while living at No.24 Montague Street, in those days when he was still learning his craft. I always enjoyed hearing of those times, and as he spoke I made notes for my journals.

As he talked into the early evening, I would occasionally glance at the package of Brett's writings, looking forward to later, when I could enjoy those tales as well.

J.H.W.
June 1929

24 Montague Street
Mr. Sherlock Holmes lived here
from early August 1874 to January 3rd, 1881,
when he moved to 221b Baker Street

The Holford Will Case

At one time, in common, perhaps, with most people, I took a sort of languid, amateur interest in questions of psychology, and was impelled there-by to plunge into the pages of the many curious and rather abstruse books which attempt to deal with phenomena of mind, soul and sense. Three things of the real nature of which, I am convinced, no man will ever learn more than we know at present — which is nothing.

From these I strayed into the many volumes of *Transactions* of the Psychical Research Society, with an occasional by-excursion into mental telepathy and theosophy; the last, a thing whereof my Philistine intelligence obstinately refused to make head or tail.

It was while these things were occupying part of my attention that I chanced to ask Holmes whether, in the course of his divers odd and out-of-the-way experiences, he had met with any such weird adventures as were detailed in such profusion in the books of "authenticated" spooks, doppelgangers, poltergeists, clairvoyance, and so forth.

"Well," Holmes answered, with reflection, "I haven't been such a wallower in the uncanny as some of the worthy people who talk at large in those books of yours, and, as a matter of fact, my little adventures, curious as some of them may seem, have been on the whole of the most solid and matter-of-fact description. One or two things have happened that perhaps your 'psychical' people might be interested in, but they've mostly been found to be capable of a disappointingly simple explanation. One case of some genuine psychological interest, however, I have had; although there's nothing even in that which isn't a matter of well-known scientific possibility." And he proceeded to tell me the story that I have set down here, as well as I can, from recollection.

"I think I have already said, in another place, that one of Holmes's early cases was the famous will case of Bartley *v.* Bartley and others, in which Messrs. Crellan, Hunt & Crellan, chiefly through Holmes's exertions, established their extremely high reputation as solicitors. It was several years or so after this case that Mr. Crellan senior — the head of the firm — retired into private life, and by an odd chance Holmes's first meeting with him after that event was occasioned by another will difficulty.

These were the terms of the telegram that brought Holmes again into personal relations with his old principal:

> "*Can you run down at once on a matter of private business? I will be at Guildford to meet eleven thirty-five from Waterloo. If later or prevented please wire. Crellan.*"

The day and the state of Holmes's engagements suited, and there was full half an hour to catch the train. Taking, therefore, the small traveling-bag that always stood ready packed in case of any sudden excursion that presented the possibility of a night from home, he got early to Waterloo, and by half-past twelve was alighting at Guildford Station. Mr. Crellan, a hale, white-haired old gentleman, wearing gold-rimmed spectacles, was waiting with a covered carriage.

"How d'ye do, Mr. Holmes, how d'ye do?" the old gentleman exclaimed as soon as they met, grasping Holmes's hand, and hurrying him toward the carriage. "I'm glad you've come, very glad. It isn't raining, and you might have preferred something more open, but I brought the brougham because I want to talk privately. I've been vegetating to such an extent for the last few years down here that any little occurrence out of the ordinary excites me, and I'm sure I couldn't have kept quiet till we had got indoors. It's been bad enough, keeping the thing to myself, already."

The door shut, and the brougham started. Mr. Crellan laid his hand on Holmes's knee, "I hope," he said, "I haven't dragged you away from any important business?"

"No," Holmes replied, "you have chosen a most excellent time. Indeed, I did think of making a small holiday today, but your telegram — "

"Yes, yes. Do you know, I was almost ashamed of having sent it after it had gone. Because, after all, the matter is, probably, really a very simple sort of affair that you can't possibly help me in. A few years ago I should have thought nothing of it, nothing at all. But as I have told you, I've got into such a dull, vegetable state of mind since I retired and have nothing to do that a little thing upsets me, and I haven't mental energy enough to make up my mind to go to dinner sometimes. But you're an old friend, and I'm sure you'll forgive my dragging you all down here on a matter that will, perhaps, seem ridiculously simple to you, a man in the thick of active business. If I hadn't known you so well I wouldn't have had the impudence to bother you. But never mind all that. I'll tell you.

"Do you ever remember my speaking of an intimate friend, a Mr. Holford? No. Well, it's a long time ago, and perhaps I never happened to mention him. He was a most excellent man — old fellow, like me, you know; two or three years older, as a matter of fact. We were chums many years ago; in fact, we lodged in the same house when I was an articled clerk and he was a student at Guy's. He retired from the medical profession early, having come into a fortune, and came down here to live at the house we're going to; as a matter of fact, Wedbury Hall.

"When I retired I came down and took up my quarters not far off, and we were a very excellent pair of old chums till last Monday — the day before yesterday — when my poor old friend died. He was pretty well in years — seventy-three — and a man can't live for ever. But I assure you it has upset me terribly, made a greater fool of me than ever, in fact, just when I ought to have my wits about me.

"The reason I particularly want my wits just now, and the reason I have requisitioned yours, is this: that I can't find poor old Holford's will. I drew it up for him years ago, and by it I was appointed his sole executor. I am perfectly convinced that he cannot have destroyed it, because he told me everything concerning his affairs. I have always been his only adviser, in fact, and I'm sure he would have consulted me as to any change in his testamentary intentions before he made it. Moreover, there are reasons why I know he could not have wished to die intestate."

"Which are — ?" queried Holmes as Mr. Crellan paused in his statement.

"Which are these: Holford was a widower, with no children of his own. His wife, who has been dead nearly fifteen years now, was a most excellent woman, a model wife, and would have been a model mother if she had been one at all. As it was she adopted a little girl, a poor little soul who was left an orphan at two years of age. The child's father, an unsuccessful man of business of the name of Garth, maddened by a sudden and ruinous loss, committed suicide, and his wife died of the shock occasioned by the calamity.

"The child, as I have said, was taken by Mrs. Holford and made a daughter of, and my old friend's daughter she has been ever since, practically speaking. The poor old fellow couldn't possibly have been more attached to a daughter of his own, and on her part she couldn't possibly have been a better daughter than she was. She stuck by him night and day during his last illness, until she became rather ill herself, although of course there was a regular nurse always in attendance.

"Now, in his will, Mr. Holford bequeathed rathermore than half of his very large property to this Miss Garth; that is to say, as residuary legatee, her interest in the will came to about that. The rest was distributed in various ways. Holford had largely spent the leisure of his retirement in scientific pursuits. So there were a few legacies to learned societies; all his servants were remembered; he left me a certain number of his books; and there was a very fair sum of money for his nephew, Mr. Cranley Mellis, the only near relation of Mr. Holford's still living. So that you see what the loss of this will may mean. Miss Garth, who was to have taken the greater part of her adoptive father's property, will not have one shilling's worth of claim on the estate and will be turned out into the world without a cent. One or two very old servants will be very awkwardly placed, too, with nothing to live on, and very little prospect of doing more work."

"Everything will go to this nephew," said Holmes, "of course?"

"Of course. That is unless I attempt to prove a rough copy of the will which I may possibly have by me. But even if I have such a thing and find it, long and costly litigation would be called for, and the result would probably be all against us."

"You say you feel sure Mr. Holford did not destroy the will himself?"

"I am quite sure he would never have done so without telling me of it; indeed, I am sure he would have consulted me first. Moreover, it can never have been his intention to leave Miss Garth utterly unprovided for; it would be the same thing as disinheriting his only daughter."

"Did you see him frequently?"

"There's scarcely been a day when I haven't seen him since I have lived down here. During his illness — it lasted a month — I saw him every day."

"And he said nothing of destroying his will?"

"Nothing at all. On the contrary, soon after his first seizure — indeed, on the first visit at which I found him in bed — he said, after telling me how he felt, 'Everything's as I want it, you know, in case I go under.' That seemed to me to mean his will was still as he desired it to be."

"Well, yes, it would seem so. But counsel on the other side (supposing there were another side) might quite as plausibly argue that he meant to die intestate, and had destroyed his will so that everything should be as he wanted it, in that sense. But what do you want me to do — find the will?"

"Certainly, if you can. It seemed to me that you, with your clever head, might be able to form a better judgment than I as to what has happened and who is responsible for it. Because if the will *has* been taken away, some one has taken it."

"It seems probable. Have you told any one of your difficulty?"

"Not a soul. I came over as soon as I could after Mr. Holford's death, and Miss Garth gave me all the keys, because, as executor, the case being a peculiar one, I wished to see that all was in order, and, as you know, the estate is legally vested in the executor from the death of the testator, so that I was responsible for everything; although, of course, if there is no will I'm not executor. But I thought it best to keep the difficulty to myself till I saw you."

"Quite right. Is this Wedbury Hall?"

The brougham had passed a lodge gate, and approached, by a wide drive, a fine old red brick mansion carrying the heavy stone dressings and copings distinctive of early eighteenth century domestic architecture.

"Yes," said Mr. Crellan, "this is the place. We will go straight to the study, I think, and then I can explain details."

The study told the tale of the late Mr. Holford's habits and interests. It was half a library, half a scientific laboratory — pathological curiosities in spirits, a retort or two, test tubes on the writing-table, and a fossilized lizard mounted in a case, balanced the many shelves and cases of books disposed about the walls. In a recess between two book-cases stood a heavy, old-fashioned mahogany bureau.

"Now it was in that bureau," Mr. Crellan explained, indicating it with his finger, "that Mr. Holford kept every document that was in the smallest degree important or valuable. I have seen him at it a hundred times, and he always maintained it was as secure as any iron safe. That may not have been altogether the fact, but the bureau is certainly a tremendously heavy and strong one. Feel it."

Holmes took down the front and pulled out a drawer that Mr. Crellan unlocked for the purpose.

"Solid Spanish mahogany an inch thick," was his verdict, "heavy, hard, and seasoned; not the sort of thing you can buy nowadays. Locks, Chubb's patent, early pattern, but not easily to be picked by anything short of a blast of gunpowder. If there are no marks on this bureau it hasn't been tampered with."

"Well," Mr. Crellan pursued, "as I say, *that* was where Mr. Holford kept his will. I have often seen it when we have been here together, and this was the drawer, the top on the right, that he kept it in. The will was a mere single sheet of foolscap, and was kept, folded of course, in a blue envelope."

"When did you yourself last actually see the will?"

"I saw it in my friend's hand two days before he took to his bed. He merely lifted it in his hand to get at something else in the drawer, replaced it, and locked the drawer again."

"Of course there are other drawers, bureaux, and so on, about the place. You have examined them carefully, I take it?"

"I've turned out ever possible receptacle for that will in the house, I positively assure you, and there isn't a trace of it."

"You've thought of secret drawers, I suppose?"

"Yes. There are two in the bureau which I always knew of. Here they are." Mr. Crellan pressed his thumb against a partition of the pigeon-holes at the back of the bureau and a strip of mahogany flew out from below, revealing two shallow drawers with small ivory catches in lieu of knobs. "Nothing there at all. And this other, as I have said, was the drawer where the will was kept. The other papers kept in the same drawer are here as usual."

"Did anybody else know where Mr. Holford kept his will?"

"Everybody in the house, I should think. He was a frank, above-board sort of man. His adopted daughter knew, and the butler knew, and there was absolutely no reason why all the other servants shouldn't know; probably they did."

"First," said Holmes, "we will make quite sure there are no more secret drawers about this bureau. Lock the door in case anybody comes."

Holmes took out every drawer of the bureau, and examined every part of each before he laid it aside. Then he produced a small pair of silver calipers and an ivory pocket-rule and went over every inch of the heavy framework, measuring, comparing, tapping, adding, and subtracting dimensions. In the end he rose to his feet satisfied. "There is most certainly nothing concealed there," he said.

The drawers were put back, and Mr. Crellan suggested lunch. At Holmes's suggestion it was brought to the study.

"So far," Holmes said, "we arrive at this: either Mr. Holford has destroyed his will, or he has most effectually concealed it, or somebody has stolen it. The first of these possibilities you don't favor."

"I don't believe it is a possibility for a moment. I have told you why; and I knew Holford so well, you know. For the same reasons I am sure he never concealed it."

"Very well, then. Somebody has stolen it. The question is, who?"

"That is so."

"It seems to me that every one in this house had a direct and personal interest in preserving that will. The servants have all something left them, you say, and without the will that goes, of course. Miss Garth has the greatest possible interest in the will. The only person I have heard of as yet who would benefit by its loss or destruction would be the nephew, Mr. Mellis. There are no other relatives, you say, who would benefit by intestacy?"

"Not one."

"Well, what do you think yourself, now? Have you any suspicions?"

Mr. Crellan shrugged his shoulders. "I've no more right to suspicions than you have, I suppose," he said. "Of course, if there are to be suspicions they can only point one way. Mr. Mellis is the only person who can gain by the disappearance of this will."

"Just so, Now, what do you know of him?"

"I don't know much of the young man," Mr. Crellan said slowly. "I must say I never particularly took to him. He is rather a clever fellow, I believe. He was called to the bar some time ago, and afterwards studied medicine, I believe, with the idea of priming himself for a practice in medical jurisprudence. He took a good deal of interest in my old friend's researches, I am told — at any rate he *said* he did; he may have been thinking of his

28

uncle's fortune. But they had a small tiff on some medical question. I don't know exactly what it was, but Mr. Holford objected to something — a method of research or something of that kind — as being dangerous and unprofessional. There was no actual rupture between them, you understand, but Mellis's visits slacked off, and there was a coolness."

"Where is Mr. Mellis now?"

"In London, I believe."

"Has he been in this house between the day you last saw the will in that drawer and yesterday, when you failed to find it?"

"Only once. He came to see his uncle two days before his death — last Saturday, in fact. He didn't stay long."

"Did you see him?"

"Yes."

"What did he do?"

"Merely came into the room for a few minutes — visitors weren't allowed to stay long — spoke a little to his uncle, and went back to town."

"Did he do nothing else, or see anybody else?"

"Miss Garth went out of the room with him as he left, and I should think they talked for a little before he went away, to judge by the time she was gone; but I don't know."

"You are sure he went then?"

"I saw him in the drive as I looked from the window."

"Miss Garth, you say, has kept all the keys since the beginning of Mr. Holford's illness?"

"Yes, until she gave them up to me yesterday. Indeed, the nurse, who is rather a peppery customer, and was jealous of Miss Garth's presence in the sick room all along, made several difficulties about having to go to her for everything."

"And there is no doubt of the bureau having been kept locked all the time?"

"None at all. I have asked Miss Garth that — and, indeed, a good many other things — without saying why I wanted the information."

"How are Mr. Mellis and Miss Garth affected toward one another — are they friendly?"

"Oh, yes. Indeed, some while ago I rather fancied that Mellis was disposed to pay serious addresses in that quarter. He may have had a fancy that way, or he may have been attracted by the young lady's expectations. At any rate, nothing definite seems to have come of it as yet. But I must say — between ourselves, of course — I have more than once noticed a decided air of agitation, shyness perhaps, in Miss Garth when Mr. Mellis has been present. But, at any rate, that scarcely matters. She is twenty-four years of age now, and can do as she likes. Although, if I had anything to say in the matter — well, never mind."

"You, I take it, have known Miss Garth a long time?"

"Bless you, yes. Danced her on my knee twenty years ago. I've been her 'Uncle Leonard' all her life."

"Well, I think we must at least let Miss Garth know of the loss of the will. Perhaps, when they have cleared away these plates, she will come here for a few minutes."

"I'll go and ask her," Mr. Crellan answered, and having rung the bell, proceeded to find Miss Garth.

Presently he returned with the lady. She was a slight, very pale young woman; no doubt rather pretty in ordinary, but now not looking her best. She was evidently worn and nervous from anxiety and want of sleep, and her eyes were sadly inflamed. As the wind slammed a loose casement behind her she started nervously, and placed her hand to her head.

"Sit down at once, my dear," Mr. Crellan said; "sit down. This is Mr. Sherlock Holmes, whom I have taken the liberty of inviting down here to help me in a very important matter. The fact is, my dear," Mr. Crellan added gravely, "I can't find your poor father's will."

Miss Garth was not surprised. "I thought so," she said mildly, "when you asked me about the bureau yesterday."

"Of course I need not say, my dear, what a serious thing it may be for you if that will cannot be found. So I hope you'll try and tell Mr. Holmes here anything he wants to know as well as you can, without forgetting a single thing. I'm pretty sure that he will find it for us if it is to be found."

"I understand, Miss Garth," Holmes asked, "that the keys of that bureau never left your possession during the whole time of Mr. Holford's last illness, and that the bureau was kept locked?"

"Yes, that is so."

"Did you ever have occasion to go to the bureau yourself?"

"No, I have not touched it."

"Then you can answer for it, I presume, that the bureau was never unlocked by *any one* from the time Mr. Holford placed the keys in your hands till you gave them to Mr. Crellan?"

"Yes, I am sure of that."

"Very good. Now is there any place on the whole premises that you can suggest where this will may possibly be hidden?"

"There is no place that Mr. Crellan doesn't know of, I'm sure."

"It is an old house, I observe," Holmes pursued. "Do you know of any place of concealment in the structure — any secret doors, I mean, you know, or sliding panels, or hollow door frames, and so forth?"

Miss Garth shook her head. "There is not a single place of the sort you speak of in the whole building, so far as I know," she said, "and I have lived here almost all my life."

"You knew the purport of Mr. Holford's will, I take it, and understand what its loss may mean to yourself?"

"Perfectly."

"Now I must ask you to consider carefully. Take your mind back to two or three days before Mr. Holford's illness began, and tell me if you can remember any single fact, occurrence, word, or hint from that day to this in any way bearing on the will or anything connected with it?"

Miss Garth shook her head thoughtfully. "I can't remember the thing being mentioned by anybody, except perhaps by the nurse, who is rather a touchy sort of woman, and once or twice took it upon herself to hint that my recent anxiety was chiefly about my poor father's money. And that once, when I had done some small thing for him, my father — I have always called him father, you know — said that he wouldn't forget it, or that I should be rewarded, or something of that sort. Nothing else that I can remember in the remotest degree concerned the will."

"Mr. Mellis said nothing about it, then?"

Miss Garth changed color slightly, but answered, "No, I only saw him to the door."

"Thank you, Miss Garth, I won't trouble you any further just now. But if you *can* remember anything more in the course of the next few hours it may turn out to be of great service."

Miss Garth bowed and withdrew. Mr. Crellan shut the door behind her and returned to Holmes. "*That* doesn't carry us much further," he said. "The more certain it seems that the will cannot have been got at, the more difficult our position is from a legal point of view. What shall we do now?"

"Is the nurse still about the place?"

"Yes, I believe so."

"Then I'll speak to her."

The nurse came in response to Mr. Crellan's summons: a sharp-featured, pragmatical woman of forty-five. She took the seat offered her, and waited for Holmes's questions.

"You were in attendance on Mr. Holford, I believe, Mrs. Turton, since the beginning of his last illness?"

"Since October 24th."

"Were you present when Mr. Mellis came to see his uncle last Saturday?"

"Yes."

"Can you tell me what took place?"

"As to what the gentleman said to Mr. Holford," the nurse replied, bridling slightly, "of course I don't know anything, it not being my business and not intended for my ears. Mr. Crellan was there, and knows as much as I do, and so does Miss Garth. I only know that Mr. Mellis stayed for a few minutes and then went out of the room with Miss Garth."

"How long was Miss Garth gone?"

"I don't know, ten minutes or a quarter of an hour, perhaps."

"Now Mrs. Turton, I want you to tell me in confidence — it is very important — whether you, at any time, heard Mr. Holford during his illness say anything of his wishes as to how his property was to be left in case of his death?"

The nurse started and looked keenly from Holmes to Mr. Crellan and back again.

"Is it the will you mean?" she asked sharply.

"Yes. Did he mention it?"

"You mean you can't find the will, isn't that it?"

"Well, suppose it is, what then?"

"Suppose won't do," the nurse answered shortly; "I *do* know something about the will, and I believe you can't find it."

"I'm sure, Mrs. Turton, that if you know anything about the will you will tell Mr. Crellan in the interests of right and justice."

"And who's to protect me against the spite of those I shall offend if I tell you?"

Mr. Crellan interposed.

"Whatever you tell us, Mrs. Turton," he said, "will be held in the strictest confidence, and the source of our information shall not be divulged. For that I give you my word of honor. And, I need scarcely add, I will see that you come to no harm by anything you may say."

"Then the will *is* lost. I may understand that?"

Holmes's features were impassive and impenetrable. But in Mr. Crellan's disturbed face the nurse saw a plain answer in the affirmative.

"Yes," she said, "I see that's the trouble. Well, I know who took it."

"Then who was it?"

"*Miss Garth!*"

"Miss Garth! Nonsense!" cried Mr. Crellan, starting upright. "Nonsense!"

"It may be nonsense," the nurse replied slowly, with a monotonous emphasis on each word. "It may be nonsense, but it's a fact. I saw her take it."

Mr. Crellan simply gasped. Holmes drew his chair a little nearer.

"If you saw her take it," he said gently, closely watching the woman's face the while, "then, of course, there's no doubt."

"I tell you I saw her take it," the nurse repeated. "What was in it, and what her game was in taking it, I don't know. But it was in that bureau, wasn't it?"

"Yes — probably."

"In the right hand top drawer?"

"Yes."

"A white paper in a blue envelope?"

"Yes."

"Then I saw her take it, as I said before. She unlocked that drawer before my eyes, took it out, and locked the drawer again."

Mr. Crellan turned blankly to Holmes, but Holmes kept his eyes on the nurse's face.

"When did this occur?" he asked, "and how?"

"It was on Saturday night, rather late. Everybody was in bed but Miss Garth and myself, and she had been down to the dining-room for something. Mr. Holford was asleep, so as I wanted to re-fill the water-bottle, I took it up and went. As I was passing the door of this room that we are in now, I heard a noise, and looked in at the door, which was open. There was a candle on the table which had been left there earlier in the evening. Miss Garth was opening the top right hand drawer of *that* bureau" — Mrs. Turton stabbed her finger spitefully toward the piece of furniture, as though she owed it a personal grudge — "and I saw her take out a blue foolscap envelope, and as the flap was open, I could see the enclosed paper was white. She shut the drawer, locked it, and came out of the room with the envelope in her hand."

"And what did you do?"

"I hurried on, and she came away without seeing me, and went in the opposite direction — toward the small staircase."

"Perhaps," Mr. Crellan ventured at a blurt, "perhaps she was walking in her sleep?"

"That she wasn't!" the nurse replied, "for she came back to Mr. Holford's room almost as soon as I returned there, and asked some questions about the medicine — which was nothing new, for I must say she was very fond of interfering in things that were part of my business."

"That is quite certain, I suppose," Holmes remarked, "that she could not have been asleep?"

"Quite certain. She talked for about a quarter of an hour, and wanted to kiss Mr. Holford, which might have wakened him, before she went to bed. In fact, I may say we had a disagreement."

Holmes did not take his steady gaze from the nurse's face for some seconds after she had finished speaking. Then he only said, "Thank you, Mrs. Turton. I need scarcely assure you, after what Mr. Crellan has said, that your confidence shall not be betrayed. I think that is all, unless you have more to tell us."

Mrs. Turton bowed and rose. "There is nothing more," she said, and left the room.

As soon as she had gone, "Is Mrs. Turton at all interested in the will," Holmes asked.

"No, there is nothing for her. She is a new-comer, you see. Perhaps," Mr. Crellan went on, struck by an idea, "she may be jealous, or something. She seems a spiteful woman — and really, I can't believe her story for a moment."

"Why?"

"Well, you see, it's absurd. Why should Miss Garth go to all this secret trouble to do herself an injury — to make a beggar of herself? And besides, she's not in the habit of telling barefaced lies. She distinctly assured us, you remember, that she had never been to the bureau for any purpose whatever."

"But the nurse has an honest character, hasn't she?"

"Yes, her character is excellent. Indeed, from all accounts, she is a very excellent woman, except for a desire to govern everybody, and a habit of spite if she is thwarted. But, of course, that sort of thing sometimes leads people rather far."

"So it does," Holmes replied. "But consider now. Is it not possible that Miss Garth, completely infatuated with Mr. Mellis, thinks she is doing a noble thing for him by destroying the will and giving up her whole claim to his uncle's property? Devoted women do just such things, you know."

Mr. Crellan stared, bent his head to his hand, and considered. "So they do, so they do," he said. "Insane foolery.

Really, it's the sort of thing I can imagine her doing — she's honor and generosity itself. But then those lies," he resumed, sitting up and slapping his leg; "I can't believe she'd tell such tremendous lies as that for anybody. And with such a calm face, too — I'm sure she couldn't."

"Well, that's as it may be. You can scarcely set a limit to the lengths a woman will go on behalf of a man she loves. I suppose, by the bye, Miss Garth is not exactly what you would call a 'strong-minded' woman?"

"No, she's not that. She'd never get on in the world by herself. She's a good little soul, but nervous — very; and her month of anxiety, grief, and want of sleep seems to have broken her up."

"Mr. Mellis knows of the death, I suppose?"

"I telegraphed to him at his chambers in London the first thing yesterday — Tuesday — morning, as soon as the telegraph office was open. He came here (as I've forgotten to tell you as yet) the first thing this morning — before I was over here myself, in fact. He had been staying not far off — at Ockham, I think — and the telegram had been sent on. He saw Miss Garth, but couldn't stay, having to get back to London. I met him going away as I came, about eleven o'clock. Of course I said nothing about the fact that I couldn't find the will, but he will probably be down again soon, and may ask questions."

"Yes," Holmes replied. "And speaking of that matter, you can no doubt talk with Miss Garth on very intimate and familiar terms?"

"Oh yes — yes; I've told you what old friends we are."

"I wish you could manage, at some favorable opportunity today, to speak to her alone, and without referring to the will in any way, get to know, as circumspectly and delicately as you can, how she stands in regard to Mr. Mellis. Whether he is an accepted lover, or likely to be one, you know. Whatever answer you may get, you may judge, I expect, by her manner how things really are."

"Very good — I'll seize the first chance. Meanwhile what to do?"

"Nothing, I'm afraid, except perhaps to examine other pieces of furniture as closely as we have examined this bureau."

Other bureaux, desks, tables, and chests were examined fruitlessly. It was not until after dinner that Mr. Crellan saw a favorable opportunity of sounding Miss Garth as he had promised. Half an hour later he came to Holmes in the study, more puzzled than ever.

"There's no engagement between them," he reported, "secret or open, nor ever has been. It seems, from what I can make out, going to work as diplomatically as possible, that Mellis *did* propose to her, or something very near it, a time ago, and was point-blank refused. Altogether, Miss Garth's sentiment for him appears to be rather dislike than otherwise."

"That rather knocks a hole in the theory of self-sacrifice, doesn't it?" Holmes remarked. "I shall have to think over this, and sleep on it. It's possible that it may be necessary tomorrow for you to tax Miss Garth, point-blank, with having taken away the will. Still, I hope not."

"I hope not, too," Mr. Crellan said, rather dubious as to the result of such an experiment. "She has been quite upset enough already. And, by the bye, she didn't seem any the better or more composed after Mellis' visit this morning."

"Still, *then* the will was gone."

"Yes."

And so Holmes and Mr. Crellan talked on late into the evening, turning over every apparent possibility and finding reason in none. The household went to bed at ten, and, soon after, Miss Garth came to bid Mr. Crellan good night. It had been settled that both Sherlock Holmes and Mr. Crellan should stay the night at Wedbury Hall.

Soon all was still, and the ticking of the tall clock in the hall below could be heard as distinctly as though it were in the study, while the rain without dropped from eaves and sills in regular splashes. Twelve o'clock struck, and Mr. Crellan was about to suggest retirement, when the sound of a light footstep startled Holmes's alert ear. He raised his hand to enjoin silence, and stepped to the door of the room, Mr. Crellan following him.

There was a light over the staircase, seven or eight yards away, and down the stairs came Miss Garth in dressing gown and slippers; she turned at the landing and vanished in a passage leading to the right.

"Where does that lead to?" Holmes whispered hurriedly.

"Toward the small staircase — other end of house," Mr. Crellan replied in the same tones.

"Come quietly," said Holmes, and stepped lightly after Miss Garth, Mr. Crellan at his heels.

She was nearing the opposite end of the passage, walking at a fair pace and looking neither to right nor left. There was another light over the smaller staircase at the end. Without hesitation Miss Garth turned down the stairs till about half down the flight, and then stopped and pressed her hand against the oak wainscot.

Immediately the vertical piece of framing against which she had placed her hand turned on central pivots top and bottom, revealing a small recess, three feet high and little more than six inches wide. Miss Garth stooped and felt about at the bottom of this recess for several seconds. Then with every sign of extreme agitation and horror she withdrew her hand empty, and sank on the stairs. Her head rolled from side to side on her shoulders, and beads of perspiration stood on her forehead. Holmes with difficulty restrained Mr. Crellan from going to her assistance.

Presently, with a sort of shuddering sigh, Miss Garth rose, and after standing irresolute for a moment, descended the flight of stairs to the bottom. There she stopped again, and pressing her hand to her forehead, turned and began to re-ascend the stairs.

Holmes touched his companion's arm, and the two hastily but noiselessly made their way back along the passage to the study. Miss Garth left the open framing as it was, reached the top of the landing, and without stopping proceeded along the passage and turned up the main staircase, while Holmes and Mr. Crellan still watched her from the study door.

At the top of the flight she turned to the right, and up three or four more steps toward her own room. There she stopped, and leaned thoughtfully on the handrail.

"Go up," whispered Holmes to Mr. Crellan, "as though you were going to bed. Appear surprised to see her; ask if she isn't well, and, if you can, manage to repeat that question of mine about secret hiding-places in the house."

Mr. Crellan nodded and started quickly up the stairs. Half-way up he turned his head, and, as he went on, "Why, Nelly, my dear," he said, "what's the matter? Aren't you well?"

Mr. Crellan acted his part well, and waiting below, Holmes heard this dialogue:

"No, uncle, I don't feel very well, but it's nothing. I think my room seems close. I can scarcely breathe."

"Oh, it isn't close tonight. You'll be catching cold, my dear. Go and have a good sleep; you mustn't worry that wise little head of yours, you know. Mr. Holmes and I have been making quite a night of it, but I'm off to bed now."

"I hope they've made you both quite comfortable, uncle?"

"Oh, yes; capital, capital. We've been talking over business, and, no doubt, we shall put that matter all in order soon. By the bye, I suppose since you saw Mr. Holmes you haven't happened to remember anything more to tell him?"

"No."

"You still can't remember any hiding-places or panels, or that sort of thing in the wainscot or anywhere?"

"No, I'm sure I don't know of any, and I don't believe for a moment that any exist."

"Quite sure of that, I suppose?"

"Oh yes."

"All right. Now go to bed. You'll catch *such* a cold in these draughty landings. Come, I won't move a step till I see your door shut behind you. Good night."

"Good night, uncle."

Mr. Crellan came downstairs again with a face of blank puzzlement.

"I wouldn't have believed it," he assured Sherlock Holmes; "positively I wouldn't have believed she'd have told such a lie, and with such confidence, too. There's something deep and horrible here, I'm afraid. What does it mean?"

"We'll talk of that afterwards," Holmes replied. "Come now and take a look at that recess."

They went, quietly still, to the small staircase, and there, with a candle, closely examined the recess. It was a mere box, three feet high, a foot or a little more deep, and six or seven inches wide. The piece of oak framing, pivoted to the stair at the bottom and to a horizontal piece of framing at the top, stood edge forward, dividing the opening down the centre. There was nothing whatever in the recess.

Holmes ascertained that there was no catch, the plank simply remaining shut by virtue of fitting tightly, so that nothing but pressure on the proper part was requisite to open it. He had closed the plank and turned to speak to Mr. Crellan, when another interruption occurred.

On each floor the two staircases were joined by passages, and the ground-floor passage, from the foot of the flight they were on, led to the entrance hall. Distinct amid the loud clicking of the hall clock, Holmes now heard a sound, as of a person's foot shifting on a stone step.

Mr. Crellan heard it too, and each glanced at the other. Then Holmes, shading the candle with his hand, led the way to the hall. There they listened for several seconds — almost an hour — it seemed — and then the noise was repeated. There was no doubt of it. It was at the other side of the front door.

In answer to Holmes's hurried whispers, Mr. Crellan assured him that there was no window from which, in the dark, a view could be got of a person standing outside the door. Also that any other way out would be equally noisy, and would entail the circuit of the house. The front door was fastened by three heavy bolts, an immense old-fashioned lock, and a bar. It would take nearly a minute to open at least, even if everything went easily. But, as there was no other way, Holmes determined to try it. Handing the candle to his companion, he first lifted the bar, conceiving that it might be done with the least noise. It went easily, and, handling it carefully, Holmes let it hang from its rivet without a sound. Just then, glancing at Mr. Crellan, he saw that he was forgetting to shade the candle, whose rays extended through the fanlight above the door, and probably through the wide crack under it. But it was too late. At the same moment the light was evidently perceived from outside; there was a hurried jump from the steps, and for an instant a sound of running on gravel. Holmes tore back the bolts, flung the door open, and dashed out into the darkness, leaving Mr. Crellan on the doorstep with the candle.

Holmes was gone, perhaps, five or ten minutes, although to Mr. Crellan — standing there at the open door in a state of high nervous tension, and with no notion of what was happening or what it all meant — the time seemed an eternity. When at last Holmes reached the door again, "What was it?" asked Mr. Crellan, much agitated. "Did you see? Have you caught them?"

Holmes shook his head.

"I hadn't a chance," he said. "The wall is low over there, and there's a plantation of trees at the other side. But I think — yes, I begin to think — that I may possibly be able to see my way through this business in a little while. See this?"

On the top step in the sheltered porch there remained the wet prints of two feet. Holmes took a letter from his pocket, opened it out, spread it carefully over the more perfect of the two marks, pressed it lightly and lifted it. Then, when the door was shut, he produced his pocket scissors, and with great care cut away the paper round the wet part, leaving a piece, of course, the shape of a boot sole.

"Come," said Holmes, "we may get at something after all. Don't ask me to tell you anything now; I don't know anything, as a matter of fact. I hope this is the end of the night's entertainment, but I'm afraid the case is rather an unpleasant business. There is nothing for us to do now but to go to bed, I think. I suppose there's a handy man kept about the place?"

"Yes, he's gardener and carpenter and carpet-beater, and so on."

"Good! Where's his sanctum? Where does he keep his shovels and carpet sticks?"

"In the shed by the coach house, I believe. I think it's generally unlocked."

"Very good. We've earned a night's rest, and now we'll have it."

The next morning, after breakfast, Holmes took Mr. Crellan into the study.

"Can you manage," he said, "to send Miss Garth out for a walk this morning — with somebody?"

"I can send her out for a ride with the groom — unless she thinks it wouldn't be the thing to go riding so soon after her bereavement."

"Never mind, that will do. Send her at once, and see that she goes. Call it doctor's orders; say she must go for her health's sake — anything."

Mr. Crellan departed, used his influence, and in half an hour Miss Garth had gone.

"I was up pretty early this morning," Holmes remarked on Mr. Crellan's return to the study, "and, among other things, I sent a telegram to London. Unless my eyes deceive me, a boy with a peaked cap — a telegraph boy, in fact — is coming up the drive this moment. Yes, he is. It is probably my answer."

In a few minutes a telegram was brought in. Holmes read it and then asked, "Your friend Mr. Mellis, I understand, was going straight to town yesterday morning?"

"Yes."

"Read that, then."

Mr. Crellan took the telegram and read:

> "*Mellis did not sleep at chambers last night. Been out of town for some days past.*"

Mr. Crellan looked up.

"Who sent it?" he asked.

"Lad back in London; sharp fellow. You see, Mellis didn't go to town after all. As a matter of fact, I believe he was nearer this place than we thought. You said he had a disagreement with his uncle because of scientific practices which the old gentleman considered 'dangerous and unprofessional,' I think?"

"Yes, that was the case."

"Ah, then the key to all the mystery of the will is in this room."

"Where?"

"There." Holmes pointed to the book-cases. "Read Bernheim's *Suggestive Therapeutics*, and one or two books of Heidenhain's and Björnström's and you'll see the thing more clearly than you can without them; but that would be rather a long sort of job, so — but why, who's this? Somebody coming up the drive in a fly, isn't it?"

"Yes," Mr. Crellan replied, looking out of the window. Presently he added, "It's Cranley Mellis."

"Ah," said Holmes, "he won't trouble us for a little. I'll bet you a penny cake he goes first by himself to the small staircase and tries that secret recess. If you get a little way along the passage you will be able to see him; but that will scarcely matter — I can see you don't guess now what I am driving at."

"I don't in the least."

"I told you the names of the books in which you could read the matter up; but that would be too long for the present purpose. The thing is fairly well summarized, I see, in that encyclopædia there in the corner. I have put a marker in volume seven. Do you mind opening it at that place and seeing for yourself?"

Mr. Crellan, doubtful and bewildered, reached the volume. It opened readily, and in the place where it opened lay a blue foolscap envelope. The old gentleman took the envelope, drew from it a white paper, stared first at the paper, then at Holmes, then at the paper again, let the volume slide from his lap, and gasped, "Why — why — it's the will!"

"Ah, so I thought," said Holmes, catching the book as it fell. "But don't lose this place in the encyclopædia. Read the name of the article. What is it?"

Mr. Crellan looked absent-mindedly at the title, holding the will before him all the time. Then, mechanically, he read aloud the word, "*Hypnotism*."

"Hypnotism it is," Holmes answered. "A dangerous and terrible power in the hands of an unscrupulous man."

"But — but how? I don't understand it. This — this is the real will, I suppose?"

"Look at it; you know best."

Mr. Crellan looked.

"Yes," he said, "this certainly is the will. But where did it come from? It hasn't been in this book all the time, has it?"

"No. Didn't I tell you I put it there myself as a marker? But come, you'll understand my explanation better if I first read you a few lines from this article. See here now:

Although hypnotism has power for good when properly used by medical men, it is an exceedingly dangerous weapon in the hands of the unskillful or unscrupulous. Crimes have been committed by persons who have been hypnotized. Just as a person when hypnotized is rendered extremely impressionable, and therefore capable of receiving beneficial suggestions, so he is nearly as liable to receive suggestions for evil; and it is quite possible for an hypnotic subject, while under hypnotic influence, to be impressed with the belief that he is to commit some act after the influence is removed, and that act he is safe to commit, acting at the time as an automaton. Suggestions may be thus made of which the subject, in his subsequent uninfluenced moments, has no idea, but which he will proceed to carry out automatically at the time appointed. In the case of a complete state of hypnotism the subject has subsequently no recollection whatever of what has happened. Persons whose will or nerve power has been weakened by fear or other similar causes can be hypnotized without consent on their part.

"There now, what do you make of that?"

"Why, do you mean that Miss Garth has been hypnotized by — by — Cranley Mellis?"

"I think that is the case; indeed, I am pretty sure of it. Notice, on the occasion of each of his last two visits, he was alone with Miss Garth for some little time. On the evening following each of those visits she does something which she afterwards knows nothing about — something connected with the disappearance of this will, the only thing standing between Mr. Mellis and the whole of his uncle's property. Who could have been in a weaker nervous state than Miss Garth has been lately? Remember, too, on the visit of last Saturday, while Miss Garth says she only showed Mellis to the door, both you and the nurse speak of their being gone some little time. Miss Garth must have forgotten what took place then, when Mellis hypnotized her, and impressed on her the suggestion that she should take Mr. Holford's will that night, long after he — Mellis — had gone, and when he could not be suspected of knowing anything of it. Further, that she should, at that time when her movements would be less likely to be observed, secrete that will in a place of hiding known only to himself."

"Dear, dear, what a rascal! Do you really think he did that?"

"Not only that, but I believe he came here yesterday morning while you were out to get the will from the recess. The recess, by the bye, I expect he discovered by accident on one of his visits (he has been here pretty often, I suppose, altogether), and kept the secret in case it might be useful. Yesterday, not finding the will there, he hypnotized Miss Garth once again, and conveyed the suggestion that, at midnight last night, she should take the will from wherever she had put it and pass it to him under the front door."

"What, do you mean it was he you chased across the grounds last night?"

"That is a thing I am pretty certain of. If we had Mr. Mellis's boot here we could make sure by comparing it with the piece of paper I cut out, as you will remember, in the entrance hall. As we have the will, though, that will scarcely be necessary. What he will do now, I expect, will be to go to the recess again on the vague chance of the will being there now, after all, assuming that his second dose of mesmerism has somehow miscarried. If Miss Garth were here he might try his tricks again, and that is why I got you to send her out."

"And where did you find the will?"

"Now you come to practical details. You will remember that I asked about the handyman's tool-house? Well, I paid it a visit at six o'clock this morning, and found therein some very excellent carpenter's tools in a chest. I took a selection of them to the small staircase, and took out the tread of a stair — the one that the pivoted framing-plank rested on."

"And you found the will there?"

"The will, as I rather expected when I examined the recess last night, had slipped down a rather wide crack at the end of the stair timber, which, you know, formed, so to speak, the floor of the recess. The fact was, the stair-tread didn't quite reach as far as the back of the recess. The opening wasn't very distinct to see, but I soon felt it with my fingers. When Miss Garth, in her hypnotic condition on Saturday night, dropped the will into the recess, it shot straight to the back corner and fell down the slit. That was why Mellis found it empty, and why Miss Garth also found it empty on returning there last night under hypnotic influence. You observed her terrible state of nervous agitation when she failed to carry out the command that haunted her. It was frightful. Something like what happens to a suddenly awakened somnambulist, perhaps. Anyway, that is all over. I found the will under the end of the stair-tread, and here it is. If you will come to the small staircase now you shall see where the paper slipped out of sight. Perhaps we shall meet Mr. Mellis."

"He's a scoundrel," said Mr. Crellan. "It's a pity we can't punish him."

"That's impossible, of course. Where's your proof? And if you had any I'm not sure that a hypnotist is responsible at law for what his subject does. Even if he were, moving a will from one part of the house to another is scarcely a legal crime. The explanation I have given you accounts entirely for the disturbed manner of Miss Garth in the presence of Mellis. She merely felt an indefinite sense of his power over her. Indeed, there is all the possibility that, finding her an easy subject, he had already practiced his influence by way of experiment. A hypnotist, as you will see in the books, has always an easier task with a person he has hypnotized before."

As Holmes had guessed, in the corridor they met Mr. Mellis. He was a thin, dark man of about thirty-five, with large, bony features, and a slight stoop. Mr. Crellan glared at him ferociously.

"Well, sir, and what do you want?" he asked.

Mr. Mellis looked surprised. "Really, that's a very extraordinary remark, Mr. Crellan," he said. "This is my late uncle's house. I might, with at least as much reason, ask you what you want."

"I'm here, sir, as Mr. Holford's executor."

"Appointed by will?"

"Yes."

"And is the will in existence?"

"Well — the fact is — we couldn't find it — "

"Then, what do you mean, sir, by calling yourself an executor with no will to warrant you?" interrupted Mellis. "Get out of this house. If there's no will, I administrate."

"But there *is* a will," roared Mr. Crellan, shaking it in his face. "There is a will. I didn't say we hadn't found it yet, did I? There *is* a will, and here it is in spite of all your diabolical tricks, with your scoundrelly hypnotism and secret holes, and the rest of it! Get out of this place, sir, or I'll have you thrown out of the window!"

Mr. Mellis shrugged his shoulders with an appearance of perfect indifference. "If you've a will appointing you executor it's all right, I suppose, although I shall take care to hold you responsible for any irregularities. As I don't in the least understand your conduct, unless it is due to drink, I'll leave you." And with that he went.

Mr. Crellan boiled with indignation for a minute, and then turning to Holmes, "I say, I hope it's all right," he said, "connecting him with all this queer business?"

"We shall soon see," replied Holmes, "if you'll come and look at the pivoted plank."

They went to the small staircase, and Holmes once again opened the recess. Within lay a blue foolscap envelope, which Holmes picked up. "See," he said, "it is torn at the corner. He has been here and opened it. It's a fresh envelope, and I left it for him this morning, with the corner gummed down a little so that he would have to tear it in opening. This is what was inside," Holmes added, and laughed aloud as he drew forth a rather crumpled piece of white paper. "It was only a childish trick after all," he concluded, "but I always liked a small practical joke on occasion." He held out the crumpled paper, on which was inscribed in large capital letters the single word — "SOLD."

The Case of the Missing Hand

I think I have recorded in another place Holmes's frequent aphorism that "there is nothing in this world that is at all possible that has not happened or is not happening in London." But there are many strange happenings in this matter-of-fact country and in these matter-of-fact times that occur far enough from London. Fantastic crimes, savage revenges, mediæval superstitions, horrible cruelty, though less in sight, have been no more extinguished by the advent of the nineteenth century than have the ancient races who practiced them in the dark ages. Some of the races have become civilized, and some of the savageries are heard of no more. But there are survivals in both cases. I say these things having in my mind a particular case that came under the personal notice of both Holmes and myself — an affair that brought one up standing with a gasp and a doubt of one's era.

My good uncle, the Colonel, was not in the habit of gathering large house parties at his place at Ratherby, partly because the place was not a great one, and partly because the Colonel's gout was. But there was an excellent bit of shooting for two or three guns, and even when he was unable to leave the house himself, my uncle was always pleased if some good friend were enjoying a good day's sport in his territory. As to myself, the good old soul was in a perpetual state of offence because I visited him so seldom, though whenever my scant holidays fell in a convenient time of the year I was never insensible to the attractions of the Ratherby stubble. More than once had I sat by the old gentleman when his foot was exceptionally troublesome, amusing him with accounts of some of the doings of Sherlock Holmes, and more than once had my uncle expressed his desire to meet Holmes himself, and commissioned me with an invitation to be presented to Holmes at the first likely opportunity, for a joint excursion to Ratherby. At length I persuaded Holmes to take a fortnight's rest, coincident with a little vacation of my own, and we got down to Ratherby within a few days past September the 1st, and before a gun had been fired at the Colonel's bit of shooting. The Colonel himself we found confined to the house with his foot on the familiar rest, and though ourselves were the only guests, we managed to do pretty well together. It was during this short holiday that the case I have mentioned arose.

When first I began to record some of the more interesting of Holmes's operations, I think I explained that such cases as I myself had not witnessed I should set down in impersonal narrative form, without intruding myself. The present case, so far as Holmes's work was concerned, I saw, but there were circumstances which led up to it that we only fully learned afterwards. These circumstances, however, I shall put in their proper place — at the beginning.

The Fosters were a fairly old Ratherby family, of whom Mr. John Foster had died by an accident at the age of about forty, leaving a wife twelve years younger than himself and three children, two boys and one girl, who was the youngest. The boys grew up strong, healthy, out-of-door young ruffians, with all the tastes of sportsmen, and all the qualities, good and bad, natural to lads of fairly well-disposed character allowed a great deal too much of their own way from the beginning.

Their only real bad quality was an unfortunate knack of bearing malice, and a certain savage vindictiveness towards such persons as they chose to consider their enemies. With the louts of the village they were at unceasing war, and, indeed, once got into serious trouble for peppering the butcher's son (who certainly was a great blackguard) with sparrow-shot. At the usual time they went to Oxford together, and were fraternally sent down together in their second year, after enjoying a spell of rustication in their first. The offence was never specifically mentioned about Ratherby, but was rumored of as something particularly outrageous.

It was at this time, sixteen years or thereabout after the death of their father, that Henry and Robert Foster first saw and disliked Mr. Jonas Sneathy, a director of penny banks and small insurance offices. He visited Ranworth (the Fosters' home) a great deal more than the brothers thought necessary, and, indeed, it was not for lack of rudeness on their part that Mr. Sneathy failed to understand, as far as they were concerned, his room was preferred to his company.

But their mother welcomed him, and in the end it was announced that Mrs. Foster was to marry again, and that after that her name would be Mrs. Sneathy.

Hereupon there were violent scenes at Ranworth. Henry and Robert Foster denounced their prospective father-in-law as a fortune-hunter, a snuffler, a hypocrite. They did not stop at broad hints as to the honesty of his penny banks and insurance offices, and the house straightway became a house of bitter strife. The marriage took place, and it was not long before Mr. Sneathy's real character became generally obvious. For months he was a model, if somewhat sanctimonious husband, and his influence over his wife was complete. Then he discovered that her property had been strictly secured by her first husband's will, and that, willing as she might be, she was unable to raise money for her new husband's benefit, and was quite powerless to pass to him any of her property by deed of gift. Hereupon the man's nature showed itself. Foolish woman as Mrs. Sneathy might be, she was a loving, indeed, an infatuated wife; but Sneathy repaid her devotion by vulgar derision, never hesitating to state plainly that he had married her for his own profit, and that he considered himself swindled in the result. More, he even proceeded to blows and other practical brutality of a sort only devisable by a mean and ugly nature. This treatment, at first secret, became open, and in the midst of it Mr. Sneathy's penny banks and insurance offices came to a grievous smash all at once, and everybody wondered how Mr. Sneathy kept out of gaol.

Keep out of gaol he did, however, for he had taken care to remain on the safe side of the law, though some of his co-directors learnt the taste of penal servitude. But he was beggared, and lived, as it were, a mere pensioner in his wife's house. Here his brutality increased to a frightful extent, till his wife, already broken in health in consequence, went in constant fear of her life, and Miss Foster passed a life of weeping misery. All her friends' entreaties, however, could not persuade Mrs. Sneathy to obtain a legal separation from her husband. She clung to him with the excuse — for it was no more — that she hoped to win him to kindness by submission, and with a pathetic infatuation that seemed to increase as her bodily strength diminished.

Henry and Robert, as may be supposed, were anything but silent in these circumstances. Indeed, they broke out violently again and again, and more than once went near permanently injuring their worthy father-in-law. Once especially, when Sneathy, absolutely without provocation, made a motion to strike his wife in their presence, there was a fearful scene. The two sprang at him like wild beasts, knocked him down and dragged him to the balcony with the intention of throwing him out of the window. But Mrs. Sneathy impeded them, hysterically imploring them to desist.

"If you lift your hand to my mother," roared Henry, gripping Sneathy by the throat till his fat face turned blue, and banging his head against the wall, "if you lift your hand to my mother again I'll chop it off — I will! I'll chop it off and drive it down your throat!"

"We'll do worse," said Robert, white and frantic with passion, "we'll hang you — hang you to the door! You're a proved liar and thief, and you're worse than a common murderer. I'd hang you to the front door for two-pence!"

For a few days Sneathy was comparatively quiet, cowed by their violence. Then he took to venting redoubled spite on his unfortunate wife, always in the absence of her sons, well aware that she would never inform them. On their part, finding him apparently better behaved in consequence of their attack, they thought to maintain his wholesome terror, and scarcely passed him without a menace, taking a fiendish delight in repeating the threats they had used during the scene, by way of keeping it present to his mind.

"Take care of your hands, sir," they would say. "Keep them to yourself, or, by George, we'll take 'em off with a billhook!"

But his revenge for all this Sneathy took unobserved on their mother. Truly a miserable household.

Soon, however, the brothers left home, and went to London by way of looking for a profession. Henry began a belated study of medicine, and Robert made a pretence of reading for the bar. Indeed, their departure was as much as anything a consequence of the earnest entreaty of their sister, who saw that their presence at home was an exasperation to Sneathy, and aggravated her mother's secret sufferings. They went, therefore; but at Ranworth things became worse.

Little was allowed to be known outside the house, but it was broadly said that Mr. Sneathy's behavior had now become outrageous beyond description. Servants left faster than new ones could be found, and gave their late employer the character of a raving maniac. Once, indeed, he committed himself in the village, attacking with his walking-stick an inoffensive tradesman who had accidentally brushed against him, and immediately running home. This assault had to be compounded for by a payment of fifty pounds. And then Henry and Robert Foster received a most urgent letter from their sister requesting their immediate presence at home.

They went at once, of course, and the servants' account of what occurred was this. When the brothers arrived Mr. Sneathy had just left the house. The brothers were shut up with their mother and sister for about a quarter of an hour, and then left them and came out to the stable yard together. The coachman (he was a new man, who had only arrived the day before) overheard a little of their talk as they stood by the door.

Mr. Henry said that "the thing must be done, and at once. There are two of us, so that it ought to be easy enough." And afterwards Mr. Robert said, "You'll know best how to go about it, as a doctor." After which Mr. Henry came towards the coachman and asked in what direction Mr. Sneathy had gone. The coachman replied that it was in the direction of Ratherby Wood, by the winding footpath that led through it. But as he spoke he distinctly with the corner of his eye saw the other brother take a halter from a hook by the stable door and put it into his coat pocket.

So far for the earlier events, whereof I learned later bit by bit. It was on the day of the arrival of the brothers Foster at their old home, and, indeed, little more than two hours after the incident last set down, that news of Mr. Sneathy came to Colonel Brett's place, where Holmes and I were sitting and chatting with the Colonel. The news was that Mr. Sneathy had committed suicide — had been found hanging, in fact, to a tree in Ratherby Wood, just by the side of the footpath.

Holmes and I had of course at this time never heard of Sneathy, and the Colonel told us what little he knew. He had never spoken to the man, he said — indeed, nobody in the place outside Ranworth would have anything to do with him. "He's certainly been an unholy scoundrel over those poor people's banks," said my uncle, "and if what they say's true, he's been about as bad as possible to his wretched wife. He must have been pretty miserable, too, with all his scoundrelism, for he was a completely ruined man, without a chance of retrieving his position, and detested by everybody. Indeed, some of his recent doings, if what I have heard is to be relied on, have been very much those of a madman. So that, on the whole, I'm not much surprised. Suicide's about the only crime, I suppose, that he has never experimented with till now, and, indeed, it's rather a service to the world at large — his only service, I expect."

The Colonel sent a man to make further inquiries, and presently this man returned with the news that now it was said that Mr. Sneathy had not committed suicide, but had been murdered. And hard on the man's heels came Mr. Hardwick, a neighbor of my uncle's and a fellow J. P. He had had the case reported to him, it seemed, as soon as the body had been found, and had at once gone to the spot. He had found the body hanging — *and with the right hand cut off.*

"It's a murder, Brett," he said, "without doubt — a most horrible case of murder and mutilation. The hand is cut off and taken away, but whether the atrocity was committed before or after the hanging of course I can't say. But the missing hand makes it plainly a case of murder, and not suicide. I've come to consult you about issuing a warrant, for I think there's no doubt as to the identity of the murderers."

"That's a good job," said the Colonel, "else we should have had some work for Mr. Sherlock Holmes here, which wouldn't be fair, as he's taking a rest. Whom do you think of having arrested?"

"The two young Fosters. It's plain as it can be — and a most revolting crime too, bad as Sneathy may have been. They came down from London today and went out deliberately to it, it's clear. They were heard talking of it, asked as to the direction in which he had gone, and followed him — and with a rope."

"Isn't that rather an unusual form of murder — hanging?" Holmes remarked.

"Perhaps it is," Mr. Hardwick replied; "but it's the case here plain enough. It seems, in fact, that they had a way of threatening to hang him and even to cut off his hand if he used it to strike their mother. So that they appear to have carried out what might have seemed mere idle threats in a diabolically savage way. Of course they *may* have strangled him first and hanged him after, by way of carrying out their threat and venting their spite on the mutilated body. But that they did it is plain enough for me. I've spent an hour or two over it, and feel I am certainly more than justified in ordering their apprehension. Indeed, they were with him at the time, as I have found by their tracks on the footpath through the wood."

The Colonel turned to Sherlock Holmes. "Mr. Hardwick, you must know," he said, "is by way of being an amateur in your particular line — and a very good amateur, too, I should say, judging by a case or two I have known in this county."

Holmes bowed, and laughingly expressed a fear lest Mr. Hardwick should come to London and supplant him altogether. "This seems a curious case," he added. "If you don't mind, I think I should like to take a glance at the tracks and whatever other traces there may be, just by way of keeping my hand in."

"Certainly," Mr. Hardwick replied, brightening. "I should of all things like to have Mr. Holmes's opinions on the observations

I have made — just for my own gratification. As to his opinion — there can be no room for doubt; the thing is plain."

With many promises not to be late for dinner, we left my uncle and walked with Mr. Hardwick in the direction of Ratherby Wood. It was an unfrequented part, he told us, and by particular care he had managed, he hoped, to prevent the rumor spreading to the village yet, so that we might hope to find the trails not yet overlaid. It was a man of his own, he said, who, making a short cut through the wood, had come upon the body hanging, and had run immediately to inform him. With this man he had gone back, cut down the body, and made his observations. He had followed the trail backward to Ranworth, and there had found the new coachman, who had once been in his own service. From him he had learned the doings of the brothers Foster as they left the place, and from him he had ascertained that they had not then returned. Then, leaving his man by the body, he had come straight to my uncle's.

Presently we came on the footpath leading from Ranworth across the field to Ratherby Wood. It was a mere trail of bare earth worn by successive feet amid the grass. It was damp, and we all stooped and examined the footmarks that were to be seen on it. They all pointed one way — towards the wood in the distance.

"Fortunately it's not a greatly frequented path," Mr. Hardwick said. "You see, there are the marks of three pairs of feet only, and as first Sneathy and then both of the brothers came this way, these footmarks must be theirs. Which are Sneathy's is plain — they are these large flat ones. If you notice, they are all distinctly visible in the centre of the track, showing plainly that they belong to the man who walked alone, which was Sneathy. Of the others, the marks of the *outside* feet — the left on the left side and the right on the right — are often not visible. Clearly they belong to two men walking side by side, and more often than not treading, with their outer feet, on the grass at the side. And where these happen to drop on the same spot as the marks in the middle they cover them. Plainly they are the footmarks of

Henry and Robert Foster, made as they followed Sneathy. Don't you agree with me Mr. Holmes?"

"Oh yes, that's very plain. You have a better pair of eyes than most people, Mr. Hardwick, and a good idea of using them, too. We will go into the wood now. As a matter of fact I can pretty clearly distinguish most of the other footmarks — those on the grass; but that's a matter of much training."

We followed the footpath, keeping on the grass at its side, in case it should be desirable to refer again to the foot-tracks. For some little distance into the wood the tracks continued as before, those of the brothers overlaying those of Sneathy. Then there was a difference. The path here was broader and muddy, because of the proximity of trees, and suddenly the outer footprints separated, and no more overlay the larger ones in the centre, but proceeded at an equal distance on either side of them.

"See there," cried Mr. Hardwick, pointing triumphantly to the spot, "this is where they over took him, and walked on either side. The body was found only a little farther on — you could see the place now if the path didn't zigzag about so."

Holmes said nothing, but stooped and examined the tracks at the sides with great care and evident thought, spanning the distances between them comparatively with his arms. Then he rose and stepped lightly from one mark to another, taking care not to tread on the mark itself. "Very good," he said shortly on finishing his examination. "We'll go on."

We went on, and presently came to the place where the body lay. Here the ground sloped from the left down towards the right, and a tiny streamlet, a mere trickle of a foot or two wide, ran across the path. In rainy seasons it was probably wider, for all the earth and clay had been washed away for some feet on each side, leaving flat, bare and very coarse gravel, on which the trail was lost. Just beyond this, and to the left, the body lay on a grassy knoll under the limb of a tree, from which still depended a part of the cut rope. It was not a pleasant sight. The man was a soft, fleshy creature, probably rather under than over the medium height, and he lay there, with his stretched neck and protruding tongue, a revolting object. His right arm lay by his side, and the stump of the wrist was clotted with black blood. Mr. Hardwick's man was still in charge, seemingly little pleased with his job, and a few yards off stood a couple of countrymen looking on.

Holmes asked from which direction these men had come, and having ascertained and noticed their footmarks, he asked them to stay exactly where they were, to avoid confusing such other tracks as might be seen. Then he addressed himself to his examination. "*First*," he said, glancing up at the branch, that was scarce a yard above his head, "this rope has been here for some time."

"Yes," Mr. Hardwick replied, "it's an old swing rope. Some children used it in the summer, but it got partly cut away, and the odd couple of yards has been hanging since."

"Ah," said Holmes, "then if the Fosters did this they were saved some trouble by the chance, and were able to take their halter back with them — and so avoid *one* chance of detection." He very closely scrutinized the top of a tree stump, probably the relic of a tree that had been cut down long before, and then addressed himself to the body.

"When you cut it down," he said, "did it fall in a heap?"

"No, my man eased it down to some extent."

"Not on to its face?"

"Oh no. On to its back, just as it is now." Mr. Hardwick saw that Holmes was looking at muddy marks on each of the corpse's knees, to one of which a small leaf clung, and at one or two other marks of the same sort on the fore part of the dress. "That seems to show pretty plainly," he said, "that he must have struggled with them and was thrown forward, doesn't it?"

Holmes did not reply, but gingerly lifted the right arm by its sleeve. "Is either of the brothers Foster left-handed?" he asked.

"No, I think not. Here, Bennett, you have seen plenty of their doings — cricket, shooting, and so on — do you remember if either is left-handed?"

"Nayther, sir," Mr. Hardwick's man answered. "Both on 'em's right-handed."

Holmes lifted the lapel of the coat and attentively regarded a small rent in it. The dead man's hat lay near, and after a few glances at that, Holmes dropped it and turned his attention to the hair. This was coarse and dark and long, and brushed straight back with no parting.

"This doesn't look very symmetrical, does it?" Holmes remarked, pointing to the locks over the right ear. They were shorter just there than on the other side, and apparently very clumsily cut, whereas in every other part the hair appeared to be rather well and carefully trimmed. Mr. Hardwick said nothing, but fidgeted a little, as though he considered that valuable time was being wasted over irrelevant trivialities.

Presently, however, he spoke. "There's very little to be learned from the body, is there?" he said. "I think I'm quite justified in ordering their arrest, eh? — indeed, I've wasted too much time already."

Holmes was groping about among some bushes behind the tree from which the corpse had been taken. When he answered, he said, "I don't think I should do anything of the sort just now, Mr. Hardwick. As a matter of fact, I *fancy*" — this word with an emphasis — "that the brothers Foster may not have seen this man Sneathy at all today."

"Not seen him? Why, my dear sir, there's no question of it. It's certain, absolutely. The evidence is positive. The fact of the threats and of the body being found treated so is pretty well enough, I should think. But that's nothing — look at those footmarks. They've walked along with him, one each side, without a possible doubt; plainly they were the last people with him, in any case. And you don't mean to ask anybody to believe that the dead man, even if he hanged himself, cut off his own hand first. Even if you do, where's the hand? And even putting aside all these considerations, each a complete case in itself, the Fosters *must* at least have seen the body as they came past, and yet nothing has been heard of them yet. Why didn't they spread the alarm? They went straight away in the opposite direction from home — there are their footmarks, which you've not seen yet, beyond the gravel."

Holmes stepped over to where the patch of clean gravel ceased, at the opposite side to that from which we had approached the brook, and there, sure enough, were the now familiar footmarks of the brothers leading away from the scene of Sneathy's end. "Yes," Holmes said, "I see them. Of course, Mr. Hardwick, you'll do what seems right in your own eyes, and in any case not much harm will be done by the arrest beyond a terrible fright for that unfortunate family. Nevertheless, if you care for my impression, it is, as I have said, that the Fosters have not seen Sneathy today."

"But what about the hand?"

"As to that I have a conjecture, but as yet it is only a conjecture, and if I told it you would probably call it absurd — certainly you'd disregard it, and perhaps quite excusably. The case is a complicated one, and, if there is anything at all in my conjecture, one of the most remarkable I have ever had to do with. It interests me intensely, and I shall devote a little time now to following up the theory I have formed. You have, I suppose, already communicated with the police?"

"I wired to Shopperton at once, as soon as I heard of the matter. It's a twelve miles drive, but I wonder the police have not arrived yet. They can't be long; I don't know where the village constable has got to, but in any case *he* wouldn't be much good. But as to your idea that the Fosters can't be suspected — well, nobody could respect your opinion, Mr. Holmes, more than myself, but really, just think. The notion's impossible — fifty-fold impossible. As soon as the police arrive I shall have that trail followed and the Fosters apprehended. I should be a fool if I didn't."

"Very well, Mr. Hardwick," Holmes replied; "you'll do what you consider your duty, of course, and quite properly, though I *would* recommend you to take another glance at those three trails in the path. I shall take a look in this direction." And he turned up by the side of the streamlet, keeping on the gravel at its side.

I followed. We climbed the rising ground, and presently, among the trees, came to the place where the little rill emerged from the broken ground in the highest part of the wood. Here the clean ground ceased, and there was a large patch of wet clayey earth. Several marks left by the feet of cattle were there, and one or two human footmarks. Two of these (a pair), the newest and the most distinct, Holmes studied carefully, and measured each direction.

"Notice these marks," he said. "They may be of importance or they may not — that we shall see. Fortunately they are very distinctive — the right boot is a badly worn one, and a small tag of leather, where the soul is damaged, is doubled over and trodden into the soft earth. Nothing could be luckier. Clearly they are the most recent footsteps in this direction — from the main road, which lies right ahead, through the rest of the wood."

"Then you think somebody else has been on the scene of the tragedy, beside the victim and the brothers?" I said.

"Yes, I do. But hark; there is a vehicle in the road. Can you see between the trees? Yes, it is the police cart. We shall be able to report its arrival to Mr. Hardwick as we go down."

We turned and walked rapidly down the incline to where we had come from. Mr. Hardwick and his man were still there, and another rustic had arrived to gape. We told Mr. Hardwick that he might expect the police presently, and proceeded along the gravel skirting the stream, toward the lower part of the wood.

Here Holmes proceeded very cautiously, keeping a sharp look-out on either side for footprints on the neighboring soft ground. There were none, however, for the gravel margin of the stream made a sort of footpath of itself, and the trees and undergrowth were close and thick on each side. At the bottom we emerged from the wood on a small piece of open ground skirting a lane, and here, just by the side of the lane, where the stream fell into a trench, Holmes suddenly pounced on another footmark. He was unusually excited.

"See," he said, "here it is — the right foot with its broken leather, and the corresponding left foot on the damp edge of the lane itself. He — the man with the broken shoe — has walked on the hard gravel all the way down from the source of the stream, and his is the only trail unaccounted for near the body. Come, Brett, we've an adventure on foot. Do you care to let your uncle's dinner go by the board, and follow?"

"Can't we go back and tell him?"

"No — there's no time to lose; we must follow up this man — or at least I must. You go or stay, of course, as you think best."

I hesitated a moment, picturing to myself the excellent Colonel as he would appear after waiting dinner an hour or two for us, but decided to go. "At any rate," I said, "if the way lies along the roads we shall probably meet somebody going in the direction of Ratherby who will take a message. But what is your theory? I don't understand at all. I must say everything Hardwick said seemed to me to be beyond question. There were the tracks to prove that the three had walked together to the spot, and that the brothers had gone on alone; and every other circumstance pointed the same way. Then, what possible motive could anybody else about here have for such a crime? Unless, indeed, it were one of the people defrauded by Sneathy's late companies."

"The motive," said Holmes, "is, I fancy, a most extraordinary — indeed, a weird one. A thing as of centuries ago. Ask me no questions — I think you will be a little surprised before very long. But come, we must move." And we mended our pace along the lane.

The lane, by the bye, was hard and firm, with scarcely a spot where a track might be left, except in places at the sides; and at these places Holmes never gave a glance. At the end the lane turned into a by-road, and at the turning Holmes stopped and scrutinized the ground closely. There was nothing like a recognizable footmark to be seen; but almost immediately Holmes turned off to the right, and we continued our brisk march without a glance at the road.

"How did you judge which way to turn then?" I asked.

"Didn't you see?" replied Holmes; "I'll show you at the next turning."

Half a mile farther on the road forked, and here Holmes stooped and pointed silently to a couple of small twigs, placed crosswise, with the longer twig of the two pointing down the branch of the road to the left. We took the branch to the left, and went on.

"Our man's making a mistake," Holmes observed. "He leaves his friends' messages lying about for his enemies to read."

We hurried forward with scarcely a word. I was almost too bewildered by what Holmes had said and done to formulate anything like a reasonable guess as to what our expedition tended, or even to make an effective inquiry — though, after what Holmes had said, I knew that would be useless. Who was this mysterious man with the broken shoe? What had he to do with the murder of Sneathy? What did the mutilation mean? And who were his friends who left him signs and messages by means of crossed twigs?

We met a man, by whom I sent a short note to my uncle, and soon after we turned into a main road. Here again, at the corner, was the curious message of twigs. A cart-wheel had passed over and crushed them, but it had not so far displaced them as to cause any doubt that the direction to take was to the right. At an inn a little farther along we entered, and Holmes bought a pint of Irish whisky and a flat bottle to hold it in, as well as a loaf of bread and some cheese, which we carried away wrapped in paper.

"This will have to do for our dinner," Holmes said as we emerged.

"But we're not going to drink a pint of common whisky between us?" I asked in some astonishment.

"Never mind," Holmes answered with a smile. "Perhaps we'll find somebody to help us — somebody not so fastidious as yourself as to quality."

Now we hurried — hurried more than ever, for it was beginning to get dusk, and Holmes feared a difficulty in finding and reading the twig signs in the dark. Two more turnings we made, each with its silent direction — the crossed twigs. To me there was something almost weird and creepy in this curious hunt for the invisible and incomprehensible, guided faithfully and persistently at every turn by this now unmistakable signal. After the second turning we broke into a trot along a long, winding lane, but presently Holmes's hand fell on my shoulder, and we stopped. He pointed ahead, where some large object, round a bend of the hedge was illuminated as though by a light from below.

"We will walk now," Holmes said. "Remember that we are on a walking tour, and have come along here entirely by accident."

We proceeded at a swinging walk, Holmes whistling gaily. Soon we turned the bend, and saw that the large object was a traveling van drawn up with two others on a space of grass by the side of the lane. It was a gipsy encampment, the caravan having apparently only lately stopped, for a man was still engaged in tugging at the rope of a tent that stood near the vans. Two or three sullen-looking ruffians lay about a fire which burned in the space left in the middle of the encampment. A woman stood at the door of one van with a large kettle in her hand, and at the foot of the steps below her a more pleasant-looking old man sat on an inverted pail. Holmes swung towards the fire from the road, and with an indescribable mixture of slouch, bow, and smile addressed the company generally with "*Kooshto bock, pals!* "[1]

The men on the ground took no notice, but continued to stare doggedly before them. The man working at the tent looked round quickly for a moment, and the old man on the bucket looked up and nodded.

Quick to see the most likely friend, Holmes at once went up to the old man, extending his hand, "*Sarshin, daddo?*" he said; "*Dell mandy tooty's varst.*"[2]

The old man smiled and shook hands, though without speaking. Then Holmes proceeded, producing the flat bottle of whisky, "*Tatty for pawny, chals. Dell mandy the pawny, and lell posh the tatty.*"[3]

The whisky did it. We were Romany ryes in twenty minutes or less, and had already been taking tea with the gypsies for half the time. The two or three we had found about the fire were still reserved, but these, I found, were only half-gypsies, and understood very little Romany. One or two others, however, including the old man, were of purer breed, and talked freely, as did one of the women. They were Lees, they said, and expected to be on Wirksby racecourse in three days' time. We, too, were *pirimengroes*, or travelers, Holmes explained, and might look to see them on the course.

Then he fell to telling gipsy stories, and they to telling others back, to my intense mystification. Holmes explained afterwards that they were mostly stories of poaching, with now and again a horse-coping anecdote thrown in. Since then I have learned enough of Romany to take my part in such a conversation, but at the time a word or two here and there was all I could understand. In all this talk the man we had first noticed stretching the tent-rope took very little interest, but lay, with his head away from the fire, smoking his pipe. He was a much darker man than any other present — had, in fact, the appearance of a man of even a swarthier face than that of the others about us.

Presently, in the middle of a long and, of course, to me unintelligible story by the old man, I caught Holmes's eye. He lifted one eyebrow almost imperceptibly, and glanced for a single moment at his walking-stick. Then I saw that it was pointed toward the feet of the very dark man, who had not yet spoken. One leg was thrown over the others as he lay, with the soles of his shoes presented toward the fire, and in its glare I saw — that the right sole was worn and broken, and that a small triangular tag of leather was doubled over beneath in just the place we knew of from the prints in Ratherby Wood.

I could not take my eyes off that man with his broken shoe. There lay the secret, the whole mystery of the fantastic crime in Ratherby Wood centered in that shabby ruffian. What was it?

But Holmes went on, talking and joking furiously. The men who were not speaking mostly smoked gloomily, but whenever one spoke, he became animated and lively. I had attempted once or twice to join in, though my efforts were not particularly successful, except in inducing one man to offer me tobacco from his box — tobacco that almost made me giddy in the smell. He tried some of mine in exchange, and though he praised it with native politeness, and smoked the pipe through, I could see that my Hignett mixture was poor stuff in his estimation, compared with the awful tobacco in his own box.

Presently the man with the broken shoe got up, slouched over to his tent, and disappeared. Then said Holmes (I translate):

"You're not all Lees here, I see?"

"Yes, *pal*, all Lees."

"But *he's* not a Lee?" and Holmes jerked his head towards the tent.

"Why not a Lee, *pal*? We be Lees, and he is with us. Thus he is a Lee."

"Oh yes, of course. But I know he is from over the *pawny*. Come, I'll guess the *tem*[4] he comes from — it's from Roumania, eh? Perhaps the Wallachian part?"

The men looked at one another, and then the old Lee said:

"You're right, pal. You're cleverer than we took you for. That is what they calls his *tem*. He is a petulengro,[5] and he comes with us to shoe the *gries*[6] and mend the *vardoes*.[7] But he is with us, and so he is a Lee."

The talk and the smoke went on, and presently the man with the broken shoe returned, and lay down again. Then, when the whisky had all gone, and Holmes, with some excuse that I did not understand, had begged a piece of cord from one of the men, we left in a chorus of *kooshto rardies*.[8]

By this time it was nearly ten o'clock. We walked briskly till we came back again to the inn where we had bought the whisky. Here Holmes, after some little trouble, succeeded in hiring a village cart, and while the driver was harnessing the horse, cut a couple of short sticks from the hedge. These, being each divided into two, made four short, stout pieces of something less than six inches long apiece. Then Holmes joined them together in pairs, each pair being connected from centre to centre by about nine or ten inches of the cord he had brought from the gypsies' camp. These done, he handed one pair to me. "Handcuffs," he explained, "and no bad ones either. See — you use them so." And he passed the cord round my wrist, gripping the two handles, and giving them a slight twist that sufficiently convinced me of the excruciating pain that might be inflicted by a vigorous turn, and the utter helplessness of a prisoner thus secured in the hands of captors prepared to use their instruments.

"Whom are these for?" I asked. "The man with the broken shoe?"

Holmes nodded.

"Yes," he said. "I expect we shall find him out alone about midnight. You know how to use these now."

It was fully eleven before the cart was ready and we started. A quarter of a mile or so from the gipsy encampment Holmes stopped the cart and gave the driver instructions to wait. We got through the hedge, and made our way on the soft ground behind it in the direction of the vans and the tent.

"Roll up your handkerchief," Holmes whispered, "into a tight pad. The moment I grab him, ram it into his mouth — *well* in, mind, so that it doesn't easily fall out. Probably he will be stooping — that will make it easier; we can pull him suddenly backward. Now be quiet."

We kept on till nothing but the hedge divided us from the space whereon stood the encampment. It was now nearer twelve o'clock than eleven, but the time we waited seemed endless. But time is not eternity after all, and at last we heard a move in the tent. A minute after, the man we sought was standing before us. He made straight for a gap in the hedge which we had passed on our way, and we crouched low and waited. He emerged on our side of the hedge with his back towards us, and began walking, as we had walked, behind the hedge, but in the opposite direction. We followed.

He carried something in his hand that looked like a large bundle of sticks and twigs, and he appeared to be as anxious to be secret as we ourselves. From time to time he stopped and listened; fortunately there was no moon, or in turning about, as he did once or twice, he would probably have observed us. The field sloped downward just before us, and there was another hedge at right angles, leading down to a slight hollow. To this hollow the man made his way, and in the shade of the new hedge we followed. Presently he stopped suddenly, stooped, and deposited his bundle on the ground before him. Crouching before it, he produced matches from his pocket, struck one, and in a moment had a fire of twigs and small branches, that sent up a heavy white smoke. What all this portended I could not imagine, but a sense of the weirdness of the whole adventure came upon me unchecked. The horrible corpse in the wood, with its severed wrist, Holmes's enigmatical forebodings, the mysterious tracking of the man with the broken shoe, the scene round the gypsies' fire, and now the strange behavior of this man, whose connection with the tragedy was so intimate and yet so inexplicable — all these things contributed to make up a tale of but a few hours' duration, but of an inscrutable impressiveness that I began to feel in my nerves.

The man bent a thin stick double, and using it as a pair of tongs, held some indistinguishable object over the flames before him. Excited as I was, I could not help noticing that he bent and held the stick with his left hand. We crept stealthily nearer, and as I stood scarcely three yards behind him and looked over his shoulder, the form of the object stood out clear and black against the dull red of the flame. It was a *human hand*.

I suppose I may have somehow betrayed my amazement and horror to my companion's sharp eyes, for suddenly I felt his hand tightly grip my arm just above the elbow. I turned, and found his face close by mine and his finger raised warningly. Then I saw him produce his wrist-grip and make a motion with his palm toward his mouth, which I understood to be intended to remind me of the gag. We stepped forward.

The man turned his horrible cookery over and over above the crackling sticks, as though to smoke and dry it in every part. I saw Holmes's hand reach out toward him, and in a flash we had pulled him back over his heels and I had driven the gag between his teeth as he opened his mouth. We seized his wrists in the cords at once, and I shall never forget the man's look of ghastly, frantic terror as he lay on the ground. When I knew more I understood the reason of this.

Holmes took both wrist-holds in one hand and drove the gag entirely into the man's mouth, so that he almost choked. A piece of sacking lay near the fire, and by Holmes's request I dropped that awful hand from the wooden twigs upon it and rolled it up in a parcel — it was, no doubt, what the sacking had been brought for. Then we lifted the man to his feet and hurried him in the direction of the cart. The whole capture could not have occupied thirty seconds, and as I stumbled over the rough field at the man's left elbow I could only think of the thing as one thinks of a dream that one knows all the time *is* a dream.

But presently the man, who had been walking quietly, though gasping, sniffing and choking because of the tightly rolled handkerchief in his mouth — presently he made a sudden dive, thinking doubtless to get his wrists free by surprise. But Holmes was alert, and gave them a twist that made him roll his head with a dismal, stifled yell, and with the opening of his mouth, by some chance the gag fell away. Immediately the man roared aloud for help.

"Quick," said Holmes, "drag him along — they'll hear in the vans. Bring the hand!"

I seized the fallen handkerchief and crammed it over the man's mouth as well as I might, and together we made as much of a trot as we could, dragging the man between us, while Holmes checked any reluctance on his part by a timely wrench of the wristholds. It was a hard two hundred and fifty yards to the lane even for us — for the gipsy it must have been a bad minute and a half indeed. Once more as we went over the uneven ground he managed to get out a shout, and we thought we heard a distinct reply from somewhere in the direction of the encampment.

We pulled him over a stile in a tangle; and dragged and pushed him through a small hedge-gap all in a heap. Here we were but a short distance from the cart, and into that we flung him without wasting time or tenderness, to the intense consternation of the driver, who, I believe, very nearly set up a cry for help on his own account. Once in the cart, however, I seized the reins and the whip myself and, leaving Holmes to take care of the prisoner, put the turn-out along toward Ratherby at as near ten miles an hour as it could go.

We made first for Mr. Hardwick's, but he, we found, was with my uncle, so we followed him. The arrest of the Fosters had been effected, we learned, not very long after we had left the wood, as they returned by another route to Ranworth. We brought our prisoner into the Colonel's library, where he and Mr. Hardwick were sitting.

"I'm not quite sure what we can charge him with unless it's anatomical robbery," Holmes remarked, "but here's the criminal."

The man only looked down, with a sulkily impenetrable countenance. Holmes spoke to him once or twice, and at last he said, in a strange accent, something that sounded like "*kekin jin-navvy.*"

"*Keck jin?*"[9] asked Holmes, in the loud, clear tone one instinctively adopts in talking to a foreigner, "*Keckeno jinny?*"

The man understood and shook his head, but not another word would he say or another question answer.

"He's a foreign gipsy," Holmes explained, "just as I thought — a Wallachian, in fact. Theirs is an older and purer dialect than that of the English gypsies, and only some of the root-words are alike. But I think we can make him explain tomorrow that the Fosters at least had nothing to do with, at any rate, cutting off Sneathy's hand. Here it is, I think." And he gingerly lifted the folds of sacking from the ghastly object as it lay on the table, and then covered it up again.

"But what — what does it all mean?" Mr. Hardwick said in bewildered astonishment. "Do you mean this man was an accomplice?"

"Not at all — the case was one of suicide, as I think you'll agree, when I've explained. This man simply found the body hanging and stole the hand."

"But what in the world for?"

"For the Hand of Glory. Eh?" He turned to the gipsy and pointed to the hand on the table: "*Yag-varst,*[10] eh?"

There was a quick gleam of intelligence in the man's eye, but he said nothing. As for myself I was more than astounded. Could it be possible that the old superstition of the Hand of Glory remained alive in a practical shape at this day?

"You know the superstition, of course," Holmes said. "It did exist in this country in the last century, when there were plenty of dead men hanging at cross-roads, and so on. On the Continent, in some places, it has survived later. Among the Wallachian gypsies it has always been a great article of belief, and the superstition is quite active still. The belief is that the right hand of a hanged man, cut off and dried over the smoke of certain wood and herbs, and then provided with wicks at each finger made of the dead man's hair, becomes, when lighted at each wick (the wicks are greased, of course), a charm, whereby a thief may walk without hindrance where he pleases in a strange house, push open all doors and take what he likes. Nobody can stop him, for everybody the Hand of Glory approaches is made helpless, and can neither move nor speak. You may remember there was some talk of 'thieves' candles' in connection with the horrible series of Whitechapel murders not long ago. That is only one form of the cult of the Hand of Glory."

"Yes," my uncle said, "I remember reading so. There is a story about it in the Ingoldsby Legends, too, I believe."

"There is — it is called 'The Hand of Glory,' in fact. You remember the spell, 'Open lock to the dead man's knock,' and so on. But I think you'd better have the constable up and get this man into safe quarters for the night. He should be searched, of course. I expect they will find on him the hair I noticed to have been cut from Sneathy's head."

The village constable arrived with his iron handcuffs in substitution for those of cord which had so sorely vexed the wrists of our prisoner, and marched him away to the little lock-up on the green.

Then my uncle and Mr. Hardwick turned on Sherlock Holmes with doubts and many questions:

"Why do you call it suicide?" Mr. Hardwick asked. "It is plain the Fosters were with him at the time from the tracks. Do you mean to say that they stood there and watched Sneathy hang himself without interfering?"

"No, I don't," Holmes replied, lighting a cigar. "I think I told you that they never saw Sneathy."

"Yes, you did, and of course that's what they said themselves when they were arrested. But the thing's impossible. Look at the tracks!"

"The tracks are exactly what revealed to me that it was *not* impossible," Holmes returned. "I'll tell you how the case unfolded itself to me from the beginning. As to the information you gathered from the Ranworth coachman, to begin with. The conversation between the Fosters which he overheard might well mean something less serious than murder. What did they say? They had been sent for in a hurry and had just had a short consultation with their mother and sister. Henry said that 'the thing must be done at once'; also that as there were two of them it should be easy. Robert said that Henry, as a doctor, would know best what to do.

"Now you, Colonel Brett, had been saying — before we learned these things from Mr. Hardwick — that Sneathy's behavior of late had become so bad as to seem that of a madman. Then there was the story of his sudden attack on a tradesman in the village, and equally sudden running away — exactly the sort of impulsive, wild thing that madmen do. Why then might it not be reasonable to suppose that Sneathy *had* become mad — more especially considering all the circumstances of the case, his commercial ruin and disgrace and his horrible life with his wife and her family? — had become suddenly much worse and quite uncontrollable, so that the two wretched women left alone with him were driven to send in haste for Henry and Robert to help them? That would account for all.

"The brothers arrive just after Sneathy had gone out. They are told in a hurried interview how affairs stand, and it is decided that Sneathy must be at once secured and confined in an asylum before something serious happens. He has just gone out — something terrible may be happening at this moment. The brothers determine to follow at once and secure him wherever he may be. Then the meaning of their conversation is plain. The thing that 'must be done, and at once,' is the capture of Sneathy and his confinement in an asylum. Henry, as a doctor, would 'know what to do' in regard to the necessary formalities. And they took a halter in case a struggle should ensue and it were found necessary to bind him. Very likely, wasn't it?"

"Well, yes," Mr. Hardwick replied, "it certainly is. It never struck me in that light at all."

"That was because you believed, to begin with, that a murder had been committed, and looked at the preliminary circumstances which you learned after in the light of your conviction. But now, to come to my actual observations. I saw the footmarks across the fields, and agreed with you (it was indeed obvious) that Sneathy had gone that way first, and that the brothers had followed, walking over his tracks. This state of the tracks continued until well into the wood, when suddenly the tracks of the brothers opened out and proceeded on each side of Sneathy's. The simple inference would seem to be, of course, the one you made — that the Fosters had here overtaken Sneathy, and walked one at each side of him.

"But of this I felt by no means certain. Another very simple explanation was available, which might chance to be the true one. It was just at the spot where the brothers' tracks separated that the path became suddenly much muddier, because of the closer overhanging of the trees at the spot. The path was, as was to be expected, wettest in the middle. It would be the most natural thing in the world for two well-dressed young men, on arriving here, to separate so as to walk one on each side of the mud in the middle.

"On the other hand, a man in Sneathy's state (assuming him, for the moment, to be mad and contemplating suicide) would walk straight along the centre of the path, taking no note of mud or anything else. I examined all the tracks very carefully, and my theory was confirmed. The feet of the brothers had everywhere alighted in the driest spots, and the steps were of irregular lengths — which meant, of course, that they were picking their way; while Sneathy's footmarks had never turned aside even for the dirtiest puddle. Here, then, were the rudiments of a theory.

"At the watercourse, of course, the footmarks ceased, because of the hard gravel. The body lay on a knoll at the left — a knoll covered with grass. On this the signs of footmarks were almost undiscoverable, although I am often able to discover tracks in grass that are invisible to others. Here, however, it was almost useless to spend much time in examination, for you and your man had been there, and what slight marks there might be would be indistinguishable one from another.

"Under the branch from which the man had hung there was an old tree stump, with a flat top, where the tree had been sawn off. I examined this, and it became fairly apparent that Sneathy had stood on it when the rope was about his neck — his muddy footprint was plain to see; the mud was not smeared about, you see, as it probably would have been if he had been stood there forcibly and pushed off. It was a simple, clear footprint — another hint at suicide.

"But then arose the objection that you mentioned yourself. Plainly the brothers Foster were following Sneathy, and came this way. Therefore, if he hanged himself before they arrived, it would seem that they must have come across the body. But now I examined the body itself. There was mud on the knees, and clinging to one knee was a small leaf. It was a leaf corresponding to those on the bush behind the tree, and it was not a dead leaf, so must have been just detached.

"After my examination of the body I went to the bush, and there, in the thick of it, were, for me, sufficiently distinct knee-marks, in one of which the knee had crushed a spray of the bush against the ground, and from that spray a leaf was missing. Behind the knee-marks were the indentations of boot-toes in the soft, bare earth under the bush, and thus the thing was plain. The poor lunatic had come in sight of the dangling rope, and the temptation to suicide was irresistible. To people in a deranged state of mind the mere sight of the means of self-destruction is often a temptation impossible to withstand. But at that moment he must have heard the steps — probably the voices — of the brothers behind him on the winding path. He immediately hid in the bush till they had passed. It is probable that seeing who the men were, and conjecturing that they were following him — thinking also, perhaps, of things that had occurred between them and himself — his inclination to self-destruction became completely ungovernable, with the result that you saw.

"But before I inspected the bush I noticed one or two more things about the body. You remember I inquired if either of the brothers Foster was left-handed, and was assured that neither was. But clearly the hand had been cut off by a left-handed man, with a large, sharply pointed knife. For well away to the *right* of where the wrist had hung the knife-point had made a tiny triangular rent in the coat, so that the hand must have been held in the mutilator's right hand, while he used the knife with his left — clearly a left-handed man.

"But most important of all about the body was the jagged hair over the right ear. Everywhere else the hair was well cut and orderly — here it seemed as though a good piece had been, so to speak, *sawn* off. What could anybody want with a dead man's right hand and certain locks of his hair? Then it struck me suddenly — the man was hanged; it was the Hand of Glory!

"Then you will remember I went, at your request, to see the footprints of the Fosters on the part of the path *past* the watercourse. Here again it was muddy in the middle, and the two brothers had walked as far apart as before, although nobody had walked between them. A final proof, if one were needed, of my theory as to the three lines of footprints.

"Now I was to consider how to get at the man who had taken his hand. He should be punished for the mutilation, but beyond that he would be required as a witness. Now all the foot-tracks in the vicinity had been accounted for. There were those of the brothers and of Sneathy, which we have been speaking of; those of the rustics looking on, which, however, stopped a little way off, and did not interfere with our sphere of observation; those of your man, who had cut straight through the wood when he first saw the body, and had come back the same way with you; and our own, which we had been careful to keep away from the others. Consequently there was *no* track of the man who had cut off the hand; therefore it was certain that he must have come along the hard gravel by the watercourse, for that was the only possible path which would not tell the tale. Indeed, it seemed quite a likely path through the wood for a passenger to take, coming from the high ground by the Shopperton road.

"Brett and I left you and traversed the watercourse, both up and down. We found a footprint at the top, left lately by a man with a broken shoe. Right down to the bottom of the watercourse where it emerged from the wood there was no sign on either side of this man having left the gravel. (Where the body was, as you will remember, he would simply have stepped off the gravel on to the grass, which I thought it useless to examine, as I have explained.) But at the bottom, by the lane, the footprint appeared again.

"This then was the direction in which I was to search for a left-handed man with a broken-soled shoe, probably a gipsy — and most probably a foreign gipsy — because a foreign gipsy would be the most likely still to hold the belief in the Hand of Glory. I conjectured the man to be a straggler from a band of gypsies — one who probably had got behind the caravan and had made a short cut across the wood after it; so at the end of the lane I looked for a *patrin*. This is a sign that gypsies leave to guide stragglers following up. Sometimes it is a heap of dead leaves, sometimes a few stones, sometimes a mark on the ground, but more usually a couple of twigs crossed, with the longer twig pointing the road.

"Guided by these *patrins* we came in the end on the gipsy camp just as it was settling down for the night. We made ourselves agreeable (as Brett will probably describe to you better than I can), we left them, and after they had got to sleep we came back and watched for the gentleman who is now in the lock-up. He would, of course, seize the first opportunity of treating his ghastly trophy in the prescribed way, and I guessed he would choose midnight, for that is the time the superstition teaches that the hand should be prepared. We made a few small preparations, collared him, and now you've got him. And I should think the sooner you let the brothers Foster go the better."

"But why didn't you tell me all the conclusions you had arrived at at the time?" asked Mr. Hardwick.

"Well, really," Holmes replied, with a quiet smile, "you were so positive, and some of the traces I relied on were so small, that it would probably have meant a long argument and a loss of time. But more than that, confess, if I had told you bluntly that Sneathy's hand had been taken away to make a mediæval charm to enable a thief to pass through a locked door and steal plate calmly under the owner's nose, what *would* you have said?"

"Well, well, perhaps I *should* have been a little skeptical. Appearances combined so completely to point to the Fosters as murderers that any other explanation almost would have seemed unlikely to me, and *that* — well no, I confess, I shouldn't have believed in it. But it is a startling thing to find such superstitions alive now-a-days."

"Yes, perhaps it is. Yet we find survivals of the sort very frequently. The Wallachians, however, are horribly superstitious still — the gypsies among them are, of course, worse. Don't you remember the case reported a few months ago, in which a child was drowned as a sacrifice in Wallachia in order to bring rain? And that was not done by gypsies either. Even in England, as late as 1865, a poor paralyzed Frenchman was killed by being 'swum' for witchcraft — that was in Essex. And less atrocious cases of belief in wizardry occur again and again even now."

Then Mr. Hardwick and my uncle fell into a discussion as to how the gipsy in the lock-up could be legally punished. Mr. Hardwick thought it should be treated as a theft of a portion of a dead body, but my uncle fancied there was a penalty for mutilation of a dead body *per se*, though he could not point to the statute. As it happened, however, they were saved the trouble of arriving at a decision, for in the morning he was discovered to have escaped. He had been left, of course, with free hands, and had occupied the night in wrenching out the bars at the top of the back wall of the little prison-shed (it had stood on the green for a hundred and fifty years) and climbing out. He was not found again, and a month or two later the Foster family left the district entirely.

[1] "Good luck, brothers!"
[2] "How do you do, father? Give me your hand."
[3] "Spirits for water, lads. Give me the water and take your share of the spirits."
[4] Country
[5] Smith
[6] Horses
[7] Vans
[8] Good night
[9] "Not understand?"
[10] Fire-hand

The Case of Laker, Absconded

There were several of the larger London banks and insurance offices from which Holmes held a sort of general retainer as detective adviser, in fulfillment of which he was regularly consulted as to the measures to be taken in different cases of fraud, forgery, theft, and so forth, which it might be the misfortune of the particular firms to encounter. The more important and intricate of these cases were placed in his hands entirely, with separate commissions, in the usual way. One of the most important companies of the sort was the General Guarantee Society, an insurance corporation which, among other risks, took those of the integrity of secretaries, clerks, and cashiers. In the case of a cash-box elopement on the part of any person guaranteed by the society, the directors were naturally anxious for a speedy capture of the culprit, and more especially of the booty, before too much of it was spent, in order to lighten the claim upon their funds, and in work of this sort Holmes was times engaged, either in general advice and direction, or in the actual pursuit of the plunder and the plunderer.

One morning, Holmes received an urgent message from the General Guarantee Society, requesting his attention to a robbery which had taken place on the previous day. He had gleaned some hint of the case from the morning paper, wherein appeared a short paragraph, which ran thus:

> *Serious Bank Robbery. In the course of yesterday a clerk employed by Messrs. Liddle, Neal & Liddle, the well-known bankers, disappeared, having in his possession a large sum of money, the property of his employers — a sum reported to be rather over £15,000. It would seem that he had been entrusted to collect the money in his capacity of "walk-clerk" from various other banks and trading concerns during the morning, but failed to return*

at the usual time. A large number of the notes which he received had been cashed at the Bank of England before suspicion was aroused. We understand that Detective-Inspector Plummer, of Scotland Yard, has the case in hand.

The clerk, whose name was Charles William Laker, had, it appeared from the message, been guaranteed in the usual way by the General Guarantee Society, and Holmes's presence at the office was at once desired, in order that steps might quickly be taken for the man's apprehension, and in the recovery, at any rate, of as much of the booty as possible.

A smart hansom brought Holmes to Threadneedle Street in a bare quarter of an hour, and there a few minutes' talk with the manager, Mr. Lyster, put him in possession of the main facts of the case, which appeared to be simple. Charles William Laker was twenty-five years of age, and had been in the employ of Messrs. Liddle, Neal & Liddle for something more than seven years — since he left school, in fact — and until the previous day there had been nothing in his conduct to complain of. His duties as walk-clerk consisted in making a certain round, beginning at about half-past ten each morning. There were a certain number of the more important banks between which and Messrs. Liddle, Neal & Liddle there were daily transactions, and a few smaller semi-private banks and merchant firms acting as financial agents, with whom there was business intercourse of less importance and regularity; and each of these, as necessary, he visited in turn, collecting cash due on bills and other instruments of a like nature. He carried a wallet, fastened securely to his person by a chain, and this wallet contained the bills and the cash. Usually at the end of his round, when all his bills had been converted into cash, the wallet held very large sums. His work and responsibilities, in fine, were those common to walk-clerks in all banks.

On the day of the robbery he had started out as usual — possibly a little earlier than was customary — and the bills and other securities in his possession represented considerably more

80

than £15,000. It had been ascertained that he had called in the usual way at each establishment on the round, and had transacted his business at the last place by about a quarter-past one, being then, without doubt, in possession of cash to the full value of the bills negotiated. After that, Mr. Lyster said, yesterday's report was that nothing more had been heard of him. But this morning there had been a message to the effect that he had been traced out of the country — to Calais, at least, it was thought. The directors of the society wished Holmes to take the case in hand personally and at once, with a view of recovering what was possible from the plunder by way of salvage; also, of course, of finding Laker, for it is an important moral gain to guarantee societies, as an example, if a thief is caught and punished. Therefore Holmes and Mr. Lyster, as soon as might be, made for Messrs. Liddle, Neal & Liddle's, that the investigation might be begun.

The bank premises were quite near — in Leadenhall Street. Having arrived there, Holmes and Mr. Lyster made their way to the firm's private rooms. As they were passing an outer waiting-room, Holmes noticed two women. One, the elder, in widow's weeds, was sitting with her head bowed in her hand over a small writing-table. Her face was not visible, but her whole attitude was that of a person overcome with unbearable grief; and she sobbed quietly. The other was a young woman of twenty-two or twenty-three. Her thick black veil revealed no more than that her features were small and regular, and that her face was pale and drawn. She stood with a hand on the elder woman's shoulder, and she quickly turned her head away as the two men entered.

Mr. Neal, one of the partners, received them in his own room. "Good morning, Mr. Holmes," he said, when Mr. Lyster had introduced the detective. "This is a serious business — very. I think I am sorrier for Laker himself than for anybody else, ourselves included — or, at any rate, I am sorrier for his mother. She is waiting now to see Mr. Liddle, as soon as he arrives — Mr. Liddle has known the family for a long time. Miss Shaw is with her, too, poor girl. She is a governess, or something of that sort, and I believe she and Laker were engaged to be married. It's all very sad."

"Inspector Plummer, I understand," Holmes remarked, "has the affair in hand, on behalf of the police?"

"Yes," Mr. Neal replied; "in fact, he's here now, going through the contents of Laker's desk, and so forth; he thinks it possible Laker may have had accomplices. Will you see him?"

"Presently. Inspector Plummer and I are acquainted. We met last, I think, in the case of the Stanway cameo, some months ago. But, first, will you tell me how long Laker has been a walk-clerk?"

"Barely four months, although he has been with us altogether seven years. He was promoted to the walk soon after the beginning of the year."

"Do you know anything of his habits — what he used to do in his spare time, and so forth?"

"Not a great deal. He went in for boating, I believe, though I have heard it whispered that he had one or two more expensive tastes — expensive, that is, for a young man in his position," Mr. Neal explained, with a dignified wave of the hand that he peculiarly affected. He was a stout old gentleman, and the gesture suited him.

"You have had no reason to suspect him of dishonesty before, I take it?"

"Oh, no. He made a wrong return once, I believe, that went for some time undetected, but it turned out, after all, to be a clerical error — a mere clerical error."

"Do you know anything of his associates out of the office?"

"No, how should I? I believe Inspector Plummer has been making inquiries as to that, however, of the other clerks. Here he is, by the bye, I expect. Come in!"

It was Plummer who had knocked, and he came in at Mr. Neal's call. He was a middle-sized, small-eyed, impenetrable-looking man, as yet of no great reputation in the force. Some of my readers may remember his connection with that case, so long a public mystery, that I have elsewhere fully set forth and explained under the title of "The Stanway Cameo Mystery." Plummer carried his billy-cock hat in one hand and a few papers in the other. He gave Holmes good morning, placed his hat on a chair, and spread the papers on the table.

"There's not a great deal here," he said, "but one thing's plain — Laker had been betting. See here, and here, and here" — he took a few letters from the bundle in his hand — "two letters from a bookmaker about settling — wonder he trusted a clerk — several telegrams from tipsters, and a letter from some friend — only signed by initials — asking Laker to put a sovereign on a horse for the friend 'with his own.' I'll keep these, I think. It may be worth while to see that friend, if we can find him. Ah, we often find it's betting, don't we, Mr. Holmes? Meanwhile, there's no news from France yet."

"You are sure that is where he is gone?" asked Holmes.

"Well, I'll tell you what we've done as yet. First, of course, I went round to all the banks. There was nothing to be got from that. The cashiers all knew him by sight, and one was a personal friend of his. He had called as usual, said nothing in particular, cashed his bills in the ordinary way, and finished up at the Eastern Consolidated Bank at about a quarter-past one. So far there was nothing whatever. But I had started two or three men meanwhile making inquiries at the railway stations, and so on. I had scarcely left the Eastern Consolidated when one of them came after me with news. He had tried Palmer's Tourist Office, although that seemed an unlikely place, and there struck the track."

"Had he been there?"

"Not only had he been there, but he had taken a tourist ticket for France. It was quite a smart move, in a way. You see it was the sort of ticket that lets you do pretty well what you like; you have the choice of two or three different routes to begin with, and you can break your journey where you please, and make all sorts of variations. So that a man with a ticket like that, and a few hours' start, could twist about on some remote branch route, and strike off in another direction altogether, with a new ticket, from some out-of-the-way place, while we were carefully sorting out and inquiring along the different routes he *might* have taken. Not half a bad move for a new hand; but he made one bad mistake, as new hands always do — as old hands do, in fact, very often. He was fool enough to give his own name, C. Laker! Although that didn't matter much, as the description was enough to fix him. There he was, wallet and all, just as he had come from the Eastern Consolidated Bank. He went straight from there to Palmer's, by the bye, and probably in a cab. We judge that by the time. He left the Eastern Consolidated at a quarter-past one, and was at Palmer's by twenty-five-past — ten minutes. The clerk at Palmer's remembered the time because he was anxious to get out to his lunch, and kept looking at the clock, expecting another clerk in to relieve him. Laker didn't take much in the way of luggage, I fancy. We inquired carefully at the stations, and got the porters to remember the passengers for whom they had been carrying luggage, but none appeared to have had any dealings with our man. That, of course, is as one would expect. He'd take as little as possible with him, and buy what he wanted on the way, or when he'd reached his hiding-place. Of course, I wired to Calais (it was a Dover to Calais route ticket) and sent a couple of smart men off by the 8.15 mail from Charing Cross. I expect we shall hear from them in the course of the day. I am being kept in London in view of something expected at headquarters, or I should have been off myself."

"That is all, then, up to the present? Have you anything else in view?"

"That's all I've absolutely ascertained at present. As for what I'm going to do" — a slight smile curled Plummer's lip — "well, I shall see. I've a thing or two in my mind."

Holmes smiled slightly himself; he recognized Plummer's touch of professional jealousy. "Very well," he said, rising, "I'll make an inquiry or two for myself at once. Perhaps, Mr. Neal, you'll allow one of your clerks to show me the banks, in their regular order, at which Laker called yesterday. I think I'll begin at the beginning."

Mr. Neal offered to place at Holmes's disposal anything or anybody the bank contained, and the conference broke up. As Holmes, with the clerk, came through the rooms separating Mr.

Neal's sanctum from the outer office, he fancied he saw the two veiled women leaving by a side door.

The first bank was quite close to Liddle, Neal & Liddle's. There the cashier who had dealt with Laker the day before remembered nothing in particular about the interview. Many other walk-clerks had called during the morning, as they did every morning, and the only circumstances of the visit that he could say anything definite about were those recorded in figures in the books. He did not know Laker's name till Plummer had mentioned it in making inquiries on the previous afternoon. As far as he could remember, Laker behaved much as usual, though really he did not notice much; he looked chiefly at the bills. He described Laker in a way that corresponded with the photograph that Holmes had borrowed from the bank; a young man with a brown moustache and ordinary-looking, fairly regular face, dressing much as other clerks dressed — tall hat, black cutaway coat, and so on. The numbers of the notes handed over had already been given to Inspector Plummer, and these Holmes did not trouble about.

The next bank was in Cornhill, and here the cashier was a personal friend of Laker's — at any rate, an acquaintance — and he remembered a little more. Laker's manner had been quite as usual, he said; certainly he did not seem preoccupied or excited in his manner. He spoke for a moment or two — of being on the river on Sunday, and so on — and left in his usual way.

"Can you remember *everything* he said?" Holmes asked. "If you can tell me, I should like to know exactly what he did and said to the smallest particular."

"Well, he saw me a little distance off — I was behind there, at one of the desks — and raised his hand to me, and said, 'How d'ye do?' I came across and took his bills, and dealt with them in the usual way. He had a new umbrella lying on the counter — rather a handsome umbrella — and I made a remark about the handle. He took it up to show me, and told me it was a present he had just received from a friend. It was a gorse-root handle, with two silver bands, one with his monogram C.W.L. I said it was a very nice handle, and asked him whether it was fine in his district

85

on Sunday. He said he had been up the river, and it was very fine there. And I think that was all."

"Thank you. Now about this umbrella. Did he carry it rolled? Can you describe it in detail?"

"Well, I've told you about the handle, and the rest was much as usual, I think; it wasn't rolled — just flapping loosely, you know. It was rather an odd-shaped handle, though. I'll try and sketch it, if you like, as well as I can remember." He did so, and Holmes saw in the result rough indications of a gnarled crook, with one silver band near the end, and another, with the monogram, a few inches down the handle. Holmes put the sketch in his pocket, and bade the cashier good day.

At the next bank the story was the same as at the first — there was nothing remembered but the usual routine. Holmes and the clerk turned down a narrow paved court, and through into Lombard Street for the next visit. The bank — that of Buller, Clayton, Ladds & Co. — was just at the corner at the end of the court, and the imposing stone entrance-porch was being made larger and more imposing still, the way being almost blocked by ladders and scaffold-poles. Here there was only the usual tale, and so on through the whole walk. The cashiers knew Laker only by sight, and that not always very distinctly. The calls of walk-clerks were such matters of routine that little note was taken of the persons of the clerks themselves, who were called by the names of their firms, if they were called by any names at all. Laker had behaved much as usual, so far as the cashiers could remember, and when finally the Eastern Consolidated was left behind, nothing more had been learnt than the chat about Laker's new umbrella.

Holmes had taken leave of Mr. Neal's clerk, and was stepping into a hansom, when he noticed a veiled woman in widow's weeds hailing another hansom a little way behind. He recognized the figure again, and said to the driver, "Drive fast to Palmer's Tourist Office, but keep your eye on that cab behind, and tell me presently if it is following us."

The cabman drove off, and after passing one or two turnings, opened the lid above Holmes's head, and said, "That there other keb *is* a-follerin' us, sir, an' keepin' about even distance all along."

"All right; that's what I wanted to know. Palmer's now."

At Palmer's the clerk who had attended to Laker remembered him very well, and described him. He also remembered the wallet, and *thought* he remembered the umbrella — was practically sure of it, in fact, upon reflection. He had no record of the name given, but remembered it distinctly to be Laker. As a matter of fact, names were never asked in such a transaction, but in this case Laker appeared to be ignorant of the usual procedure, as well as in a great hurry, and asked for the ticket and gave his name all in one breath, probably assuming that the name would be required.

Holmes got back to his cab, and started for Charing Cross. The cabman once more lifted the lid and informed him that the hansom with the veiled woman in it was again following, having waited while Holmes had visited Palmer's. At Charing Cross Holmes discharged his cab and walked straight to the lost property office. The man in charge knew him very well, for his business had carried him there frequently before.

"I fancy an umbrella was lost in the station yesterday," Holmes said. "It was a new umbrella, silk, with a gnarled gorse-root handle and two silver bands, something like this sketch. There was a monogram on the lower band — 'C. W. L.' were the letters. Has it been brought here?"

"There was two or three yesterday," the man said; "let's see." He took the sketch and retired to a corner of his room. "Oh, yes — here it is, I think; isn't this it? Do you claim it?"

"Well, not exactly that, but I think I'll take a look at it, if you'll let me. By the way, I see it's rolled up. Was it found like that?"

"No; the chap rolled it up what found it — porter he was. It's a fad of his, rolling up umbrellas close and neat, and he's rather proud of it. He often looks as though he'd like to take a man's umbrella away and roll it up for him when it's a bit clumsy done. Rum fad, eh?"

"Yes; everybody has his little fad, though. Where was this found — close by here?"

"Yes, sir; just there, almost opposite this window, in the little corner."

"About two o'clock?"

"Ah, about that time, more or less."

Holmes took the umbrella up, unfastened the band, and shook the silk out loose. Then he opened it, and as he did so a small scrap of paper fell from inside it. Holmes pounced on it like lightning. Then, after examining the umbrella thoroughly, inside and out, he handed it back to the man, who had not observed the incident of the scrap of paper.

"That will do, thanks," he said. "I only wanted to take a peep at it — just a small matter connected with a little case of mine. Good morning."

He turned suddenly and saw, gazing at him with a terrified expression from a door behind, the face of the woman who had followed him in the cab. The veil was lifted, and he caught but a mere glance of the face ere it was suddenly withdrawn. He stood for a moment to allow the woman time to retreat, and then left the station.

Scarcely thirty yards along the Strand he met Plummer.

"I'm going to make some much closer inquiries all down the line as far as Dover," Plummer said. "They wire from Calais that they have no clue as yet, and I mean to make quite sure, if I can, that Laker hasn't quietly slipped off the line somewhere between here and Dover. There's one very peculiar thing," Plummer added confidentially. "Did you see the two women who were waiting to see a member of the firm at Liddle, Neal & Liddle's?"

"Yes. Laker's mother and his *fiancée*, I was told."

"That's right. Well, do you know that girl — Shaw her name is — has been shadowing me ever since I left the Bank. Of course I spotted it from the beginning — these amateurs don't know how to follow anybody — and, as a matter of fact, she's just inside that jeweler's shop door behind me now, pretending to look at the things in the window. But it's odd, isn't it?"

"Well," Holmes replied, "of course it's not a thing to be neglected. If you'll look very carefully at the corner of Villiers Street, without appearing to stare, I think you will possibly observe some signs of Laker's mother. She's shadowing *me*."

Plummer looked casually in the direction indicated, and then immediately turned his eyes in another direction.

"I see her," he said; "she's just taking a look round the corner. That's a thing not to be ignored. Of course, the Lakers' house is being watched — we set a man on it at once, yesterday. But I'll put some one on now to watch Miss Shaw's place, too. I'll send a message through to Liddle's — probably they'll be able to say where it is. And the women themselves must be watched, too. As a matter of fact, I had a notion that Laker wasn't alone in it. And it's just possible, you know, that he has sent an accomplice off with his tourist ticket to lead us a dance while he looks after himself in another direction. Have you done anything?"

"Well," Holmes replied, with a faint reproduction of the secretive smile with which Plummer had met an inquiry of his earlier in the morning, "I've been to the station here, and I've found Laker's umbrella in the lost property office."

"Oh! Then probably he *has* gone. I'll bear that in mind, and perhaps have a word with the lost property man."

Plummer made for the station and Holmes for his rooms. He mounted the stairs and reached his door just as I myself, who had been disappointed in not finding him in, was leaving. I had called with the idea of taking Holmes to lunch with me at my club, but he declined lunch. "I have an important case in hand," he said. "Look here, Brett. See this scrap of paper. You know the types of the different newspapers. Do you agree that this is from the *Chronicle*?"

He handed me a small piece of paper. It was part of a cutting containing an advertisement, which had been torn in half.

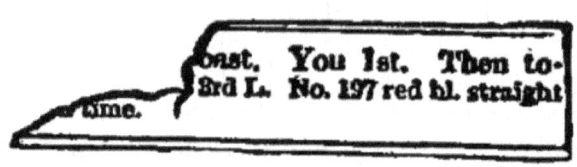

"I *think*," I said, "this is from the *Daily Chronicle*, judging by the paper. It is plainly from the 'agony column,' but all the papers use pretty much the same type for these advertisements, except the *Times*. If it were not torn I could tell you at once, because the *Chronicle* columns are rather narrow."

"Never mind — I'll send for them all." He rang, and sent the page boy for a copy of each morning paper of the previous day. Then he took from a large wardrobe cupboard a decent but well-worn and rather roughened tall hat. Also a coat a little worn and shiny on the collar. He exchanged these for his own hat and coat, and then substituted an old necktie for his own clean white one, and encased his legs in mud-spotted leggings. This done, he produced a very large and thick pocket-book, fastened by a broad elastic band, and said, "Well, what do you think of this? Will it do for Queen's taxes, or sanitary inspection, or the gas, or the water-supply?"

"Very well indeed, I should say," I replied. "What's the case?"

"Oh, I'll tell you all about that when it's over — no time now. Oh, here is the boy now. Listen closely, lad. By the bye, I'm going out presently by the back way. Wait for about ten minutes or a quarter of an hour after I am gone, and then just go across the road and speak to that lady in black, with the veil, who is waiting in that little foot-passage opposite. Say Mr. Sherlock Holmes sends his compliments, and he advises her not to wait, as he has already left his rooms by another door, and has been gone some little time. That's all; it would be a pity to keep the poor woman waiting all day for nothing. Now the papers. *Daily News, Standard, Telegraph, Chronicle* — yes, here it is, in the Chronicle."

The whole advertisement read thus:

YOB. — H.R. Shop roast. You 1st. Then tonight. 02. 2nd top 3rd L. No. 197 red bl. straight mon. One at a time.

"What's this," I asked, "a cryptogram?"

"I'll see," Holmes answered. "But I won't tell you anything about it till afterwards, so you get your lunch. Hand me the directory."

This was all I actually saw of this case myself, and I have written the rest in its proper order from Holmes's information, as I have written some other cases entirely.

To resume at the point where, for the time I lost sight of the matter. Holmes left by the back way and stopped an empty cab as it passed. "Abney Park Cemetery" was his direction to the driver. In little more than twenty minutes the cab was branching off down the Essex Road on its way to Stoke Newington, and in twenty minutes more Holmes stopped it in Church Street, Stoke Newington. He walked through a street or two, and then down another, the houses of which he scanned carefully as he passed. Opposite one which stood by itself he stopped, and, making a pretence of consulting and arranging his large pocket-book, he took a good look at the house. It was rather larger, neater, and more pretentious than the others in the street, and it had a natty little coach-house just visible up the side entrance. There were red blinds hung with heavy lace in the front windows, and behind one of these blinds Holmes was able to catch the glint of a heavy gas chandelier.

He stepped briskly up the front steps and knocked sharply at the door. "Mr. Merston?" he asked, pocket-book in hand, when a neat parlor-maid opened the door.

"Yes."

"Ah!" Holmes stepped into the hall and pulled off his hat; "it's only the meter. There's been a deal of gas running away somewhere here, and I'm just looking to see if the meters are right. Where is it?"

The girl hesitated. "I'll — I'll ask master," she said.

"Very well. I don't want to take it away, you know — only to give it a tap or two, and so on."

The girl retired to the back of the hall, and without taking her eyes off Sherlock Holmes, gave his message to some invisible person in a back room, whence came a growling reply of "All right."

Holmes followed the girl to the basement, apparently looking straight before him, but in reality taking in every detail of the place. The gas meter was in a very large lumber cupboard under the kitchen stairs. The girl opened the door and lit a candle. The meter stood on the floor, which was littered with hampers and boxes and odd sheets of brown paper. But a thing that at once arrested Holmes's attention was a garment of some sort of bright blue cloth, with large brass buttons, which was lying in a tumbled heap in a corner, and appeared to be the only thing in the place that was not covered with dust. Nevertheless, Holmes took no apparent notice of it, but stooped down and solemnly tapped the meter three times with his pencil, and listened with great gravity, placing his ear to the top. Then he shook his head and tapped again. At length he said: —

"It's a bit doubtful. I'll just get you to light the gas in the kitchen a moment. Keep your hand to the burner, and when I call out shut it off *at once*; see?"

The girl turned and entered the kitchen, and Holmes immediately seized the blue coat — for a coat it was. It had a dull red piping in the seams, and was of the swallow-tail pattern — a livery coat, in fact. He held it for a moment before him, examining its pattern and color, and then rolled it up and flung it again into the corner.

"Right!" he called to the servant. "Shut off!"

The girl emerged from the kitchen as he left the cupboard.

"Well," she asked, "are you satisfied now?"

"Quite satisfied, thank you," Holmes replied.

"Is it all right?" she continued, jerking her hand toward the cupboard.

"Well, no, it isn't; there's something wrong there, and I'm glad I came. You can tell Mr. Merston, if you like, that I expect his gas bill will be a good deal less next quarter." And there was a suspicion of a chuckle in Holmes's voice as he crossed the hall to leave. For a gas inspector is pleased when he finds at length what he has been searching for.

Things had fallen out better than Holmes had dared to expect. He saw the key of the whole mystery in that blue coat; for it was the uniform coat of the hall porters at one of the banks that he had visited in the morning, though which one he could not for the moment remember. He entered the nearest post-office and dispatched a telegram to Plummer, giving certain directions and asking the inspector to meet him; then he hailed the first available cab and hurried toward the City.

At Lombard Street he alighted, and looked in at the door of each bank till he came to Buller, Clayton, Ladds & Co.'s. This was the bank he wanted. In the other banks the hall porters wore mulberry coats, brick-dust coats, brown coats, and what not, but here, behind the ladders and scaffold poles which obscured the entrance, he could see a man in a blue coat, with dull red piping and brass buttons. He sprang up the steps, pushed open the inner swing door, and finally satisfied himself by a closer view of the coat, to the wearer's astonishment. Then he regained the pavement and walked the whole length of the bank premises in front, afterwards turning up the paved passage at the side, deep in thought. The bank had no windows or doors on the side next the court, and the two adjoining houses were old and supported in places by wooden shores. Both were empty, and a great board announced that tenders would be received in a month's time for the purchase of the old materials of which they were constructed; also that some part of the site would be let on a long building lease.

Holmes looked up at the grimy fronts of the old buildings. The windows were crusted thick with dirt — all except the bottom window of the house nearer the bank, which was fairly clean, and seemed to have been quite lately washed. The door, too, of this house was cleaner than that of the other, though the paint was worn. Holmes reached and fingered a hook driven into the left-hand doorpost about six feet from the ground. It was new, and not at all rusted; also a tiny splinter had been displaced when the hook was driven in, and clean wood showed at the spot.

Having observed these things, Holmes stepped back and read at the bottom of the big board the name, "Winsor & Weekes, Surveyors and Auctioneers, Abchurch Lane." Then he stepped into Lombard Street.

Two hansoms pulled up near the post-office, and out of the first stepped Inspector Plummer and another man. This man and the two who alighted from the second hansom were unmistakably plain-clothes constables — their air, gait, and boots proclaimed it.

"What's all this?" demanded Plummer, as Holmes approached.

"You'll soon see, I think. But, first, have you put the watch on No. 197, Hackworth Road?"

"Yes; nobody will get away from there alone."

"Very good. I am going into Abchurch Lane for a few minutes. Leave your men out here, but just go round into the court by Buller, Clayton & Ladds's, and keep your eye on the first door on the left. I think we'll find something soon. Did you get rid of Miss Shaw?"

"No, she's behind now, and Mrs. Laker's with her. They met in the Strand, and came after us in another cab. Rare fun, eh! They think we're pretty green! It's quite handy, too. So long as they keep behind me it saves all trouble of watching *them*." And Inspector Plummer chuckled and winked.

"Very good. You don't mind keeping your eye on that door, do you? I'll be back very soon," and with that Holmes turned off into Abchurch Lane.

At Winsor & Weekes's information was not difficult to obtain. The houses were destined to come down very shortly, but a week or so ago an office and a cellar in one of them was let temporarily to a Mr. Westley. He brought no references; indeed, as he paid a fortnight's rent in advance, he was not asked for any, considering the circumstances of the case. He was opening a London branch for a large firm of cider merchants, he said, and just wanted a rough office and a cool cellar to store samples in

94

for a few weeks till the permanent premises were ready. There was another key, and no doubt the premises might be entered if there were any special need for such a course. Sherlock Holmes gave such excellent reasons that Winsor & Weekes's managing clerk immediately produced the key and accompanied Holmes to the spot.

"I think you'd better have your men handy," Holmes remarked to Plummer when they reached the door, and a whistle quickly brought the men over.

The key was inserted in the lock and turned, but the door would not open; the bolt was fastened at the bottom. Holmes stooped and looked under the door.

"It's a drop bolt," he said. "Probably the man who left last let it fall loose, and then banged the door, so that it fell into its place. I must try my best with a wire or a piece of string."

A wire was brought, and with some maneuvering Holmes contrived to pass it round the bolt, and lift it little by little, steadying it with the blade of a pocket-knife. When at length the bolt was raised out of the hole, the knife-blade was slipped under it, and the door swung open.

They entered. The door of the little office just inside stood open, but in the office there was nothing, except a board a couple of feet long in a corner. Holmes stepped across and lifted this, turning its downward face toward Plummer. On it, in fresh white paint on a black ground, were painted the words:

BULLER, CLAYTON, LADDS & CO.,
TEMPORARY ENTRANCE

Holmes turned to Winsor & Weekes's clerk and asked, "The man who took this room called himself Westley, didn't he?"

"Yes."

"Youngish man, clean-shaven, and well-dressed?"

"Yes, he was."

"I fancy," Holmes said, turning to Plummer, "I *fancy* an old friend of yours is in this — Mr. Sam Gunter."

"What, the 'Hoxton Yob'?"

"I think it's possible he's been Mr. Westley for a bit, and somebody else for another bit. But let's come to the cellar."

Winsor & Weekes's clerk led the way down a steep flight of steps into a dark underground corridor, wherein they lighted their way with many successive matches. Soon the corridor made a turn to the right, and as the party passed the turn, there came from the end of the passage before them a fearful yell.

"Help! help! Open the door! I'm going mad — mad! O my God!"

And there was a sound of desperate beating from the inside of the cellar door at the extreme end. The men stopped, startled.

"Come," said Holmes, "more matches!" and he rushed to the door. It was fastened with a bar and padlock.

"Let me out, for God's sake!" came the voice, sick and hoarse, from the inside. "Let me out!"

"All right!" Holmes shouted. "We have come for you. Wait a moment."

The voice sank into a sort of sobbing croon, and Holmes tried several keys from his own bunch on the padlock. None fitted. He drew from his pocket the wire he had used for the bolt of the front door, straightened it out, and made a sharp bend at the end.

"Hold a match close," he ordered shortly, and one of the men obeyed. Three or four attempts were necessary, and several different bendings of the wire were effected, but in the end Holmes picked the lock, and flung open the door.

From within a ghastly figure fell forward among them fainting, and knocked out the matches.

"Hullo!" cried Plummer. "Hold up! Who are you?"

"Let's get him up into the open," said Holmes. "He can't tell you who he is for a bit, but I believe he's Laker."

"Laker! What, here?"

"I think so. Steady up the steps. Don't bump him. He's pretty sore already, I expect."

Truly the man was a pitiable sight. His hair and face were caked in dust and blood, and his finger-nails were torn and bleeding. Water was sent for at once, and brandy.

"Well," said Plummer hazily, looking first at the unconscious prisoner and then at Holmes, "but what about the swag?"

"You'll have to find that yourself," Holmes replied. "I think my share of the case is about finished. I only act for the Guarantee Society, you know, and if Laker's proved innocent — "

"Innocent! How?"

"Well, this is what took place, as near as I can figure it. You'd better undo his collar, I think" — this to the men. "What I believe has happened is this. There has been a very clever and carefully prepared conspiracy here, and Laker has not been the criminal, but the victim."

"Been robbed himself, you mean? But how? Where?"

"Yesterday morning, before he had been to more than three banks — here, in fact."

"But then how? You're all wrong. We *know* he made the whole round, and did all the collection. And then Palmer's office, and all, and the umbrella; why — "

The man lay still unconscious. "Don't raise his head," Holmes said. "And one of you had best fetch a doctor. He's had a terrible shock." Then turning to Plummer he went on, "As to *how* they managed the job I'll tell you what I think. First it struck some very clever person that a deal of money might be got by robbing a walk-clerk from a bank. This clever person was one of a clever gang of thieves — perhaps the Hoxton Row gang, as I think I hinted. Now you know quite as well as I do that such a gang will spend any amount of time over a job that promises a big haul, and that for such a job they can always command the necessary capital. There are many most respectable persons living in good style in the suburbs whose chief business lies in financing such ventures, and taking the chief share of the proceeds. Well, this is their plan, carefully and intelligently carried out. They watch Laker, observe the round he takes, and his habits. They find that there is only one of the clerks with whom he does business that he is much acquainted with, and that this clerk is in a bank which is commonly second in Laker's round. The sharpest man among them — and I don't think there's a man in London could do this as well as young Sam Gunter — studies Laker's dress and habits just as an actor studies a character. They take this office and cellar, as we have seen, *because it is next door to a bank whose front entrance is being altered* — a fact which Laker must know from his daily visits. The smart man — Gunter, let us say, and I have other reasons for believing it to be he — makes up precisely like Laker, false moustache, dress, and everything, and waits here with the rest of the gang. One of the gang is dressed in a blue coat with brass buttons, like a hall-porter in Buller's bank. Do you see?"

"Yes, I think so. It's pretty clear now."

"A confederate watches at the top of the court, and the moment Laker turns in from Cornhill — having already been, mind, at the only bank where he was so well known that the disguised thief would not have passed muster — as soon as he turns in from Cornhill, I say, a signal is given, and that board" — pointing to that with the white letters — "is hung on the hook in the doorpost. The sham porter stands beside it, and as Laker approaches says, 'This way in, sir, this morning. The front way's shut for the alterations.' Laker, suspecting nothing, and supposing that the firm have made a temporary entrance through the empty house, enters. He is seized when well along the corridor, the board is taken down and the door shut. Probably he is stunned by a blow on the head — see the blood now. They take his wallet and all the cash he has already collected. Gunter takes the wallet and also the umbrella, since it has Laker's initials, and is therefore distinctive. He simply completes the walk in the character of Laker, beginning with Buller, Clayton & Ladds's just round the corner. It is nothing but routine work, which is quickly done, and nobody notices him particularly — it is the bills they examine. Meanwhile this unfortunate fellow is locked up in the cellar here, right at the end of the underground corridor, where he can never make himself heard in the street, and where next him are only the empty cellars of the deserted house next door. The thieves shut the front door and vanish. The rest is plain. Gunter, having completed the round, and bagged some £15,000 or more, spends a few pounds in a tourist ticket at Palmer's as a blind, being careful to give Laker's name. He leaves the umbrella at Charing Cross in a conspicuous place right opposite the lost property office, where it is sure to be seen, and so completes his false trail."

"Then who are the people at 197, Hackworth Road?"

"The capitalist lives there — the financier, and probably the directing spirit of the whole thing. Merston's the name he goes by there, and I've no doubt he cuts a very imposing figure in chapel every Sunday. He'll be worth picking up — this isn't the first thing he's been in, I'll warrant."

"But — but what about Laker's mother and Miss Shaw?"

"Well, what? The poor women are nearly out of their minds with terror and shame, that's all, but though they may think Laker a criminal, they'll never desert him. They've been following us about with a feeble, vague sort of hope of being able to baffle us in some way or help him if we caught him, or something, poor things. Did you ever hear of a real woman who'd desert a son or a lover merely because he was a criminal? But here's the doctor. When he's attended to him will you let your men take Laker home? I must hurry and report to the Guarantee Society, I think."

"But," said the perplexed Plummer, "where did you get your clue? You must have had a tip from some one, you know — you can't have done it by clairvoyance. What gave you the tip?"

"The *Daily Chronicle*."

"The *what*?"

"The *Daily Chronicle*. Just take a look at the 'agony column' in yesterday morning's issue, and read the message to 'Yob' — to Gunter, in fact. That's all."

By this time a cab was waiting in Lombard Street, and two of Plummer's men, under the doctor's directions, carried Laker to it. No sooner, however, were they in the court than the two watching women threw themselves hysterically upon Laker, and it was long before they could be persuaded that he was not being taken to gaol. The mother shrieked aloud, "My boy — my boy! Don't take him! Oh, don't take him! They've killed my boy!

Look at his head — oh, his head!" and wrestled desperately with the men, while Holmes attempted to soothe her, and promised to allow her to go in the cab with her son if she would only be quiet. The younger woman made no noise, but she held one of Laker's limp hands in both hers.

Holmes and I dined together that evening, and he gave me a full account of the occurrences which I have here set down. Still, when he was finished I was not able to see clearly by what process of reasoning he had arrived at the conclusions that gave him the key to the mystery, nor did I understand the "agony column" message, and I said so.

"In the beginning," Holmes explained, "the thing that struck me as curious was the fact that Laker was said to have given his own name at Palmer's in buying his ticket. Now, the first thing the greenest and newest criminal thinks of is changing his name, so that the giving of his own name seemed unlikely to begin with. Still, he *might* have made such a mistake, as Plummer suggested when he said that criminals usually make a mistake somewhere — as they do, in fact. Still, it was the least likely mistake I could think of — especially as he actually didn't wait to be asked for his name, but blurted it out when it wasn't really wanted. And it was conjoined with another rather curious mistake, or what would have been a mistake if the thief were Laker. Why should he conspicuously display his wallet — such a distinctive article — for the clerk to see and note? Why rather had he not got rid of it before showing himself? Suppose it should be somebody personating Laker? In any case I determined not to be prejudiced by what I had heard of Laker's betting. A man may bet without being a thief.

"But, again, supposing it *were* Laker? Might he not have given his name, and displayed his wallet, and so on, while buying a ticket for France, in order to draw pursuit after himself in that direction while he made off in another, in another name, and disguised? Each supposition was plausible. And, in either case, it might happen that whoever was laying this trail would probably lay it a little farther. Charing Cross was the next point, and there I went. I already had it from Plummer that Laker had not been recognized there. Perhaps the trail had been laid in some other manner. Something left behind with Laker's name on it, perhaps? I at once thought of the umbrella with his monogram, and, making a long shot, asked for it at the lost property office, as you know. The guess was lucky. In the umbrella, as you know, I found that scrap of paper. That, I judged, had fallen in from the hand of the man carrying the umbrella. He had torn the paper in half in order to fling it away, and one piece had fallen into the loosely flapping umbrella. It is a thing that will often happen with an omnibus ticket, as you may have noticed. Also, it was proved that the umbrella *was* unrolled when found, and rolled immediately after. So here was a piece of paper dropped by the person who had brought the umbrella to Charing Cross and left it. I got the whole advertisement, as you remember, and I studied it. 'Yob' is back-slang for 'boy,' and it is often used in nicknames to denote a young smooth-faced thief. Gunter, the man I suspect, as a matter of fact, is known as the 'Hoxton Yob.' The message, then, was addressed to some one known by such a nickname. Next, 'H.R. shop roast.' Now, in thieves' slang, to 'roast' a thing or a person is to watch it or him. They call any place a shop — notably, a thieves' den. So that this meant that some resort — perhaps the 'Hoxton Row shop' — was watched. 'You 1st then tonight' would be clearer, perhaps, when the rest was understood. I thought a little over the rest, and it struck me that it must be a direction to some other house, since one was warned of as being watched. Besides, there was the number, 197, and 'red bl.,' which would be extremely likely to mean 'red blinds,' by way of clearly distinguishing the house. And then the plan of the thing was plain. You have noticed, probably, that the map of London which accompanies the Post Office Directory is divided, for convenience of reference, into numbered squares?"

"Yes. The squares are denoted by letters along the top margin and figures down the side. So that if you consult the directory, and find a place marked as being in D 5, for instance, you find vertical divisions D, and run your finger down it till it intersects horizontal division 5, and there you are."

"Precisely. I got my Post Office Directory, and looked for 'O 2.' It was in North London, and took in parts of Abney Park Cemetery and Clissold Park; '2nd top' was the next sign. Very well, I counted the second street intersecting the top of the square — counting, in the usual way, from the left. That was Lordship Road. Then, '3rd L.' From the point where Lordship Road crossed the top of the square, I ran my finger down the road till it came to '3rd L,' or, in other words, the third turning on the left — Hackworth Road. So there we were, unless my guesses were altogether wrong. 'Straight mon' probably meant 'straight moniker' — that is to say, the proper name, a thief's *real* name, in contradistinction to that he may assume. I turned over the directory till I found Hackworth Road, and found that No. 197 was inhabited by a Mr. Merston. From the whole thing I judged this. There was to have been a meeting at the 'H.R. shop,' but that was found, at the last moment, to be watched by the police for some purpose, so that another appointment was made for this house in the suburbs. 'You 1st. Then tonight' — the person addressed was to come first, and the others in the evening. They were to ask for the householder's 'straight moniker' — Mr. Merston. And they were to come one at a time.

"Now, then, what was this? What theory would fit it? Suppose this were a robbery, directed from afar by the advertiser. Suppose, on the day before the robbery, it was found that the place fixed for division of spoils were watched. Suppose that the principal thereupon advertised (as had already been agreed in case of emergency) in these terms. The principal in the actual robbery — the 'Yob' addressed — was to go first with the booty. The others were to come after, one at a time. Anyway, the thing was good enough to follow a little further, and I determined to try No. 197, Hackworth Road. I have told you what I found there, and how it opened my eyes. I went, of course, merely on chance, to see what I might chance to see. But luck favored, and I happened on that coat — brought back rolled up, on the evening after the robbery, doubtless by the thief who had used it, and flung carelessly into the handiest cupboard. *That* was this gang's mistake."

"Well, I congratulate you," I said. "I hope they'll catch the rascals."

"I rather think they will, now they know where to look. They can scarcely miss Merston, anyway. There has been very little to go upon in this case, but I stuck to the thread, however slight, and it brought me through. The rest of the case, of course, is Plummer's. It was a peculiarity of my commission that I could equally well fulfill it by catching the man with all the plunder, or by proving him innocent. Having done the latter, my work was at an end, but I left it where Plummer will be able to finish the job handsomely."

Plummer did. Sam Gunter, Merston, and one accomplice were taken — the first and last were well known to the police — and were identified by Laker. Merston, as Holmes had suspected, had kept the lion's share for himself, so that altogether, with what was recovered from him and the other two, nearly £11,000 was saved for Messrs. Liddle, Neal & Liddle. Merston, when taken, was in the act of packing up to take a holiday abroad, and there cash his notes, which were found, neatly packed in separate thousands, in his portmanteau. As Holmes had predicted, his gas bill *was* considerably less next quarter, for less than half-way through it he began a term in gaol.

As for Laker, he was reinstated, of course, with an increase of salary by way of compensation for his broken head. He had passed a terrible twenty-six hours in the cellar, unfed and unheard. Several times he had become insensible, and again and again he had thrown himself madly against the door, shouting and tearing at it, till he fell back exhausted, with broken nails and bleeding fingers. For some hours before the arrival of his rescuers he had been sitting in a sort of stupor, from which he was suddenly aroused by the sound of voices and footsteps. He was in bed for a week, and required a rest of a month in addition before he could resume his duties. Then he was quietly lectured by Mr. Neal as to betting, and, I believe, dropped that practice in consequence. I am told that he is "at the counter" now — a considerable promotion.

The Case of the Lost Foreigner

I have already said in more than one place that Holmes's personal relations with the members of the London police force were of a cordial character. In the course of his work it has frequently been Holmes's hap to learn of matters on which the police were glad of information, and that information was always passed on at once; and so long as no infringement of regulations or damage to public service were involved, Holmes could always rely on a return in kind.

It was with a message of a useful sort that Holmes one day dropped into Vine Street police-station and asked for a particular inspector, who was not in. Holmes sat and wrote a note, and by way of making conversation said to the inspector on duty, "Anything very startling this way today?"

"Nothing *very* startling, perhaps, as yet," the inspector replied. "But one of our chaps picked up rather an odd customer a little while ago. Lunatic of some sort, I should think — in fact, I've sent for the doctor to see him. He's a foreigner — a Frenchman, I believe. He seemed horribly weak and faint; but the oddest thing occurred when one of the men, thinking he might be hungry, brought in some bread. He went into fits of terror at the sight of it, and wouldn't be pacified till they took it away again."

"That was strange."

"Odd, wasn't it? And he *was* hungry too. They brought him some more a little while after, and he didn't funk it a bit, — pitched into it, in fact, like anything, and ate it all with some cold beef. It's the way with some lunatics — never the same five minutes together. He keeps crying like a baby, and saying things we can't understand. As it happens, there's nobody in just now who speaks French."

"I speak French," Holmes replied. "Shall I try him?"

"Certainly, if you will. He's in the men's room below. They've been making him as comfortable as possible by the fire until the doctor comes. He's a long time. I expect he's got a case on."

Holmes found his way to the large mess-room, where three or four policemen in their shirt-sleeves were curiously regarding a young man of very disordered appearance who sat on a chair by the fire. He was pale, and exhibited marks of bruises on his face, while over one eye was a scarcely healed cut. His figure was small and slight, his coat was torn, and he sat with a certain indefinite air of shivering suffering. He started and looked round apprehensively as Holmes entered. Holmes bowed smilingly, wished him good day, speaking in French, and asked him if he spoke the language.

The man looked up with a dull expression, and after an effort or two, as of one who stutters, burst out with, "*Je le nie!*"

"That's strange," Holmes observed to the men. "I ask him if he speaks French, and he says he denies it — speaking *in* French."

"He's been saying that very often, sir," one of the men answered, "as well as other things we can't make anything of."

Holmes placed his hand kindly on the man's shoulder and asked his name. The reply was for a little while an inarticulate gurgle, presently merging into a meaningless medley of words and syllables — "*Qu'est ce qu'* — *il n'a* — Leystar Squarr — *sacré nom* — not spik it — *quel chemin* — sank you ver' mosh — *je le nie! je le nie!*" He paused, stared, and then, as though realizing his helplessness, he burst into tears.

"He's been a-cryin' two or three times," said the man who had spoken before. "He was a-cryin' when we found him."

Several more attempts Holmes made to communicate with the man, but though he seemed to comprehend what was meant, he replied with nothing but meaningless gibber, and finally gave up the attempt, and, leaning against the side of the fireplace, buried his head in the bend of his arm.

Then the doctor arrived and made *his* examination. While it was in progress Holmes took aside the policeman who had been

105

speaking before and questioned him further. He had himself found the Frenchman in a dull back street by Golden Square, where the man was standing helpless and trembling, apparently quite bewildered and very weak. He had brought him in, without having been able to learn anything about him. One or two shopkeepers in the street where he was found were asked, but knew nothing of him — indeed, had never seen him before.

"But the curiousest thing," the policeman proceeded, "was in this 'ere room, when I brought him a loaf to give him a bit of a snack, seein' he looked so weak an' 'ungry. You'd 'a thought we was a-goin' to poison 'im. He fair screamed at the very sight o' the bread, an' he scrouged hisself up in that corner an' put his hands in front of his face. I couldn't make out what was up at first — didn't tumble to it's bein' the bread he was frightened of, seein' as he looked like a man as 'ud be frightened at anything else afore *that*. But the nearer I came with it the more he yelled, so I took it away an' left it outside, an' then he calmed down. An' s'elp me, when I cut some bits off that there very loaf an' brought 'em in, with a bit o' beef, he just went for 'em like one o'clock. *He* wasn't frightened o' no bread then, you bet. Rum thing, how the fancies takes 'em when they're a bit touched, ain't it? All one way one minute, all the other the next."

"Yes, it is. By the way, have you another uncut loaf in the place?"

"Yes, sir. Half a dozen if you like."

"One will be enough. I am going over to speak to the doctor. Wait awhile until he seems very quiet and fairly comfortable; then bring a loaf in quietly and put it on the table, not far from his elbow. Don't attract his attention to what you are doing."

The doctor stood looking thoughtfully down on the Frenchman, who, for his part, stared gloomily, but tranquilly, at the fireplace. Holmes stepped quietly over to the doctor and, without disturbing the man by the fire, said interrogatively, "Aphasia?"

The doctor tightened his lips, frowned, and nodded significantly. "Motor," he murmured, just loudly enough for Holmes to hear; "and there's a general nervous break-down as well, I should say. By the way, perhaps there's no agraphia. Have you tried him with pen and paper?"

Pen and paper were brought and set before the man. He was told, slowly and distinctly, that he was among friends, whose only object was to restore him to his proper health. Would he write his name and address, and any other information he might care to give about himself, on the paper before him?

The Frenchman took the pen and stared at the paper; then slowly, and with much hesitation, he traced these marks: —

The man paused after the last of these futile characters, and his pen stabbed into the paper with a blot, as he dazedly regarded his work. Then with a groan he dropped it, and his face sank again into the bend of his arm.

The doctor took the paper and handed it to Holmes. "Complete agraphia, you see," he said. "He can't write a word. He begins to write 'Monsieur' from sheer habit in beginning letters thus; but the word tails off into a scrawl. Then his attempts become mere scribble, with just a trace of some familiar word here and there — but quite meaningless all."

Although he had never before chanced to come across a case of aphasia (happily a rare disease), Holmes was acquainted with its general nature. He knew that it might arise either from some physical injury to the brain, or from a break-down consequent on some terrible nervous strain. He knew that in the case of motor aphasia the sufferer, though fully conscious of all that goes on about him, and though quite understanding what is said to him is entirely powerless to put his own thoughts into spoken words — has lost, in fact, the connection between words and their spoken symbols. Also that in most bad cases agraphia — the loss of ability to write words with any reference to their meaning — is commonly an accompaniment.

"You will have him taken to the infirmary, I suppose?" Holmes asked.

"Yes," the doctor replied. "I shall go and see about it at once."

The man looked up again as they spoke. The policeman had, in accordance with Holmes's request, placed a loaf of bread on the table near him, and now as he looked up he caught sight of it. He started visibly and paled, but gave no such signs of abject terror as the policeman had previously observed. He appeared nervous and uneasy, however, and presently reached stealthily toward the loaf. Holmes continued to talk to the doctor, while closely watching the Frenchman's behavior from the corner of his eye.

The loaf was what is called a "plain cottage," of solid and regular shape. The man reached it and immediately turned it bottom up on the table. Then he sank back in his chair with a more contented expression, though his gaze was still directed toward the loaf. The policeman grinned silently at this curious maneuver.

The doctor left, and Holmes accompanied him to the door of the room. "He will not be moved just yet, I take it?" Holmes asked as they parted.

"It may take an hour or two," the doctor replied. "Are you anxious to keep him here?"

"Not for long; but I think there's a curious inside to the case, and I may perhaps learn something of it by a little watching. But I can't spare very long."

At a sign from Holmes the loaf was removed. Then Holmes pulled the small table closer to the Frenchman and pushed the pen and sheets of paper toward him. The maneuver had its result. The man looked up and down the room vacantly once or twice and then began to turn the papers over. From that he went to dipping the pen in the inkpot, and presently he was scribbling at random on the loose sheets. Holmes affected to leave him entirely alone, and seemed to be absorbed in a contemplation of a photograph of a police-division brass band that hung on the wall, but he saw every scratch the man made.

108

At first there was nothing but meaningless scrawls and attempted words. Then rough sketches appeared, of a man's head, a chair or what not. On the mantelpiece stood a small clock — apparently a sort of humble presentation piece, the body of the clock being set in a horse-shoe frame, with crossed whips behind it. After a time the Frenchman's eyes fell on this, and he began a crude sketch of it. That he relinquished, and went on with other random sketches and scribblings on the same piece of paper, sketching and scribbling over the sketches in a half-mechanical sort of way, as of one who trifles with a pen during a brown study. Beginning at the top left-hand corner of the paper, he traveled all round it till he arrived at the left-hand bottom corner. Then dashing his pen hastily across his last sketch he dropped it, and with a great shudder turned away again and hid his face by the fireplace.

Holmes turned at once and seized the papers on the table. He stuffed them all into his coat-pocket, with the exception of the last which the man had been engaged on, and this, a facsimile of which is subjoined, he studied earnestly for several minutes.

Holmes wished the men good day, and made his way to the inspector.

"Well," the inspector said, "not much to be got out of him, is there? The doctor will be sending for him presently."

"I fancy," said Holmes, "that this may turn out a very important case. Possibly — quite possibly — I may not have guessed correctly, and so I won't tell you anything of it till I know a little more. But what I want now is a messenger. Can I send somebody at once in a cab to my friend Brett at his chambers?"

"Certainly. I'll find somebody. Want to write a note?"

Holmes wrote and dispatched a note, which reached me in less than ten minutes. Then he asked the inspector, "Have you searched the Frenchman?"

"Oh, yes. We went all over him, when we found he couldn't explain himself, to see if we could trace his friends or his address. He didn't seem to mind. But there wasn't a single thing in his pocket — not a single thing, barring a rag of a pocket-handkerchief with no marking on it."

"You noticed that somebody had stolen his watch, I suppose?"

"Well, he hadn't got one."

"But he had one of those little vertical button-holes in his waistcoat, used to fasten a watchguard to, and it was much worn and frayed, so that he must be in the habit of carrying a watch; and it is gone."

"Yes, and everything else too, eh? Looks like robbery. He's had a knock or two in the face — notice that?"

"I saw the bruises and the cut, of course; and his collar has been broken away, with the back button; somebody has taken him by the collar or throat. Was he wearing a hat when he was found?"

"No."

"That would imply that he had only just left a house. What street was he found in?"

"Henry Street — a little off Golden Square. Low street, you know."

"Did the constable notice a door open near by?"

The inspector shook his head. "Half the doors in the street are open," he said, "pretty nearly all day."

"Ah, then there's nothing in that. I don't think he lives there, by the bye. I fancy he comes from more in the Seven Dials or Drury Lane direction. Did you notice anything about the man that gave you a clue to his occupation — or at any rate to his habits?"

"Can't say I did."

"Well, just take a look at the back of his coat before he goes away — just over the loins. Good day."

As I have said, Holmes's messenger was quick. I happened to be in — having lately returned from a latish lunch — when he arrived with this note:

> *My dear B.,*
>
> *I meant to have lunched with you today, but have been kept. I expect you are idle this afternoon, and I have a case that will interest you — perhaps be useful to you from a journalistic point of view. If you care to see anything of it, cab away at once to Fitzroy Square, south side, where I'll meet you. I will wait no later than 3.30.*
>
> *Yours, S.H.*

I had scarce a quarter of an hour, so I seized my hat and left my chambers at once. As it happened, my cab and Holmes's burst into Fitzroy Square from opposite sides almost at the same moment, so that we lost no time.

"Come," said Holmes, taking my arm and marching me off, "we are going to look for some stabling. Try to feel as though you'd just set up a brougham and had come out to look for a place to put it in. I fear we may have to delude some person with that belief presently."

"Why — what do you want stables for? And why make me your excuse?"

"As to what I want the stables for — really I'm not altogether sure myself. As to making you an excuse — well, even the humblest excuse is better than none. But come, here are some stables. Not good enough, though, even if any of them were empty. Come on."

We had stopped for an instant at the entrance to a small alley of rather dirty stables, and Holmes, paying apparently but small attention to the stables themselves, had looked sharply about him with his gaze in the air.

"I know this part of London pretty well," Holmes observed, "and I can only remember one other range of stabling near by; we must try that. As a matter of fact, I'm coming here on little more than conjecture, though I shall be surprised if there isn't something in it. Do you know anything of aphasia?"

"I have heard of it, of course, though I can't say I remember ever knowing a case."

"I've seen one today — very curious case. The man's a Frenchman, discovered helpless in the street by a policeman. The only thing he can say that has any meaning in it at all is '*je le nie*,' and that he says mechanically, without in the least knowing what he is saying. And he can't write. But he got sketching and scrawling various things on some paper, and his scrawls — together with another thing or two — have given me an idea. We're following it up now. When we are less busy, and in a quiet place, I'll show you the sketches and explain things generally; there's no time now, and I *may* want your help for a bit, in which case ignorance may prevent you spoiling things, you clumsy ruffian. Hullo! here we are, I think!"

We had stopped at the end of another stable-yard, rather dirtier than the first. The stables were sound but inelegant sheds, and one or two appeared to be devoted to other purposes, having low chimneys, on one of which an old basket was rakishly set by way of cowl. Beside the entrance a worn-out old board was nailed, with the legend, "Stabling to Let," in letters formerly white on a ground formerly black.

"Come," said Holmes, "we'll explore."

112

We picked our way over the greasy cobble-stones and looked about us. On the left was the wall enclosing certain back-yards, and on the right the stables. Two doors in the middle of these were open, and a butcher's young man, who with his shiny bullet head would have been known for a butcher's young man anywhere, was wiping over the new-washed wheel of a smart butcher's cart.

"Good day," Holmes said pleasantly to the young man. "I notice there's some stabling to let here. Now, where should I inquire about it?"

"Jones, Whitfield Street," the young man answered, giving the wheel a final spin. "But there's only one little place to let now, I think, and it ain't very grand."

"Oh, which is that?"

"Next but one to the street there. A chap 'ad it for wood-choppin', but 'e chucked it. There ain't room for more'n a donkey an' a barrow."

"Ah, that's a pity. We're not particular, but want something big enough, and we don't mind paying a fair price. Perhaps we might make an arrangement with somebody here who has a stable?"

The young man shook his head.

"I shouldn't think so," he said doubtfully; "they're mostly shop-people as wants all the room theirselves. My guv'nor couldn't do nothink, I know. These 'ere two stables ain't scarcely enough for all 'e wants as it is. Then there's Barkett the greengrocer 'ere next door. *That* ain't no good. Then, next to that, there's the little place as is to let, and at the end there's Griffith's at the butter-shop."

"And those the other way?"

"Well, this 'ere first one's Curtis's, Euston Road — that's a butter-shop, too, an' 'e 'as the next after that. The last one, up at the end — I dunno quite whose that is. It ain't been long took, but I b'lieve it's some foreign baker's. I ain't ever see anythink come out of it, though; but there's a 'orse there, I know — I seen the feed took in."

Holmes turned thoughtfully away.

"Thanks," he said. "I suppose we can't manage it, then. Good day."

We walked to the street as the butcher's young man wheeled in his cart and flung away his pail of water.

"Will you just hang about here, Brett," he asked, "while I hurry round to the nearest iron-monger's? I shan't be gone long. We're going to work a little burglary. Take note if anybody comes to that stable at the farther end."

He hurried away and I waited. In a few moments the butcher's young man shut his doors and went whistling down the street, and in a few moments more Holmes appeared.

"Come," he said, "there's nobody about now; we'll lose no time. I've bought a pair of pliers and a few nails."

We re-entered the yard at the door of the last stable. Holmes stooped and examined the padlock. Taking a nail in his pliers he bent it carefully against the brick wall. Then using the nail as a key, still held by the pliers, and working the padlock gently in his left hand, in an astonishingly few seconds he had released the hasp and taken off the padlock. "I'm not altogether a bad burglar," he remarked. "Not so bad, really."

The padlock fastened a bar which, when removed, allowed the door to be opened. Opening it, Holmes immediately seized a candle stuck in a bottle which stood on a shelf, pulled me in, and closed the door behind us.

"We'll do this by candle-light," he said, as he struck a match. "If the door were left open it would be seen from the street. Keep your ears open in case anybody comes down the yard."

The part of the shed that we stood in was used as a coach-house, and was occupied by a rather shabby tradesman's cart, the shafts of which rested on the ground. From the stall adjoining came the sound of the shuffling and trampling of an impatient horse.

We turned to the cart. On the name-board at the side were painted in worn letters the words, "Schuyler, Baker." The address, which had been below, was painted out.

Holmes took out the pins and let down the tail board. Within the cart was a new bed-mattress which covered the whole surface at the bottom. I felt it, pressed it from the top, and saw that it was an ordinary spring mattress — perhaps rather unusually soft in the springs. It seemed a curious thing to keep in a baker's cart.

Holmes, who had set the candle on a convenient shelf, plunged his arm into the farthermost recesses of the cart and brought forth a very long French loaf, and then another. Diving again he produced certain loaves of the sort known as the "plain cottage " — two sets of four each, each set baked together in a row. "Feel this bread," said Holmes, and I felt it. It was stale — almost as hard as wood.

Holmes produced a large pocket-knife, and with what seemed to me to be superfluous care and elaboration, cut into the top of one of the cottage loaves. Then he inserted his fingers in the gap he had made and firmly but slowly tore the hard bread into two pieces. He pulled away the crumb from within till there was nothing left but a rather thick outer shell.

"No," he said, rather to himself than to me, "there's nothing in *that*." He lifted one of the very long French loaves and measured it against the interior of the cart. It had before been propped diagonally, and now it was noticeable that it was just a shade longer than the inside of the cart was wide. Jammed in, in fact, it held firmly. Holmes produced his knife again, and divided this long loaf in the centre; there was nothing but bread in *that*. The horse in the stall fidgeted more than ever.

"That horse hasn't been fed lately, I fancy," Holmes said. "We'll give the poor chap a bit of this hay in the corner."

"But," I said, "what about this bread? What did you expect to find in it? I can't see what you're driving at."

"I'll tell you," Holmes replied, "I'm driving after something I expect to find, and close at hand here, too. How are your nerves today — pretty steady? The thing may try them."

Before I could reply there was a sound of footsteps in the yard outside, approaching. Holmes lifted his finger instantly for silence and whispered hurriedly, "There's only one. If he comes *here*, we grab him."

The steps came nearer and stopped outside the door. There was a pause, and then a slight drawing in of breath, as of a person suddenly surprised. At that moment the door was slightly shifted ajar and an eye peeped in.

"Catch him!" said Holmes aloud, as we sprang to the door. "He mustn't get away!"

I had been nearer the doorway, and was first through it. The stranger ran down the yard at his best, but my legs were the longer, and half-way to the street I caught him by the shoulder and swung him round. Like lightning he whipped out a knife, and I flung in my left instantly on the chance of flooring him. It barely checked him, however, and the knife swung short of my chest by no more than two inches; but Holmes had him by the wrist and tripped him forward on his face. He struggled like a wild beast, and Holmes had to stand on his forearm and force up his wrist till the bones were near breaking before he dropped his knife. But throughout the struggle the man never shouted, called for help, nor, indeed, made the slightest sound, and we on our part were equally silent. It was quickly over, of course, for he was on his face, and we were two. We dragged our prisoner into the stable and closed the door behind us. So far as we had seen, nobody had witnessed the capture from the street, though, of course, we had been too busy to be certain.

"There's a set of harness hanging over at the back," said Holmes; "I think we'll tie him up with the traces and reins — nothing like leather. We don't need a gag; I know he won't shout."

While I got the straps Holmes held the prisoner by a peculiar neck-and-wrist grip that forbade him to move except at the peril of a snapped arm. He had probably never been a person of pleasant aspect, being short, strongly and squatly built, large and ugly of feature, and wild and dirty of hair and beard. And now, his face flushed with struggling and smeared with mud from the stable-yard, his nose bleeding and his forehead exhibiting a growing bump, he looked particularly repellent. We strapped his elbows together behind, and as he sullenly ignored a demand for the contents of his pockets Holmes unceremoniously turned them out. Helpless as he was, the man struggled to prevent this, though, of course, ineffectually. There were papers, tobacco, a bunch of keys, and various odds and ends. Holmes was glancing hastily at the papers when, suddenly dropping them, he caught the prisoner by the shoulder and pulled him away from a partly-consumed hay-truss which stood in a corner, and toward which he had quietly sidled.

"Keep him still," said Holmes; "we haven't examined this place yet." And he commenced to pull away the hay from the corner.

Presently a large piece of sackcloth was revealed, and this being lifted left visible below it another batch of loaves of the same sort as we had seen in the cart. There were a dozen of them in one square batch, and the only thing about them that differed them from those in the cart was their position, for the batch lay bottom side up.

"That's enough, I think," Holmes said. "Don't touch them, for Heaven's sake!" He picked up the papers he had dropped. "That has saved us a little search," he continued. "See here, Brett; I was in the act of telling you my suspicions when this little affair interrupted me. If you care to look at one or two of these letters you'll see what I should have told you. It's Anarchism and bombs, of course. I'm about as certain as I can be that there's a reversible dynamite bomb inside each of those innocent loaves, though I assure you I don't mean meddling with them now. But see here. Will you go and bring in a four-wheeler? Bring it right down the yard. There's more to do, and we mustn't attract attention."

I hurried away and found the cab. The meaning of the loaves, the cart, and the spring-mattress was now plain. There was an Anarchist plot to carry out a number of explosions probably simultaneously, in different parts of the city. I had, of course, heard much of the terrible "reversing" bombs — those bombs which, containing a tube of acid plugged by wadding, required no fuse, and only needed to be inverted to be set going to explode in a few minutes. The loaves containing these bombs would form an effectual "blind," and they were to be distributed, probably in broad daylight, in the most natural manner possible, in a baker's cart. A man would be waiting near the scene of each contemplated explosion. He would be given a loaf taken from the inverted batch. He would take it — perhaps wrapped in paper, but still inverted, and apparently the most innocent object possible — to the spot selected, deposit it, right side up — which would reverse the inner tube and set up the action — in some quiet corner, behind a door or what not, and make his own escape, while the explosion tore down walls and — if the experiment were lucky — scattered the flesh and bones of unsuspecting people.

The infernal loaves were made and kept reversed, to begin with, in order to stand more firmly, and — if observed — more naturally, when turned over to explode. Even if a child picked up the loaf and carried it off, that child at least would be blown to atoms, which at any rate would have been something for the conspirators to congratulate themselves upon. The spring-mattress, of course, was to ease the jolting to the bombs, and obviate any random jerking loose of the acid, which might have had the deplorable result of sacrificing the valuable life of the conspirator who drove the cart. The other loaves, too, with no explosive contents, had their use. The two long ones, which fitted across the inside of the cart, would be jammed across so as to hold the bombs in the centre, and the others would be used to pack the batch on the other sides and prevent any dangerous slipping about. The thing seemed pretty plain, except that as yet I had no idea of how Holmes learned anything of the business.

I brought the four-wheeler up to the door of the stable and we thrust the man into it, and Holmes locked the stable door with its proper key. Then we drove off to Tottenham Court Road police-station, and, by Holmes's order, straight into the yard.

In less than ten minutes from our departure from the stable our prisoner was finally secured, and Holmes was deep in consultation with police officials. Messengers were sent and telegrams dispatched, and presently Holmes came to me with information.

"The name of the helpless Frenchman the police found this morning," he said, "appears to be Gérard — at least I am almost certain of it. Among the papers found on the prisoner — whose full name doesn't appear, but who seems to be spoken of as Luigi (he is Italian) — among the papers, I say, is a sort of notice convening a meeting for this evening to decide as to the 'final punishment' to be awarded the 'traitor Gérard, now in charge of comrade Pingard.'

"The place of meeting is not mentioned, but it seems more than probable that it will be at the Bakunin Club, not five minutes' walk from this place. The police have all these places under quiet observation, of course, and that is the club at which apparently important Anarchist meetings have been held lately. It is the only club that has never been raided as yet, and, it would seem, the only one they would feel at all safe in using for anything important.

"Moreover, Luigi just now simply declined to open his mouth when asked where the meeting was to be, and said nothing when the names of several other places were suggested, but suddenly found his tongue at the mention of the Bakunin Club, and denied vehemently that the meeting was to be there — it was the only thing he uttered. So that it seems pretty safe to assume that it *is* to be there. Now, of course, the matter's very serious. Men have been dispatched to take charge of the stable very quietly, and the club is to be taken possession of at once — also very quietly. It must be done without a moment's delay, and as there is a chance that the only detective officers within reach at the moment may be known by sight, I have undertaken to get in first. Perhaps you'll come? We may have to take the door with a rush."

Of course I meant to miss nothing if I could help it, and said so.

"Very well," replied Holmes, "we'll get ourselves up a bit." He began taking off his collar and tie. "It is getting dusk," he proceeded, "and we shan't want old clothes to make ourselves look sufficiently shabby. We're both wearing bowler hats, which is lucky. Make a dent in yours — if you can do so without permanently damaging it."

We got rid of our collars and made chokers of our ties. We turned our coat-collars up at one side only, and then, with dented hats worn raffishly, and our hands in our pockets, we looked disreputable enough for all practical purposes in twilight. A cordon of plain-clothes police had already been forming round the club, we were told, and so we sallied forth. We turned into Windmill Street, crossed Whitfield Street, and in a turning or two we came to the Bakunin Club. I could see no sign of anything like a ring of policemen, and said so. Holmes chuckled. "Of course not," he said; "they don't go about a job of this sort with drums beating and flags flying. But they are all there, and some are watching us. There is the house. I'll negotiate."

The house was one of the very shabby *passé* sort that abound in that quarter. The very narrow area was railed over, and almost choked with rubbish. Visible above it were three floors, the lowest indicated by the door and one window, and the other two by two windows each — mean and dirty all. A faint light appeared in the top floor, and another from somewhere behind the refuse-heaped area. Everywhere else was in darkness. Holmes looked intently into the area, but it was impossible to discern anything behind the sole grimy patch of window that was visible. Then we stepped lightly up the three or four steps to the door and rang the bell.

We could hear slippered feet mounting a stair and approaching. A latch was shifted, a door opened six inches, an indistinct face appeared, and a female voice asked, "*Qui est là?*"

"*Deux camarades*," Holmes grunted testily. "*Ouvrez vite.*"

I had noticed that the door was kept from opening further by a short chain. This chain the woman unhooked from the door, but still kept the latter merely ajar, as though intending to assure herself still further. But Holmes immediately pushed the door back, planted his foot against it, and entered, asking carelessly as he did so, "*Où se trouve Luigi?*"

I followed on his heels, and in the dark could just distinguish that Holmes pushed the woman instantly against the wall and clapped his hand to her mouth. At the same moment a file of quiet men were suddenly visible ascending the steps at my heels. They were the police.

The door was closed behind us almost noiselessly, and a match was struck. Two men stood at the bottom of the stairs, and the others searched the house. Only two men were found — both in a top room. They were secured and brought down.

The woman was now ungagged, and she used her tongue at a great rate. One of the men was a small, meek-looking slip of a fellow, and he appeared to be the woman's husband. "Eh, messieurs le police," she exclaimed vehemently, "it ees not of 'im, mon pauvre Pierre, zat you sall rrun in. 'Im and me — we are not of the clob — we work only — we housekeep."

Holmes whispered to an officer, and the two men were taken below. Then Holmes spoke to the woman, whose protests had not ceased. "You say you are not of the club," he said, "but what is there to prove that? If you are but housekeepers, as you say, you have nothing to fear. But you can only prove it by giving the police information. For instance, now, about Gérard. What have they done with him?"

"Jean Pingard — 'im you 'ave take downstairs — 'e 'ave lose 'im. Jean Pingard get last night all a-boosa — all dronk like zis" — she rolled her head and shoulders to express intoxication — "and he sleep too much today, when Émile go out, and Gérard, he go too, and nobody know. I will tell you anysing. We are not of the clob — we housekeep, me and Pierre."

"But what did they do to Gérard before he went away?"

The woman was ready and anxious to tell anything. Gérard had been selected to do something — what it was exactly she did not know, but there was a horse and cart, and he was to drive it. Where the horse and cart was also she did not know, but Gérard had driven a cart before in his work for a baker, and he was to drive one in connection with some scheme among the members of the club. But *le pauvre Gérard* at the last minute disliked to drive the cart; he had fear. He did not say he had fear, but he prepared a letter — a letter that was not signed. The letter was to be sent to the police, and it told them the whereabouts of the horse and cart, so that the police might seize these things, and then there would be nothing for Gérard, who had fear, to do in the way of driving. No, he did not betray the names of the comrades, but he told the place of the horse and the cart.

Nevertheless, the letter was never sent. There was suspicion, and the letter was found in a pocket and read. Then there was a meeting, and Gérard was confronted with his letter. He could say nothing but "*Je le nie!*" — found no explanation but that. There was much noise, and she had observed from a staircase, from which one might see through a ventilating hole, Gérard had much fear — very much fear. His face was white, and it moved; he prayed for mercy, and they talked of killing him. It was discussed how he should be killed, and the poor Gérard was more terrified. He was made to take off his collar, and a razor was drawn across his throat, though without cutting him, till he fainted.

Then water was flung over him, and he was struck in the face till he revived. He again repeated, "*Je le nie! je le nie!*" and nothing more. Then one struck him with a bottle, and another with a stick; the point of a knife was put against his throat and held there, but this time he did not faint, but cried softly, as a man who is drunk, "*Je le nie! je le nie!*" So they tied a handkerchief about his neck, and twisted it till his face grew purple and black, and his eyes were round and terrible, and then they struck his face, and he fainted again. But they took away the handkerchief, having fear that they could not easily get rid of the body if he were killed, for there was no preparation. So they decided to meet again and discuss when there would be preparation. Wherefore they took him away to the rooms of Jean Pingard — of Jean and Émile Pingard — in Henry Street, Golden Square. But Émile Pingard had gone out, and Jean was drunk and slept, and they lost him. Jean Pingard was he downstairs — the taller of the two; the other was but *le pauvre Pierre*, who, with herself, was not of the club. They worked only; they were the keepers of the house. There was nothing for which they should be arrested, and she would give the police any information they might ask.

"As I thought, you see," Holmes said to me, "the man's nerves have broken down under the terror and the strain, and aphasia is the result. I think I told you that the only articulate thing he could say was '*Je le nie!*' and now we know how those words were impressed on him till he now pronounces them mechanically, with no idea of their meaning. Come, we can do no more here now. But wait a moment."

There were footsteps outside. The light was removed, and a policeman went to the door and opened it as soon as the bell rang. Three men stepped in one after another, and the door was immediately shut behind them — they were prisoners.

We left quietly, and although we, of course, expected it, it was not till the next morning that we learned absolutely that the largest arrest of Anarchists ever made in this country was made at the Bakunin Club that night. Each man as he came was admitted — and collared.

We made our way to Luzatti's, and it was over our dinner that Holmes put me in full possession of the earlier facts of this case, which I have set down as impersonal narrative in their proper place at the beginning.

"But," I said, "what of that aimless scribble you spoke of that Gérard made in the police station? Can I see it?"

Holmes turned to where his coat hung behind him and took a handful of papers from his pocket.

"Most of these," he said, "mean nothing at all. *That* is what he wrote at first," and he handed me the first of the two papers which were presented in facsimile in the earlier part of this narrative.

"You see," he said, "he has begun mechanically from long use to write 'monsieur' — the usual beginning of a letter. But he scarcely makes three letters before tailing off into sheer scribble. He tries again and again, and although once there is something very like 'que,' and once something like a word preceded by a negative 'n,' the whole thing is meaningless.

"This" (he handed me the other paper which has been printed in facsimile) "*does* mean something, though Gérard never intended it. Can you spot the meaning? Really, I think it's pretty plain — especially now that you know as much as I about the day's adventures. The thing at the top left-hand corner, I may tell you, Gérard intended for a sketch of a clock on the mantelpiece in the police-station."

I stared hard at the paper, but could make nothing whatever of it. "I only see the horse-shoe clock," I said, "and a sort of second, unsuccessful attempt to draw it again. Then there is a horse-shoe dotted, but scribbled over, and then a sort of kite or balloon on a string, a Highlander, and — well, I don't understand it, I confess. Tell me."

"I'll explain what I learned from that," Holmes said, "and also what led me to look for it. From what the inspector told me, I judged the man to be in a very curious state, and I took a fancy to see him. Most I was curious to know why he should have a terror of bread at one moment and eat it ravenously at another. When I saw him I felt pretty sure that he was not mad, in the common sense of the term. As far as I could judge it seemed to be a case of aphasia.

"Then when the doctor came I had a chat (as I have already told you) with the policeman who found the man. He told me about the incident of the bread with rather more detail than I had had from the inspector. Thus it was plain that the man was terrified at the bread only when it was in the form of a loaf, and ate it eagerly when it was cut into pieces. That was *one* thing to bear in mind. He was not afraid of *bread*, but only of a *loaf*.

"Very well. I asked the policeman to find another uncut loaf, and to put it near the man when his attention was diverted. Meantime the doctor reported that my suspicion as to aphasia was right. The man grew more comfortable, and was assured that he was among friends and had nothing to fear, so that when at length he found the loaf near his elbow he was not so violently terrified, only very uneasy. I watched him and saw him turn it bottom up — a very curious thing to do; he immediately became less uneasy — the turning over of the loaf seemed to have set his mind at rest in some way. This was more curious still. I thought for some little while before accepting the bomb theory as the most probable.

"The doctor left, and I determined to give the man another chance with pen and paper. I felt pretty certain that if he were allowed to scribble and sketch as he pleased, sooner or later he would do something that would give me some sort of a hint. I left him entirely alone and let him do as he pleased, but I watched.

"After all the futile scribble which you have seen, he began to sketch, first a man's head, then a chair — just what he might happen to see in the room. Presently he took to the piece of paper you have before you. He observed that clock and began to sketch it, then went on to other things, such as you see, scribbling idly over most of them when finished. When he had made the last of the sketches he made a hasty scrawl of his pen over it and broke down. It had brought his terror to his mind again somehow.

"I seized the paper and examined it closely. Now just see. Ignore the clock, which was merely a sketch of a thing before him, and look at the three things following. What are they? A horse-shoe, a captive balloon, and a Highlander. Now, can't you think of something those three things in that order suggest?"

I could think of nothing whatever, and I confessed as much.

"Think, now. Tottenham Court Road!"

I started. "Of course," I said. "That never struck me. There's the Horse-shoe Hotel, with the sign outside, there's the large toy and fancy shop half-way up, where they have a captive balloon moored to the roof as an advertisement, and there's the tobacco and snuff shop on the left, toward the other end, where they have a life-size wooden Highlander at the door — an uncommon thing, indeed, nowadays."

"You are right. The curious conjunction struck me at once. There they are, all three, and just in the order in which one meets them going up from Oxford Street. Also, as if to confirm the conjecture, note the *dotted* horse-shoe. Don't you remember that at night the Horse-shoe Hotel sign is illuminated by two rows of gas lights?

"Now here was my clue at last. Plainly, this man, in his mechanical sketching, was following a regular train of thought, and unconsciously illustrating it as he went along. Many people in perfect health and mental soundness do the same thing if a pen and a piece of waste paper be near. The man's train of thought led him, in memory, up Tottenham Court Road, and further, to where some disagreeable recollection upset him. It was my business to trace this train of thought. Do you remember the feat of Dupin in Poe's story, 'The Murders in the Rue Morgue' — how he walks by his friend's side in silence for some distance, and then suddenly breaks out with a divination of his thoughts, having silently traced them from a fruiterer with a basket, through paving-stones, Epicurus, Dr. Nichols, the constellation Orion, and a Latin poem, to a cobbler lately turned actor?

"Well, it was some such task as this (but infinitely simpler, as a matter of fact) that was set me. This man begins by drawing the horse-shoe clock. Having done with that, and with the horse-shoe still in his mind, he starts to draw a horse-shoe simply. It is a failure, and he scribbles it out. His mind at once turns to the Horse-shoe Hotel, which he knows from frequently passing it, and its sign of gas-jets. He sketches *that*, making dots for the gas lights. Once started in Tottenham Court Road, his mind naturally follows his usual route along it. He remembers the advertising captive balloon half-way up, and down *that* goes on his paper. In imagination he crosses the road, and keeps on till he comes to the very noticeable Highlander outside the tobacconist's. *That* is sketched. Thus it is plain that a familiar route with him was from New Oxford Street up Tottenham Court Road.

"At the police-station I ventured to guess from this that he lived somewhere near Seven Dials. Perhaps before long we shall know if this was right. But to return to the sketches. After the Highlander there is something at first not very distinct. A little examination, however, shows it to be intended for a chimney-pot partly covered with a basket. Now an old basket, stuck sideways on a chimney by way of cowl, is not an uncommon thing in parts of the country, but it is very unusual in London. Probably, then, it would be in some by-street or alley. Next and last, there is a horse's head, and it was at this that the man's trouble returned to him.

"Now, when one goes to a place and finds a horse there, that place is not uncommonly a stable; and, as a matter of fact, the basket-cowl would be much more likely to be found in use in a range of back stabling than anywhere else. Suppose, then, that after taking the direction indicated in the sketches — the direction of Fitzroy Square, in fact — one were to find a range of stabling with a basket-cowl visible about it? I know my London pretty well, as you are aware, and I could remember but two likely stable-yards in that particular part — the two we looked at, in the second of which you may possibly have noticed just such a basket-cowl as I have been speaking of.

"Well, what we did you know, and that we found confirmation of my conjecture about the loaves you also know. It was the recollection of the horse and cart, and what they were to transport, and what the end of it all had been, that upset Gérard as he drew the horse's head. You will notice that the sketches have not been done in separate rows, left to right — they have simply followed one another all round the paper, which means preoccupation and unconsciousness on the part of the man who made them."

"But," I asked, "supposing those loaves to contain bombs, how were the bombs put there? Baking the bread round them would have been risky, wouldn't it?"

"Certainly. What they did was to cut the loaves, each row, down the centre. Then most of the crumb was scooped out, the explosive inserted, and the sides joined up and glued. I thought you had spotted the joins, though they certainly were neat."

"No, I didn't examine closely. Luigi, of course, had been told off for a daily visit to feed the horse, and that is how we caught him."

"One supposes so. They hadn't rearranged their plans as to going on with the outrages after Gérard's defection. By the way, I noticed that he was accustomed to driving when I first saw him. There was an unmistakable mark on his coat, just at the small of the back, that drivers get who lean against a rail in a cart."

The loaves were examined by official experts, and, as everybody now knows, were found to contain, as Holmes had supposed, large charges of dynamite. What became of some half-dozen of the men captured is also well known: their sentences were exemplary.

The Case of Mr. Geldard's Elopement

I. Many people have been surprised at the information that, in all Sherlock Holmes's wide and busy practice, the matrimonial cases whereon he has been engaged have been comparatively few. That he has had many important cases of the sort is true, but among the innumerable cases of different descriptions they make a small percentage. The reason is that so many of the persons wishing to consult him on such concerns were actuated by mere unreasoning or fanciful jealousy that Holmes would do no more in their cases than urge reconciliation and mutual trust. The common "private inquiry" offices chiefly flourish on this class of case, and their proprietors present no particular reluctance to taking it up. In any event it means fees for consultation and "watching"; and recent newspaper reports have made it plain that among some of the less scrupulous agents a case may be manufactured from beginning to end according to order. Again, Holmes had a distaste for the sort of work commonly involved in matrimonial troubles; and with the immense amount of business brought to him, rendering necessary his rejection of so many commissions, it was easy for him to avoid what went against his inclinations. Still, as I have said, matrimonial cases there were, and often of an interesting nature, taking rise in no fanciful nor unreasoning jealousy.

When, on its change of proprietorship, I accepted my appointment on the paper that now claims me, I had a week or two's holiday pending the final turning over of the property. I could not leave town, for I might have been wanted at any moment, but I made an absorbing and instructive use of my leisure as an amateur assistant to Holmes. I sat in his rooms much of the time and saw more of the daily routine of his work than I had ever done before; and I was present at one or two interviews that initiated cases that afterwards developed striking features. One of these — which indeed I saw entirely through before I resumed my more legitimate work — was the case of Mr. and Mrs. Geldard.

Holmes had stepped out for a few minutes, and I was sitting alone in his rooms when I became conscious of some disturbance in the hall. An excited female voice was audible making impatient inquiries. Presently the housekeeper came in with the message that a lady — Mrs. Geldard, was the name on the visiting card — was anxious to see Mr. Holmes at once, and failing himself had decided to see me, whom the housekeeper had calmly taken it upon herself to describe as Holmes's confidential assistant. She apologized for this, and explained that she thought, as the lady seemed excited, it would be as well to let her see me to begin with, if there was no objection, and perhaps she would begin to be coherent and intelligible by Holmes's arrival, which might occur at any moment. So the lady was shown in. She was tall, bony, and severe of face, and she began as soon as she saw me: "I've come to get you to get a watch set on my husband. I've endured this sort of thing in silence long enough. I won't have it. I'll see if there's no protection to be had for a woman treated as I am — with his goings out all day 'on business' when his office is shut up tight all the time. I wanted to see Mr. Holmes himself, but I suppose you'll do, for the present at any rate, though I'll have it sifted to the bottom, and get the best advice to be had, no matter what it costs, though I *am* only a woman with nobody to confide in or to speak a word for me, and I'm not going to be crushed like a fly, as I'll soon let him know."

Here I seized a short opportunity to offer Mrs. Geldard a chair, and to say that I expected Mr. Holmes in a few minutes.

"Very well, I'll wait and see him. But you have to do with the watching business no doubt, and you'll understand what it is I want done; and I'm sure I'm justified, and mean to sift it to the bottom, whatever happens. Am I to be kept in total ignorance of what my husband does all day when he is supposed to be at business? Is it likely I should submit to that?"

I said I didn't think it likely at all, which was a fact. Mrs. Geldard appeared to be the least submissive woman I ever saw.

"No, and I won't, that's more. Nice goings on somewhere, no doubt, with his office shut up all day and the business going to ruin. I want you to watch him. I want you to follow him tomorrow morning and find out all he does and let me know. I've followed him myself this morning and yesterday morning, but he gets away somehow from the back of his office, and I can't watch on two staircases at once, so I want you to come and do it, and I'll — "

Here fortunately Holmes's arrival checked Mrs. Geldard's flow of speech, and I rose and introduced him. I told him shortly that the lady desired a watch to be set on her husband at his office, and a report to be given her of his daily proceedings. Holmes did not appear to accept the commission with any particular delight, but he sat down to hear his visitor's story. "Stay here, Brett," he said, as he saw my hands stretched towards the door. "We've an engagement presently, you know."

The engagement, I remembered, was merely to lunch, and Holmes kept me with some notion of restricting the time which this alarming woman might be disposed to occupy. She repeated to Holmes, in the same manner, what she had already said to me, and then Holmes, seizing his first opportunity, said, "Will you please tell me, Mrs. Geldard, definitely and concisely, what evidence, or even indication, you have of unbecoming conduct on your husband's part, and substantially what case you wish me to take up?"

"Case? Why, I've been telling you." And again Mrs. Geldard repeated her vague catalogue of sufferings, assuring Holmes that she was determined to have the best advice and assistance, and that therefore she had come to him. In the end Holmes answered, "Put concisely, Mrs. Geldard, I take it that your case is simply this. Mr. Geldard is in business as, I think you told me, a general agent and broker, and keeps an office in the city. You have had various disagreements with him — not an uncommon thing, unfortunately, between married people — and you have entertained certain indefinite suspicions of his behavior. Yesterday you went so far as to go to his office soon after he should have been there, and found him absent and the

131

office shut up. You waited some time, and called again, but the door was still locked, and the caretaker of the building assured you that Mr. Geldard usually kept his office thus shut. You knocked repeatedly, and called through the keyhole, but got no answer. This morning you even followed your husband and saw him enter his office, but when, a little later, you yourself attempted to enter it you once more found it locked and apparently tenantless. From this you conclude that he must have left his rooms by some back way, and you say you are determined to find out where he goes and what he does during the day. For this purpose you, I gather, wish me to watch him and report his whole day's proceedings to you?"

"Yes, of course; as I said."

"I'm afraid the state of my other engagements just at present will scarcely admit of that. Indeed, to speak quite frankly, this mere watching, especially of husband or wife, is not a sort of business that I care to undertake, except as a necessary part of some definite, tangible case. But apart from that, will you allow me to advise you? Not professionally, I mean, but merely as a man of the world. Why come to third parties with these vague suspicions? Family divisions of this sort, with all sorts of covert mistrust and suspicion, are bad things at best, and once carried as far as you talk of carrying this, go beyond peaceable remedy. Why not deal frankly and openly with your husband? Why not ask him plainly what he has been doing during the days you were unable to get into his office? You will probably find it all capable of a very simple and innocent explanation."

"Am I to understand, then," Mrs. Geldard said, bridling, "that you refuse to help me?"

"I have not refused to help you," Holmes replied. "On the contrary, I am trying to help you now. Did your husband ever follow any other profession than the one he is now engaged in?"

"Once he was a mechanical engineer, but he got very few clients, and it didn't pay."

"There, now, is a suggestion. Would it be very unlikely that your husband, trained mechanician as he is, may have reverted so far to his old profession as to be conceiving some new invention?

And in that case, what more probable than that he would lock himself securely in his office to work out his idea, and take no notice of visitors knocking, in order to admit nobody who might learn something of what he was doing? Does he keep a clerk or office boy?"

"No, he never has since he left the mechanical engineering."

"Well, Mrs. Geldard, I'm sorry I have no more time now, but I must earnestly repeat my advice. Come to an understanding with your husband in a straightforward way as soon as you possibly can. There are plenty of private inquiry offices about where they will watch anybody, and do almost anything, without any inquiry into their clients' motives, and with a single eye to fees. I charge you no fee, and advise you to treat your husband with frankness."

Mrs. Geldard did not seem particularly satisfied, though Holmes's rejection of a consultation fee somewhat softened her. She left protesting that Holmes didn't know the sort of man she had to deal with, and that, one way or another, she must have an explanation.

"Come, we'll get to lunch," said Holmes. "I'm afraid my suggestion as to Mr. Geldard's probable occupation in his office wasn't very brilliant, but it was the pleasantest I could think of for the moment, and the main thing was to pacify the lady. One does no good by aggravating a misunderstanding of that sort."

"Can you make any conjecture," I said, "at what the trouble really is?"

Holmes raised his eyebrows and shook his head. "There's no telling," he said. "An angry, jealous, pragmatical woman, apparently, this Mrs. Geldard, and it's impossible to judge at first sight how much she really knows and how much she imagines. I don't suppose she'll take my advice. She seems to have worked herself into a state of rancor that must burst out violently somewhere. But lunch is the present business. Come."

The next day I spent at a friend's house a little way out of town, so that it was not till the following morning, about the same time, that I learned from Holmes that Mrs. Geldard had called again.

"Yes," he said; "she seems to have taken my advice in her own way, which wasn't a judicious one. When I suggested that she should speak frankly to her husband I meant her to do it in a reasonably amicable mood. Instead of that, she appears to have flown at his throat, so to speak, with all the bitterness at her tongue's disposal. The natural result was a row. The man slanged back, the woman threatened divorce, and the man threatened to leave the country altogether. And so yesterday Mrs. Geldard was here again to get me to follow and watch him. I had to decline once more, and got something rather like a slanging myself for my pains. She seemed to think I was in league with her husband in some way. In the end I promised — more to get rid of her than anything else — to take the case in hand if ever there were anything really tangible to go upon; if her husband really did desert her, you know, or anything like that. If, in fact, there were anything more for me to consider than these spiteful suspicions."

"I suppose," I said, "she had nothing more to tell you than she had before?"

"Very little. She seems to have startled Geldard, however, by a chance shot. It seems that she once employed a maid, whom she subsequently dismissed, because, as she tells me, the young woman was a great deal too good-looking, and because she observed, or fancied she observed, signs of some secret understanding between her maid and her husband. Moreover, it was her husband who discovered this maid and introduced her into the house, and furthermore, he did all he could to induce Mrs. Geldard not to dismiss her. He even hinted that her dismissal might cause serious trouble, and Mrs. Geldard says it is chiefly since this maid has left the house that his movements have become so mysterious. Well it seems that in the heat of yesterday's quarrel Mrs. Geldard, quite at random, asked tauntingly how many letters Geldard had received from Emma Trennatt lately — Emma Trennatt was the girl's name. This chance shot seemed to hit the target. Geldard (so his wife tells me at any rate) winced visibly, paled a little, and dodged the question. But for the rest of the quarrel he appeared much less at ease, and made more than one attempt to find out how much his wife really knew of the correspondence she had spoken of. But as her reference to it was of course the wildest possible fluke, he got little guidance, while his better-half waxed savage in her triumph, and they parted on wild cat terms. She came straight here and evidently thought that after Geldard's reception of her allusion to correspondence with Emma Trennatt — which she seemed to regard as final and conclusive confirmation of all her jealousies — I should take the case in hand at once. When she found me still disinclined she gave me a trifling sample of her rhetoric, as no doubt commonly supplied to Mr. Geldard. She said in effect that she had only come to me because she meant having the best assistance possible, but that she didn't think much of me after all, and one man was as bad as another, and so on. I think she was a trifle angrier because I remained calm and civil. And she went away this time without the least reference to a consultation fee one way or another."

I laughed. "Probably," I said, "she went off to some agent who'll watch as long as she likes to pay."

"Quite possibly." But we were quite wrong. Holmes took his hat and we made for the staircase. As we opened the landing door there were hurried feet on the stairs below, and as it shut behind Mrs. Geldard's bonnet-load of pink flowers hove up before us. She was in a state of fierce alarm and excitement that had oddly enough something of triumph in it, as of the woman who says, "I told you so." Holmes gave a tragic groan under his breath.

"Here's a nice state of things I'm in for now, Mr. Holmes," she began abruptly, "through your refusing to do anything for me while there was time, though I was ready to pay you well as I told your young man but no you wouldn't listen to anything and seemed to think you knew my business better than I could tell you and now you've caused this state of affairs by delay perhaps you'll take the case in hand now?"

"But you haven't told me what has happened," Holmes began, whereat the lady instantly rejoined, with a shrill pretence of a laugh, "Happened? Why what do you suppose has happened after what I have told you over and over again? My precious husband's gone clean away, that's all. He's deserted me and gone nobody knows where. That's what's happened. You said that if he did anything of that sort you'd take the case up; so now I've come to see if you'll keep your promise. Not that it's likely to be of much use *now*."

We turned back into Holmes's rooms and Mrs. Geldard told her story. Disentangled from irrelevances, repetitions, opinions and incidental observations, it was this. After the quarrel Geldard had gone to business as usual and had not been seen nor heard of since. After her yesterday's interview with Holmes Mrs. Geldard had called at her husband's office and found it shut as before. She went home again and waited, but he never returned home that evening, nor all night. In the morning she had gone to the office once more, and finding it still shut had told the caretaker that her husband was missing and insisted on his bringing his own key and opening it for her inspection. Nobody was there, and Mrs. Geldard was astonished to find folded and laid on a cupboard shelf the entire suit of clothes that her husband had worn when he left home on the morning of the previous day. She also found in the waste paper basket the fragments of two or three envelopes addressed to her husband, which she brought for Holmes's inspection. They were in the handwriting of the girl Trennatt, and with them Mrs. Geldard had discovered a small fragment of one of the letters, a mere scrap, but sufficient to show part of the signature "Emma," and two or three of a row of crosses running beneath, such as are employed to represent kisses. These things she had brought with her.

Holmes examined them slightly and then asked, "Can I have a photograph of your husband, Mrs. Geldard?"

She immediately produced, not only a photograph of her husband, but also one of the girl Trennatt, which she said belonged to the cook. Holmes complimented her on her foresight. "And now," he said, "I think we'll go and take a look at Mr. Geldard's office, if we may. Of course I shall follow him up now." Holmes made a sign to me, which I interpreted as asking whether I would care to accompany him. I assented with a nod, for the case seemed likely to be interesting.

I omit most of Mrs. Geldard's talk by the way, which was almost ceaseless, mostly compounded of useless repetition, and very tiresome.

The office was on a third floor in a large building in Finsbury Pavement. The caretaker made no difficulty in admitting us. There were two rooms, neither very large, and one of them at the back very small indeed. In this was a small locked door.

"That leads on to the small staircase, sir," the caretaker said in response to Holmes's inquiry. "The staircase leads down to the basement, and it ain't used much 'cept by the cleaners."

"If I went down this back staircase," Holmes pursued, "I suppose I should have no difficulty in gaining the street?"

"Not a bit, sir. You'd have to go a little way round to get into Finsbury Pavement, but there's a passage leads straight from the bottom of the stairs out to Moorfields behind."

"Yes," remarked Mrs. Geldard bitterly, when the caretaker had left the room, "that's the way he's been leaving the office every day, and in disguise, too." She pointed to the cupboard where her husband's clothes lay. "Pretty plain proof that he was ashamed of his doings, whatever they were."

"Come, come," Holmes answered deprecatingly, "we'll hope there's nothing to be ashamed of — at any rate till there's proof of it. There's no proof as yet that your husband has been disguising. A great many men who rent offices, I believe, keep dress clothes at them for convenience in case of an unexpected invitation, or such other eventuality. We may find that he returned here last night, put on his evening dress and went somewhere dining. Illness, or fifty accidents, may have kept him from home."

But Mrs. Geldard was not to be softened by any such suggestion, which I could see Holmes had chiefly thrown out by way of pacifying the lady, and allaying her bitterness as far as he could, in view of a possible reconciliation when things were cleared up.

"*That* isn't very likely," she said. "If he kept a dress suit here openly I should know of it, and if he kept it here unknown to me, what did he want it for? If he went out in dress clothes last night, who did he go with? Who do you suppose, after seeing those envelopes and that piece of the letter?"

"Well, well, we shall see," Holmes replied. "May I turn out the pockets of these clothes?"

"Certainly; there's nothing in them of importance," Mrs. Geldard said. "I looked before I came to you."

Nevertheless Holmes turned them out. "Here is a check-book with a number of checks remaining. No counterfoils filled in, which is awkward. Bankers, the London Amalgamated. We will call there presently. An ivory pocket paper-knife. A sovereign purse — empty." Holmes placed the articles on the table as he named them. "Gold pencil case, ivory folding rule, Russia-leather card-case." He turned to Mrs. Geldard. "There is no pocket-book," he said, "no pocket-knife and no watch, and there are no keys. Did Mr. Geldard usually carry any of these things?"

"Yes," Mrs. Geldard replied, "he carried all four." Holmes's simple methodical calmness, and his plain disregard of her former volubility, appeared by this to have disciplined Mrs. Geldard into a businesslike brevity and directness of utterance.

"As to the watch now. Can you describe it?"

"Oh, it was only a cheap one. He had a gold one stolen — or at any rate he told me so — and since then he has only carried a very common sort of silver one, without a chain."

"The keys?"

"I only know there *was* a bunch of keys. Some of them fitted drawers and bureaux at home, and others, I suppose, fitted locks in this office."

"What of the pocket-knife?"

"That was a very uncommon one. It was a present, as a matter of fact, from an engineering friend, who had had it made specially. It was large, with a tortoise-shell handle and a silver plate with his initials. There was only one ordinary knife-blade in it, all the other implements were small tools or things of that kind. There was a small pair of silver calipers, for instance."

"Like these?" Holmes suggested, producing those he used for measuring drawers and cabinets in search of secret receptacles.

"Yes, like those. And there were folding steel compasses, a tiny flat spanner, a little spirit level, and a number of other small instruments of that sort. It was very well made indeed; he used to say that it could not have been made for five pounds."

"Indeed?" Holmes cast his eyes about the two rooms. "I see no signs of books here, Mrs. Geldard — account books I mean, of course. Your husband must have kept account books, I take it?"

"Yes, naturally; he must have done. I never saw them, of course, but every business man keeps books." Then after a pause Mrs. Geldard continued: "And they're gone too. I never thought of *that*. But there, I might have known as much. Who can trust a man safely if his own wife can't? But *I* won't shield him. Whatever he's been doing with his clients' money he'll have to answer for himself. Thank heaven I've enough to live on of my own without being dependent on a creature like him! But think of the disgrace! My husband nothing better than a common thief — swindling his clients and making away with his books when he can't go on any longer! But he shall be punished, oh yes; *I'll* see he's punished, if once I find him!"

Holmes thought for a moment, and then asked: "Do you know any of your husband's clients, Mrs, Geldard?"

"No," she answered, rather snappishly, "I don't. I've told you he never let me know anything of his business — never anything at all; and very good reason he had too, that's certain."

"Then probably you do not happen to know the contents of these drawers?" Holmes pursued, tapping the writing-table as be spoke.

"Oh, there's nothing of importance in them — at any rate in the unlocked ones. I looked at all of them this morning when I first came."

The table was of the ordinary pedestal pattern with four drawers at each side and a ninth in the middle at the top, and of very ordinary quality. The only locked drawer was the third from the top on the left-hand side. Holmes pulled out one drawer after another. In one was a tin half full of tobacco; in another a few cigars at the bottom of a box; in a third a pile of notepaper headed with the address of the office, and rather dusty; another was empty; still another contained a handful of string. The top middle drawer rather reminded me of a similar drawer of my own at my last newspaper office, for it contained several pipes; but my own were mostly briars, whereas these were all clays.

"There's nothing really so satisfactory," Holmes said, as he lifted and examined each pipe by turn, "to a seasoned smoker as a well used clay. Most such men keep one or more such pipes for strictly private use." There was nothing noticeable about these pipes except that they were uncommonly dirty, but Holmes scrutinized each before returning it to the drawer. Then he turned to Mrs. Geldard and said: "As to the bank now — the London Amalgamated, Mrs. Geldard. Are you known there personally?"

"Oh, yes; my husband gave them authority to pay checks signed by me up to a certain amount, and I often do it for household expenses, or when he happens to be away."

"Then perhaps it will be best for you to go alone," Holmes responded. "Of course they will never, as a general thing, give any person information as to the account of a customer, but perhaps, as you are known to them, and hold your husband's authority to draw checks, they may tell you something. What I want to find out is, of course, whether your husband drew from the bank all his remaining balance yesterday, or any large sum. You must go alone, ask for the manager, and tell him that you have seen nothing of Mr. Geldard since he left for business yesterday morning. Mind, you are not to appear angry, or suspicious, or anything of that sort, and you mustn't say you are employing me to bring him back from an elopement. That will shut up the channel of information at once. Hostile inquiries they'll never answer, even by the smallest hint, except after legal injunction. You can be as distressed and as alarmed as you please. Your husband has disappeared since yesterday morning, and you've no notion what has become of him; that is your tale, and a perfectly true one. You would like to know whether or not he has withdrawn his balance, or a considerable sum, since that would indicate whether or not his absence was intentional and premeditated."

Mrs. Geldard understood and undertook to make the inquiry with all discretion. The bank was not far, and it was arranged that she should return to the office with the result.

As soon as she had left Holmes turned to the pedestal table and probed the keyhole of the locked drawer with the small stiletto attached to his pen knife. "This seems to be a common sort of lock," he said. "I could probably open it with a bent nail. But the whole table is a cheap sort of thing. Perhaps there is an easier way."

He drew the unlocked drawer above completely out, passed his hand into the opening and felt about. "Yes," he said, "it's just as I hoped — as it usually is in pedestal tables not of the best quality; the partition between the drawers doesn't go more than two-thirds of the way back, and I can drop my hand into the drawer below. But I can't feel anything there — it seems empty."

He withdrew his hand and we tilted the whole table backward, so as to cause whatever lay in the drawers to slide to the back. This dodge was successful. Holmes reinserted his hand and withdrew it with two orderly heaps of papers, each held together by a metal clip. The papers in each clip, on examination, proved to be all of an identical character, with the exception of dates. They were, in fact, rent receipts. Those for the office, which had been given quarterly, were put back in their place with scarcely a glance, and the others Holmes placed on 'the table before him. Each ran, apart from dates, in this fashion: "Received from Mr. J. Cookson 15s., one month's rent of stable at 3 Dragon Yard, Benton Street, to," — here followed the date. "Also rent, feed and care of horse in own stable as agreed, £2. — W. GASK." The receipts were ill-written, and here and there ill-spelt. Holmes put the last of the receipts in his pocket and returned the others to the drawer. "Either," he said, "Mr. Cookson is a client who gets Mr. Geldard to hire stables for him, which may not be likely, or Mr. Geldard calls himself Mr.

Cookson when he goes driving — possibly with Miss Trennatt. We shall see."

The pedestal table put in order again, Holmes took the poker and raked in the fireplace. It was summer, and behind the bars was a sort of screen of cartridge paper with a frilled edge, and behind this various odds and ends had been thrown — spent matches, trade-circulars crumpled up, and torn paper. There were also the remains of several cigars, some only half smoked, and one almost whole. The torn paper Holmes examined piece by piece, and finally sorted out a number of pieces which he set to work to arrange on the blotting pad. They formed a complete note, written in the same hand as were the envelopes already found by Mrs. Geldard — that of the girl Emma Trennatt. It corresponded also with the solitary fragment of another letter which had accompanied them, by way of having a number of crosses below the signature, and it ran thus:

Tuesday Night

Dear Sam,

Tomorrow, to carry. Not late because people are coming for flowers. What you did was no good. The smoke leaks worse than ever, and F. thinks you must light a new pipe or else stop smoking altogether for a bit. Uncle is anxious.

EMMA

Then followed the crosses, filling one line and nearly half the next; seventeen in all.

Holmes gazed at the fragments thoughtfully. "This is a find," he said — "most decidedly a find. It looks so much like nonsense that it must mean something of importance. The date, you see, is Tuesday night. It would be received here on Wednesday — yesterday — morning. So that it was immediately after the receipt of this note that Geldard left. It's

142

pretty plain the crosses don't mean kisses. The note isn't quite of the sort that usually carries such symbols, and moreover, when a lady fills the end of a sheet of notepaper with kisses she doesn't stop less than half way across the last line — she fills it to the end. These crosses mean something very different. I should like, too, to know what 'smoke' means. Anyway this letter would probably astonish Mrs. Geldard if she saw it. We'll say nothing about it for the present." He swept the fragments into an envelope, and put away the envelope in his breast pocket. There was nothing more to be found of the least value in the fireplace, and a careful examination of the office in other parts revealed nothing that I had not noticed before, so far as I could see, except Geldard's boots standing on the floor of the cupboard wherein his clothes lay. The whole place was singularly bare of what one commonly finds in an office in the way of papers, handbooks, and general business material.

Mrs. Geldard was not long away. At the bank she found that the manager was absent and his deputy had been very reluctant to say anything definite without his sanction. He gave Mrs. Geldard to understand, however, that there was a balance still remaining to her husband's credit; also that Mr. Geldard had drawn a check the previous morning, Wednesday, for an amount "rather larger than usual." And that was all.

"By the way, Mrs. Geldard," Holmes observed, with an air of recollecting something, "there *was* a Mr. Cookson I believe, if I remember, who knew a Mr. Geldard. You don't happen to know, do you, whether or not Mr. Geldard had a client or an acquaintance of that name?"

"No, I know nobody of the name."

"Ah, it doesn't matter. I suppose it isn't necessary for your husband to keep horses or vehicles of any description in his business?"

"No, certainly not." Mrs. Geldard looked surprised at the question.

"Of course — I should have known that. He does not drive to business, I suppose?"

"No, he goes by omnibus."

"But as to Emma Trennatt now. This photograph is most welcome, and will be of great assistance, I make no doubt. But is there anything individual by which I might identify her if I saw her — anything beyond what I see in the photograph? A peculiarity of step, for instance, or a scar, or what not."

"Yes, there is a large mole — more than a quarter of an inch across I should think — on her left cheek, an inch below the outer corner of her eye. The photograph only shows the other side of the face."

"That will be useful to know. Now has she a relative living at Crouch End, or thereabout?"

"Yes, her uncle; she's living with him now — or she was at any rate till lately. But how did you know that?"

"The Crouch End postmark was on those envelopes you found. Do you know anything of her uncle?"

"Nothing, except that he's a nurseryman, I believe."

"Not his full address?"

"No — "

"And Trennatt is his name?"

"Yes."

"Thank you. I think, Mrs. Geldard," Holmes said, taking his hat, "that I will set out after your husband at once. You, I think, can do no better than stay at home till I have news for you. I have your address. If anything comes to your knowledge please telegraph it to my rooms at once."

The office door was locked, the keys were left with the caretaker, and we saw Mrs. Geldard into a cab at the door. "Come," said Holmes, "we'll go somewhere and look at a directory, and after that to Dragon Yard. I think I know a man in Moorgate Street who'll let me see his directory."

We started to walk down Finsbury Pavement. Suddenly Holmes caught my arm and directed my eyes toward a woman who had passed hurriedly in the opposite direction. I had not seen her face, but Holmes had. "If that isn't Miss Emma Trennatt," he said, "it's uncommonly like the notion I've formed of her. We'll see if she goes to Geldard's office."

144

We hurried after the woman, who, sure enough, turned into the large door of the building we had just left. As it was impossible that she should know us we followed her boldly up the stairs and saw her stop before the door of Geldard's office and knock. We passed her as she stood there — a handsome young woman enough — and well back on her left cheek, in the place Mrs. Geldard had indicated, there was plain to see a very large mole. We pursued our way to the landing above and there we stopped in a position that commanded a view of Geldard's door. The young woman knocked again and waited.

"This doesn't look like an elopement yesterday morning, does it?" Holmes whispered. "Unless Geldard's left both this one and his wife in the lurch."

The young woman below knocked once or twice more, walked irresolutely across the corridor and back, and in the end, after a parting knock, started slowly back downstairs.

"Brett," Holmes exclaimed with suddenness, "will you do me a favor? That woman understands Geldard's secret comings and goings, as is plain from the letter. But she would appear to know nothing of where he is now, since she seems to have come here to find him. Perhaps this last absence of his has nothing to do with the others. In any case will you follow this woman? She must be watched; but I want to see to the matter in other places. Will you do it?"

Of course I assented at once. We had been descending the stairs as Holmes spoke, keeping distance behind the girl we were following. "Thank you," Holmes now said. "Do it. If you find anything urgent to communicate wire to me in care of the inspector at Crouch End Police Station. He knows me, and I will call there in case you may have sent. But if it's after five this afternoon, wire also to my rooms. If you keep with her to Crouch End, where she lives, we shall probably meet."

We parted at the door of the office we were at first bound for, and I followed the girl southward.

This new turn of affairs increased the puzzlement I already labored under. Here was the girl Trennatt — who by all evidence appeared to be well acquainted with Geldard's mysterious proceedings, and in consequence of whose letter, whatever it might mean, he would seem to have absented himself — herself apparently ignorant of his whereabouts and even unconscious that he had left his office. I had at first begun to speculate on Geldard's probable secret employment; I had heard of men keeping good establishments who, unknown to even their own wives, procured the wherewithal by begging or crossing-sweeping in London streets; I had heard also — knew in fact from Holmes's experience — of well-to-do suburban residents whose actual profession was burglary or coining. I had speculated on the possibility of Geldard's secret being one of that kind. My mind had even reverted to the case, which I have related elsewhere, in which Holmes frustrated a dynamite explosion by his timely discovery of a baker's cart and a number of loaves, and I wondered whether or not Geldard was a member of some secret brotherhood of Anarchists or Fenians. But here, it would seem, were two distinct mysteries, one of Geldard's generally unaccountable movements, and another of his disappearance, each mystery complicating the other. Again, what did that extraordinary note mean, with its crosses and its odd references to smoking? Had the dirty clay pipes anything to do with it? Or the half-smoked cigars? Perhaps the whole thing was merely ridiculously trivial after all. I could make nothing of it, however, and applied myself to my pursuit of Emma Trennatt, who mounted an omnibus at the Bank, on the roof of which I myself secured a seat.

II. Here I must leave my own proceedings to put in their proper place those of Sherlock Holmes as I subsequently learnt them. Benton Street, he found by the directory, turned out of the City Road south of Old Street, so was quite near. He was there in less than ten minutes, and had discovered Dragon Yard. Dragon Yard was as small a stable-yard as one could easily find. Only the right-hand side was occupied by stables, and there were only three of these. On the left was a high dead wall bounding a great warehouse or some such building. Across the first and second of the stables stretched a long board with the legend, "W. Gask, Corn, Hay and Straw Dealer," and underneath a shop address in Old Street. The third stable stood blank and uninscribed, and all three were shut fast. Nobody was in the yard, and Holmes at once proceeded to examine the end stable. The doors were unusually well finished and close-fitting, and the lock was a good one, of the lever variety, and very difficult to pick. Holmes examined the front of the building very carefully, and then, after a visit to the entrance of the yard, to guard against early interruption, returned and scrambled by projections and fastenings to the roof. This was a roof in contrast to those of the other stables. They were of tiles, seemed old, and carried nothing in the way of a skylight; evidently it was the habit of Mr. Gask and his helpers to do their horse and van business with gates wide open to admit light. But the roof of this third stable was newer and better made, and carried a good-sized skylight of thick fluted glass. Holmes took a good look at such few windows as happened to be in sight, and straightway began, with the strongest blade of his pocket-knife, to cut away the putty from round one pane. It was a rather long job, for the putty had hardened thoroughly in the sun, but it was accomplished at length, and Holmes, with a final glance at the windows in view, prized up the pane from the end and lifted it out.

The interior of the stable was apparently empty. Neither stall nor rack was to be seen, and the place was plainly used as a coach or van house simply. Holmes took one more look about him and dropped quietly through the hole in the skylight. The floor was thickly laid with straw. There were a few odd pieces of harness, a rope or two, a lantern, and a few sacks lying here and there, and at the darkest end there was an obscure heap covered with straw and sacking. This heap Holmes proceeded to unmask, and having cleared away a few sacks left revealed about half-a-dozen rolls of linoleum. One of these he dragged to the light, where it became evident that it had remained thus rolled and tied with cord in two places for a long period. There were cracks in the surface, and when the cords were loosened the linoleum showed no disposition to open out or to become unrolled. Others of the rolls on inspection exhibited the same peculiarities. Moreover, each roll appeared to consist of no more than a couple of yards of material at most, though all were of the same pattern. Every roll in fact was of the same length, thickness and shape as the others, containing somewhere near two yards of linoleum in a roll of some half dozen thicknesses, leaving an open diameter of some an open diameter of some four inches in the centre. Holmes looked at each in turn and then replaced the heap as he had found it. After this to regain the skylight was not difficult by the aid of a trestle. The pane was replaced as well as the absence of fresh putty permitted, and five minutes later Holmes was in a hansom bound for Crouch End.

He dismissed his cab at the police station. Within he had no difficulty in procuring a direction to Trennatt, the nurseryman, and a short walk brought him to the place. A fairly high wall topped with broken glass bounded the nursery garden next the road and in the wall were two gates, one a wide double one for the admission of vehicles, and the other a smaller one of open pales, for ordinary visitors. The garden stood sheltered by higher ground behind, whereon stood a good-sized house, just visible among the trees that surrounded it. Holmes walked along by the side of the wall. Soon he came to where the ground of the nursery garden appeared to be divided from that of the house by a most extraordinarily high hedge extending a couple of feet above the top of the wall itself. Stepping back, the better to note this hedge, Holmes became conscious of two large boards, directly facing each other, with scarcely four feet space between them, one erected on a post in the ground of the house and the other similarly elevated from that of the nursery, each being inscribed in large letters, "TRESPASSERS WILL BE PROSECUTED." Holmes smiled and passed on; here plainly was a neighbor's quarrel of long standing, for neither board was by any means new. The wall continued, and keeping by it Holmes made the entire circuit of the large house and its grounds, and arrived once more at that part of the wall that enclosed the nursery garden. Just here, and near the wider gate, the upper part of a cottage was visible, standing within the wall, and evidently the residence of the nurseryman. It carried a conspicuous board with the legend, "H.M. Trennatt, Nurseryman." The large house and the nursery stood entirely apart from other houses or enclosures, and it would seem that the nursery ground had at some time been cut off from the grounds attached to the house.

Holmes stood for a moment thoughtfully, and then walked back to the outer gate of the house on the rise. It was a high iron gate, and as Holmes perceived, it was bolted at the bottom. Within the garden showed a neglected and weed-choked appearance, such as one associates with the garden of a house that has stood long empty.

A little way off a policeman walked. Holmes accosted him and spoke of the house. "I was wondering if it might happen to be to let," he said. "Do you know?"

"No, sir," the policeman replied, "it ain't; though anyone might almost think it, to look at the garden. That's a Mr. Fuller as lives there — and a rum 'un too."

"Oh, he's a rum 'un, is he? Keeps himself shut up, perhaps?"

"Yes, sir. On'y 'as one old woman, deaf as a post, for servant, and never lets nobody into the place. It's a rare game sometimes with the milkman. The milkman, he comes and rings that there bell, but the old gal's so deaf she never 'ears it. Then the milkman, he just slips 'is 'and through the gate rails, lifts the bolt and goes and bangs at the door. Old Fuller runs out and swears a good 'un. The old gal comes out and old Fuller swears at 'er, and she turns round and swears back like anything. She don't care for 'im — not a bit. Then when he ain't 'avin' a row with the milkman and the old gal he goes down the garden and rows with the old nurseryman there down the 'ill. He jores the nurseryman from 'is side o' the hedge and the nurseryman he jores back at the top of 'is voice. I've stood out there ten minutes together and nearly bust myself a-laughin' at them gray-'eaded old fellers a-callin' each other everythink they can think of; you can 'ear 'em 'alf over the parish. Why, each of 'em's 'ad a board painted, 'Trespassers will be Prosecuted,' and stuck 'em up facin' each other, so as to keep up the row."

"Very funny, no doubt."

"Funny? I believe you, sir. Why it's quite a treat sometimes on a dull beat like this, Why, what's that? Blowed if I don't think they're beginning again now. Yes, they are. Well, my beat's the other way."

There was a sound of angry voices in the direction of the nursery ground, and Holmes made toward it. Just where the hedge peeped over the wall the altercation was plain to hear.

"You're an old vagabond, and I'll indict you for a nuisance!"

"You're an old thief, and you'd like to turn me out of house and home, wouldn't you? Indict away, you greedy old scoundrel!"

These and similar endearments, punctuated by growls and snorts, came distinctly from over the wall, accompanied by a certain scraping, brushing sound, as though each neighbor were madly attempting to scale the hedge and personally bang the other. Holmes hastened round to the front of the nursery garden and quietly tried first the wide gate and next the small one. Both were fastened securely. But in the manner of the milkman at the gate of the house above, Holmes slipped his hand between the open slats of the small gate and slid the night latch that held it. Within the quarrel ran high as Holmes stepped quietly into the garden. He trod on the narrow grass borders of the beds for quietness' sake, till presently only a line of shrubs divided him from the clamorous nurseryman. Stooping and looking through an opening which gave him a back view, Holmes observed that the brushing and scraping noise proceeded, not from angry scramblings, but from the forcing through an inadequate opening in the hedge of some piece of machinery which the nurseryman was most amicably passing to his neighbor at the same time as he assailed him with savage abuse, and received a full return in kind. It appeared to consist of a number of coils of metal pipe, not unlike those sometimes used in heating apparatus, and was as yet only a very little way through. Something else, of bright

150

copper, lay on the garden-bed at the foot of the hedge, but intervening plants concealed its shape.

Holmes turned quickly away and made towards the greenhouses, keeping tall shrubs as much as possible between himself and the cottage, and looking sharply about him. Here and there about the garden were stand-pipes, each carrying a tap at its upper end and placed conveniently for irrigation. These in particular Holmes scrutinized, and presently, as he neared a large wooden outhouse close by the large gate, turned his attention to one backed by a thick shrub. When the thick undergrowth of the shrub was pushed aside a small stone slab, black and dirty, was disclosed, and this Holmes lifted, uncovering a square hole six or eight inches across, from the fore-side of which the stand-pipe rose.

The row went cheerily on over by the hedge, and neither Trennatt nor his neighbor saw Holmes, feeling with his hand, discover two stop-cocks and a branch pipe in the hole, nor saw him try them both. Holmes, however, was satisfied, and saw his case plain. He rose and made his way back toward the small gate. He was scarce half-way there when the straining of the hedge ceased, and before he reached it the last insult had been hurled, the quarrel ceased, and Trennatt approached. Holmes immediately turned his back to the gate, and looking about him inquiringly hemmed aloud as though to attract attention. The nurseryman promptly burst round a corner crying, "Who's that? Who's that, eh? What d'ye want, eh?"

"Why," answered Holmes in a tone of mild surprise, "is it so uncommon to have a customer drop in?"

"I'd ha' sworn that gate was fastened," the old man said, looking about him suspiciously.

"That would have been rash; I had no difficulty in opening it. Come, can't you sell me a button-hole?

The old man led the way to a greenhouse, but as he went he growled again, "I'd ha' sworn I shut that gate."

"Perhaps you forgot," Holmes suggested. "You have had a little excitement with your neighbor, haven't you?"

Trennatt stopped and turned round, darting a keen glance into Holmes's face. "Yes," he answered angrily, "I have. He's an old villain. He'd like to turn me out of here, after being here all my life — and a lot o' good the ground 'ud be to him if he kep' it like he keeps his own! And look there!" He dragged Holmes toward the "Trespassers" boards. "Goes and sticks up a board like that looking over my hedge! As though I wanted to go over among his weeds! So I stuck up another in front of it, and now they can stare each other out o' countenance. Buttonhole, you said, sir, eh?"

The old man saw Holmes off the premises with great care, and the latter, flower in coat, made straight for the nearest post office and dispatched a telegram. Then he stood for some little while outside the post office deep in thought, and in the end returned to the gate of the house above the nursery.

With much circumspection he opened the gate and entered the grounds. But instead of approaching the house he turned immediately to the left, behind trees and shrubs, making for the side nearest the nursery. Soon he reached a long, low wooden shed. The door was only secured by a button, and turning this he gazed into the dark interior. Now he had not noticed that close after him a woman had entered the gate, and that that woman was Mrs. Geldard. She would have made for the house, but catching sight of Holmes, followed him swiftly and quietly over the long grass. Thus it came to pass that his first appraisal of the lady's presence was a sharp drive in the back which pitched him down the step to the low floor of what he had just perceived to be merely a tool-house, after which the door was shut and buttoned behind him.

"Perhaps you'll be more careful in future," came Mrs. Geldard's angry voice from without, "how you go making mischief between husband and wife and poking your nose into people's affairs. Such fellows as you ought to be well punished."

Holmes laughed softly. Mrs. Geldard had evidently changed her mind. The door presented no difficulty; a fairly vigorous push dislodged the button entirely, and he walked back to the outer gate chuckling quietly. In the distance he heard Mrs.

Geldard in shrill altercation with the deaf old woman. "It's no good you a-talking," the old woman was saying. "I can't hear. Nobody ain't allowed in this here place, so you must get out. Out you go, now!" Outside the gate Holmes met me.

III. My own adventures had been simple. I had secured a back seat on the roof of the omnibus wherein Emma Trennatt traveled south from the Bank, from which I could easily observe where she alighted. When she did so I followed, and found to my astonishment that her destination was no other than the Geldards' private house at Camberwell — as I remembered from the address on the visitor's slip which Mrs. Geldard had handed in at Holmes's office a couple of days before. She handed a letter to the maid who opened the door, and soon after, in response to a message by the same maid, entered the house. Presently the maid reappeared, bonneted, and hurried off, to return in a few minutes in a cab with another following behind. Almost immediately Mrs. Geldard emerged in company with Emma Trennatt. She hurried the girl into one of the cabs, and I heard her repeat loudly twice the address of Holmes's rooms, once to the girl and once to the cabman. Now it seemed plain to me that to follow Emma Trennatt farther would be waste of time, for she was off to Holmes's rooms, where the housekeeper would learn her message. And knowing where a message would find Holmes sooner than at his rooms, I judged it well to tell Mrs. Geldard of the fact. I approached, therefore, as she was entering the other cab and began to explain when she cut me short. "You can go and tell your master to attend to his own business as soon as he pleases, for not a shilling does he get from me. He ought to be ashamed of himself, sowing dissension between man and wife for the sake of what he can make out of it, and so ought you."

I bowed with what grace I might, and retired. The other cab bad gone, so I set forth to find one for myself at the nearest rank. I could think of nothing better to do than to make for Crouch End Police Station and Endeavour to find Holmes. Soon after my cab emerged north of the city I became conscious of another cab whose driver I fancied I recognized, and which kept ahead all along the route. In fact it was Mrs. Geldard's cab, and presently it dawned upon me that we must both be bound for the same place. When it became quite clear that Crouch End was the destination of the lady I instructed my driver to disregard the police station and follow the cab in front. Thus I arrived at Mr. Fuller's house just behind Mrs. Geldard, and thus, waiting at the gate, I met Holmes as he emerged.

"Hullo, Brett!" he said. "Condole with me. Mrs. Geldard has changed her mind, and considers me a pernicious creature anxious to make mischief between her and her husband; I'm very much afraid I shan't get my fee."

"No," I answered, "she told me you wouldn't."

We compared notes, and Holmes laughed heartily. "The appearance of Emma Trennatt at Geldard's office this morning is explained," he said. "She went first with a message from Geldard to Mrs. Geldard at Camberwell, explaining his absence and imploring her not to talk of it or make a disturbance. Mrs. Geldard had gone off to town, and Emma Trennatt was told that she had gone to Geldard's office. There she went, and then we first saw her. She found nobody at the office, and after a minute or two of irresolution returned to Camberwell, and then succeeded in delivering her message, as you saw. Mrs. Geldard is apparently satisfied with her husband's explanation. But I'm afraid the revenue officers won't approve of it."

"The revenue officers?"

"Yes. It's a case of illicit distilling — and a big case, I fancy. I've wired to Somerset House, and no doubt men are on their way here now. But Mrs. Geldard's up at the house, so we'd better hurry up to the police station and have a few sent from there. Come along. The whole thing's very clever, and a most uncommonly big thing. If I know all about it — and I think I do — Geldard and his partners have been turning out untaxed spirit by the hundred gallons for a long time past. Geldard is the practical man, the engineer, and probably erected the whole apparatus himself in that house on the hill. The spirit is brought down by a pipe laid a very little way under the garden surface, and carried into one of the irrigation stand-pipes in the nursery ground. There's a quiet little hole behind the pipe with a couple of stop-cocks — one to shut off the water when necessary, the other to do the same with the spirit. When the stopcocks are right you just turn the tap at the top of the pipe and you get water or whisky, as the case may be. Fuller, the man up at the house, attends to the still, with such assistance as the deaf old woman can give him. Trennatt, down below, draws off the liquor ready to be carried away. These two keep up an ostentatious appearance of being at unending feud to blind suspicion. Our as yet ungreeted friend Geldard, guiding spirit of the whole thing, comes disguised as a carter with an apparent cart-load of linoleum, and carries away the manufactured stuff. In the pleasing language of Geldard and Co., 'smoke,' as alluded to in the note you saw, means whisky. Something has been wrong with the apparatus lately, and it has been leaking badly. Geldard has been at work on it, patching, but ineffectually. 'What you did was no good' said the charming Emma in the note, as you will remember. 'Uncle was anxious.' And justifiably so, because not only does a leak of spirit mean a waste, but it means a smell, which some sharp revenue man might sniff. Moreover, if there is a leak, the liquid runs somewhere at random, and with any sudden increase in volume attention might easily be attracted. It was so bad that 'F.' (Fuller) thought Geldard must light another pipe (start another still) or give up smoking (distilling) for a bit. There is the explanation of the note. 'Tomorrow, to carry' probably means that he is to call with his cart — the cart in whose society Geldard becomes Cookson — to remove a quantity of spirit. He is not to come late because people are expected on floral business. The crosses I *think* will be found to indicate the amount of liquid to be moved. But that we shall see. Anyhow Geldard got there yesterday and had a busy day loading up, and then set to repairing. The damage was worse than supposed, and an urgent thing. Result, Geldard works into early morning, has a sleep in the place, where he may be called at any moment, and starts again early this morning. New parts have to be ordered, and these are delivered at Trennatt's today and passed through the hedge. Meantime Geldard sends a message to his wife explaining things, and the result you've seen."

At the police station a telegram had already been received from Somerset House. That was enough for Holmes, who had discharged his duty as a citizen and now dropped the case. We left the police and the revenue officers to deal with the matter and traveled back to town.

"Yes," said Holmes on the way, after each had fully described his day's experiences, "it seemed pretty plain that Geldard left his office by the back way in disguise, and there were things that hinted what that disguise was. The pipes were noticeable. They were quite unnecessarily dirty, and partly from dirty fingers. Pipes smoked by a man in his office would never look like that. They had been smoked out of doors by a man with dirty hands, and hands and pipes would be in keeping with the rest of the man's appearance. It was noticeable that he had left not only his clothes and hat but his boots behind him. They were quite plain though good boots, and would be quite in keeping with any dress but that of a laborer or some such man in his working clothes. Moreover the partly-smoked cigars were probably thrown aside because they would appear inconsistent with Geldard's changed dress. The contents of the pockets in the clothes left behind, too, told the same tale. The cheap watch and the necessary keys, pocketbook and pocket-knife were taken, but the articles of luxury, the Russia-leather card-case, the sovereign purse and so on were left. Then we came on the receipts for stable-rent. Suggestion — perhaps the disguise was that of a carter.

"Then there was the coach-house. Plainly, if Geldard took the trouble thus to disguise himself, and thus to hide his occupation even from his wife, he had some very good reason for secrecy. Now the goods which a man would be likely to carry secretly in a cart or van, as a regular piece of business, would probably be either stolen or smuggled. When I examined those pieces of linoleum I became convinced that they were intended merely as receptacles for some other sort of article altogether.

They were old, and had evidently been thus rolled for a very long period. They appeared to have been exposed to weather, but on the outside only. Moreover they were all of one size and shape, each forming a long hollow cylinder, with plenty of interior room. Now from this it was plainly unlikely that they were intended to hold *stolen* goods. Stolen goods are not apt to be always of one size and shape, adaptable to a cylindrical recess. Perhaps they were smuggled. Now the only goods profitable to be smuggled nowadays are tobacco and spirits, and plainly these rolls of linoleum would be excellent receptacles for either. Tobacco could be packed inside the rolls and the ends stopped artistically with narrow rolls of linoleum. Spirits could be contained in metal cylinders exactly fitting the cavity and the ends filled in the same way as for tobacco. But for tobacco a smart man would probably make his linoleum rolls of different sizes, for the sake of a more innocent appearance, while for spirits it would be a convenience to have vessels of uniform measure, to save trouble in quicker delivery and calculation of quantity. Bearing these things in mind I went in search of the gentle nurseryman at Crouch End. My general survey of the nursery ground and the house behind it inspired me with the notion that the situation and arrangement were most admirably adapted for the working of a large illicit still — a form of misdemeanor, let me tell you, that is much more common nowadays than is generally supposed. I remembered Geldard's engineering experience, and I heard something of the odd manners of Mr. Fuller; my theory of a traffic in untaxed spirits became strengthened. But why a nursery? Was this a mere accident of the design? There were commonly irrigation pipes about nurseries, and an extra one might easily be made to carry whisky. With this in mind I visited the nursery with the result you know of. The stand-pipe I tested (which was where I expected — handy to the vehicle entrance) could produce simple New River water or raw whisky at command of one of two stop-cocks. My duty was plain. As you know, I am a citizen first and an investigator after, and I find the advantage of it in my frequent intercourse with the police and other authorities. As soon as I

157

could get away I telegraphed to Somerset House. But then I grew perplexed on a point of conduct. I was commissioned by Mrs. Geldard. It scarcely seemed the loyal thing to put my client s husband in gaol because of what I had learnt in course of work on her behalf. I decided to give him, and nobody else, a sporting chance. If I could possibly get at him in the time at my disposal, by himself, so that no accomplice should get the benefit of my warning, I would give him a plain hint to run; then he could take his chance. I returned to the place and began to work round the grounds, examining the place as I went; but at the very first outhouse I put my head into I was surprised in the rear by Mrs. Geldard coming in hot haste to stop me and rescue her husband. She most unmistakably gave me the sack, and so now the police may catch Geldard or not, as their luck may be."

They did catch him. In the next day's papers a report of a great capture of illicit distillers occupied a prominent place. The prisoners were James Fuller, Henry Matthew Trennatt, Sarah Blatten, a deaf woman, Samuel Geldard and his wife Rebecca Geldard.

The two women were found on the premises in violent altercation when the officers arrived, a few minutes after Holmes and I had left the police station on our way home. It was considered by far the greatest haul for the revenue authorities since the seizure of the famous ship's boiler on a wagon in the East-End stuffed full of tobacco, after that same ship's boiler had made about a dozen voyages to the continent and back "for repair." Geldard was found dressed as a workman, carrying out extensive alterations and repairs to the still. And a light van was found in a shed belonging to the nursery loaded with seventeen rolls of linoleum, each enclosing a cylinder containing two gallons of spirits, and packed at each end with narrow linoleum rolls. It will be remembered that seventeen was the number of crosses at the foot of Emma Trennatt's note.

The subsequent raids on a number of obscure public-houses in different parts of London, in consequence of information gathered on the occasion of the Geldard capture, resulted in the seizure of a large quantity of secreted spirit for which no permit could be shown. It demonstrated also the extent of Geldard's connection, and indicated plainly what was done with the spirit when he had carted it away from Crouch End. Some of the public-houses in question must have acquired a notoriety among the neighbors for frequent purchases of linoleum.

The Case of the Late Mr. Rewse

I. Of this case I personally saw nothing beyond the first advent in Holmes's rooms of Mr. Horace Bowyer, who put the case in his hands, and then I merely saw Mr. Bowyer's back as I passed down stairs from my rooms. But I noted the case in full detail after Holmes's return from Ireland, as it seemed to me one not entirely without interest, if only as an exemplar of the fatal case with which a man may unwittingly dig a pit for his own feet — a pit from which there is no climbing out.

That the visitor, Mr. Horace Bowyer, was in a hurry was plain from a hasty rattling of Holmes's door. Holmes showed himself at the door and invited Mr. Bowyer to enter, which he did. He was a stout, florid gentleman with a loud voice and a large stare.

"Mr. Holmes," he said, "I must claim your immediate attention to a business of the utmost gravity. Will you please consider yourself commissioned, wholly regardless of expense, to set aside whatever you may have in hand and devote yourself to the case I shall put in your hands?"

"Certainly not," Holmes replied with a slight smile. "What I have in hand are matters which I have engaged to attend to, and no mere compensation for loss of fees could persuade me to leave my clients in the lurch, else what would prevent some other gentleman coming here to-morrow with a bigger fee than yours and bribing me away from you?"

"But this — this is a most serious thing, Mr. Holmes. A matter of life or death — it is indeed!"

"Quite so," Holmes replied: "but there are a thousand such matters at this moment pending of which you and I know nothing, and there are also two or three more of which you know nothing but on which I am at work. So that it becomes a question of practicability. If you will tell me your business I can judge whether or not I may be able to accept your commission concurrently with those I have in hand. Some operations take months of constant attention; some can be conducted intermittently; others still are a mere matter of a few days — many of hours simply."

"I will tell you then," Mr. Bowyer replied. "In the first place, will you have the kindness to read that? It is a cutting from the *Standard's* column of news from the provinces of two days ago."

Holmes took the cutting and read as follows:

> The epidemic of small-pox in County Mayo, Ireland, shows few signs of abating. The spread of the disease has been very remarkable considering the widely-scattered nature of the population, though there can be no doubt that the market towns are the centers of infection, and that it is from these that the germs of contagion are carried into the country by people from all parts who resort thither on market days. In many cases the disease has assumed a particularly malignant form, and deaths have been very rapid and numerous. The comparatively few medical men available are sadly overworked owing largely to the distances separating their different patients. Among those who have succumbed within the last few days is Mr. Algernon Rewse, a young English gentleman who has been staying with a friend at a cottage a few miles from Cullanin, on a fishing excursion.

Holmes placed the cutting on the table at his side. "Yes?" he said inquiringly. "It is to Mr. Algernon Rewse's death you wish to draw my attention?"

"It is," Mr. Bowyer answered; "and the reason I come to you is that I very much suspect — more than suspect, indeed — that Mr. Algernon Rewse has *not* died by smallpox, but has been murdered — murdered cold-bloodedly, and for the most sordid motives, by the friend who has been sharing his holiday."

"In what way do you suppose him to have been murdered?"

161

"That I cannot say — that, indeed, I want you to find out, among other things — chiefly perhaps, the murderer himself, who has made off."

"And your own status in the matter," queried Holmes, "is that of?"

"I am trustee under a will by which Mr. Rewse would have benefited considerably had he lived but a month or two longer. That circumstance indeed lies rather near the root of the matter. The thing stood thus. Under the will I speak of — that of young Rewse's uncle, a very old friend of mine in his lifetime — the money lay in trust till the young fellow should attain twenty-five years of age. His younger sister, Miss Mary Rewse, was also benefited, but to a much smaller extent. She was to come into her property also on attaining the age of twenty-five, or on her marriage, whichever event happened first. It was further provided that in case either of these young people died before coming into the inheritance, his or her share should go to the survivor. I want you particularly to remember this. You will observe that now, in consequence of young Algernon Rewse's death, barely two months before his twenty-fifth birthday, the whole of the very large property — all personality, and free from any tie or restriction — which would otherwise have been his, will, in the regular course, pass, on her twenty-fifth birthday, *or on her marriage,* to Miss Mary Rewse, whose own legacy was comparatively trifling. You will understand the importance of this when I tell you that the man whom I suspect of causing Algernon Rewse's death, and who has been his companion on his otherwise lonely holiday, is engaged to be married to Miss Rewse."

Mr. Bowyer paused at this, but Holmes only raised his eyebrows and nodded.

"I have never particularly liked the man," Mr. Bowyer went on. "He never seemed to have much to say for himself. I like a man who holds his head and opens his mouth. I don't believe in the sort of modesty that he showed so much of — it isn't genuine. A man can't afford to be genuinely meek and retiring

162

who has his way to make in the world — and he was clever enough to know *that.*"

"He is poor, then?" Holmes asked.

"Oh yes, poor enough. His name, by-the-bye, is Main — Stanley Main — and he is a medical man. He hasn't been practicing, except as assistant, since he became qualified, the reason being, I understand, that he couldn't afford to buy a good practice. He is the person who will profit by young Rewse's death — or at any rate who intended to; but we will see about that. As for Mary, poor girl, she wouldn't have lost her brother for fifty fortunes."

"As to the circumstances of the death, now?"

"Yes, yes, I am coming to that. Young Algernon Rewse, you must know, had rather run down in health, and Main persuaded him that he wanted a change. I don't know what it was altogether, but Rewse seemed to have been having his own little love troubles and that sort of thing, you know. He'd been engaged, I think, or very nearly so, and the young lady died, and so on. Well, as I said, he had run down and got into low health and spirits, and no doubt a change of some sort would have done him good. This Stanley Main always seemed to have a great influence over the poor boy — he was four or five years older than Rewse — and somehow he persuaded him to go away, the two together, to some outlandish wilderness of a place in the West of Ireland for salmon-fishing. It seemed to me at the time rather a ridiculous sort of place to go to, but Main had his way, and they went. There was a cottage — rather a good sort of cottage, I believe, for the district — which some friend of Main's, once a landowner in the district, had put up as a convenient box for salmon-fishing, and they rented it. Not long after they got there this epidemic of small-pox got about in the district — though that, I believe, has had little to do with poor young Rewse's death. All appeared to go well until a day over a week ago, when Mrs. Rewse received this letter from Main." Mr. Bowyer handed Sherlock Holmes a letter, written in an irregular and broken hand, as though of a person writing under stress of extreme agitation. It ran thus:

163

My dear Mrs. Rewse,

*You will probably have heard through the newspapers —
indeed I think Algernon has told you in his letters — that
a very bad epidemic of small-pox is abroad in this
district. I am deeply grieved to have to tell you that
Algernon himself has taken the disease in a rather bad
form. He showed the first symptoms today (Tuesday),
and he is now in bed in the cottage. It is fortunate that I,
as a medical man, happen to be on the spot, as the
nearest local doctor is five miles off at Cullanin, and he
is working and traveling night and day as it is. I have my
little medicine chest with me, and can get whatever else
is necessary from Cullanin, so that everything is being
done for Algernon that is possible, and I hope to bring
him up to scratch in good health soon, though of course
the disease is a dangerous one. Pray don't unnecessarily
alarm yourself, and don't think about coming over here,
or anything of that sort. You can do no good, and will
only run risk yourself. I will take care to let you know
how things go on, so please don't attempt to come. The
journey is long and would be very trying to you, and you
would have no place to stay at nearer than Cullanin,
which is quite a centre of infection. I will write again tomorrow.*

Yours most sincerely,

STANLEY MAIN

Not only did the handwriting of this letter show signs of
agitation, but here and there words had been repeated, and
sometimes a letter had been omitted. Holmes placed the letter on
the table by the newspaper cutting, and Mr. Bowyer proceeded.

"Another letter followed on the next day," he said, handing
it to Holmes as he spoke; "a short one, as you see; not written

with quite such signs of agitation. It merely says that Rewse is very bad, and repeats the former entreaties that his mother will not think of going to him." Holmes glanced at the letter and placed it with the other, while Mr. Bowyer continued: "Notwithstanding Main's persistent anxiety that she should stay at home, Mrs. Rewse, who was of course terribly worried about her only son, had almost made up her mind, in spite of her very delicate health, to start for Ireland, when she received a third letter announcing Algernon's death. Here it is. It is certainly the sort of letter that one might expect to be written in such circumstances, and yet there seems to me at least a certain air of disingenuousness about the wording. There are, as you see, the usual condolences, and so forth. The disease was of the malignant type, it says, which is terribly rapid in its action, often carrying off the patient even before the eruption has time to form. Then — and this is a thing I wish you especially to note — there is once more a repetition of his desire that neither the young man's mother nor his sister shall come to Ireland. The funeral must take place immediately, he says, under arrangements made by the local authorities, and before they could reach the spot. Now doesn't this obtrusive anxiety of his that no connection of young Rewse's should be near him during his illness, nor even at the funeral, strike you as rather singular?"

"Well, possibly it is: though it may easily be nothing but zeal for the health of Mrs. Rewse and her daughter. As a matter of fact what Main says is very plausible. They could do no sort of good in the circumstances, and might easily run into danger themselves, to say nothing of the fatigue of the journey and general nervous upset. Mrs. Rewse is in weak health, I think you said?"

"Yes, she's almost an invalid in fact; she is subject to heart disease. But tell me now, as an entirely impartial observer, doesn't it seem to you that there is a very forced, unreal sort of tone in all these letters?"

"Perhaps one may notice something of the sort, but fifty things may cause that. The case from the beginning may have been worse than he made it out. What ensued on the receipt of this letter?"

"Mrs. Rewse was prostrated, of course. Her daughter communicated with me as a friend of the family, and that is how I heard of the whole thing for the first time. I saw the letters, and it seemed to me, looking at all the circumstances of the case, that somebody at least ought to go over and make certain that everything was as it should be. Here was this poor young man, staying in a lonely cottage with the only man in the world who had any reason to desire his death, or any profit to gain by it, and he had a very great inducement indeed. Moreover he was a medical man, *carrying his medicine chest with him*, remember, as he says himself in his letter. In this situation Rewse suddenly dies, with nobody about him, so far as there is anything to show, but Main himself. As his medical attendant it would be Main who would certify and register the death, and no matter what foul play might have taken place he would be safe as long as nobody was on the spot to make searching inquiries — might easily escape even then, in fact. When one man is likely to profit much by the death of another a doctor's medicine chest is likely to supply but too easy a means to his end."

"Did you say anything of your suspicions to the ladies?"

"Well — well I hinted perhaps — no more than hinted, you know. But they wouldn't hear of it — got indignant, and 'took on' as people call it, worse than ever, so that I had to smooth them over. But since it seemed somebody's duty to see into the matter a little more closely, and there seemed to be nobody to do it but myself, I started off that very evening by the night mail. I was in Dublin early the next morning and spent that day getting across Ireland. The nearest station was ten miles from Cullanin, and that, as you remember, was five miles from the cottage, so that I drove over on the morning of the following day. I must say Main appeared very much taken aback at seeing me. His manner was nervous and apprehensive, and made me more suspicious than ever. The body had been buried, of course, a couple of days or more. I asked a few rather searching questions about the illness, and so forth, and his answers became positively confused. He had burned the clothes that Rewse was wearing at the time the disease first showed itself, he said, as well as all the bedclothes, since there was no really efficient means of disinfection at hand. His story in the main was that he had gone off to Cullanin one morning on foot to see about a top joint of a fishing-rod that was to be repaired. When he returned early in the afternoon he found Algernon Rewse sickening of small-pox, at once put him to bed, and there nursed him till he died. I wanted to know, of course, why no other medical man had been called in. He said that there was only one available, and it was doubtful if he could have been got at even a day's notice, so overworked was he; moreover he said this man, with his hurry and over-strain, could never have given the patient such efficient attention as he himself, who had nothing else to do. After a while I put it to him plainly that it would at any rate have been more prudent to have had the body at least inspected by some independent doctor, considering the fact that he was likely to profit so largely by young Rewse's death, and I suggested that with an exhumation order it might not be too late now, as a matter of justice to himself. The effect of that convinced me. The man gasped and turned blue with terror. It was a full minute, I should think, before he could collect himself sufficiently to attempt to dissuade me from doing what I had hinted at. He did so as soon as he could think of — entreated me in fact almost desperately. That decided me. I said that after what he had said, and particularly in view of his whole manner and bearing, I should insist, by every means in my power, on having the body properly examined, and I went off at once to Cullanin to set the telegraph going, and see whatever local authority might be proper. When I returned in the afternoon Stanley Main had packed his bag and vanished, and I have not heard nor seen anything of him since. I stayed in the neighborhood that day and the next, and left for London in the evening. By the help of my solicitors proper representations were made at the Home Office, and, especially in view of Main's flight, a prompt order was made for exhumation and medical examination preliminary to an inquest. I am expecting to hear that the disinterment has been effected today. What I want you to do of course is chiefly to find Main. The Irish constabulary in that district are fine big men, and no doubt most excellent in quelling a faction fight or shutting up a shebeen, but I doubt their efficiency in anything requiring much more finesse. Perhaps also you may be able to find out something of the means by which the murder — it is plain it is one — was committed. It is quite possible that Main may have adopted some means to give the body the appearance, even to a medical man, of death from small-pox."

"That," Holmes said, "is scarcely likely, else, indeed, why did he not take care that another doctor should see the body before the burial? That would have secured him. But that is not a thing one can deceive a doctor over. Of course in the circumstances exhumation is desirable, but if the case *is* one of small-pox, I don't envy the medical man who is to examine. At any rate the business is, I should imagine, not likely to be a very long one, and I can take it in hand at once and will leave to-night for Ireland by the 6.30 train from Euston."

"Very good. I shall go over myself, of course. If anything comes to my knowledge in the meanwhile, of course I'll let you know."

An hour or two after this a cab stopped at the door, and a young lady dressed in black sent in her name and a minute later was shown into Holmes's room. It was Miss Mary Rewse. She wore a heavy veil, and all she said she uttered in evidently deep distress of mind. Holmes did what he could to calm her, and waited patiently.

At length, she said: "I felt that I must come to you, Mr. Holmes, and yet now that I am here I don't know what to say. Is it the fact that Mr. Bowyer has commissioned you to investigate the circumstances of my poor brother's death, and to discover the whereabouts of Mr. Main?"

"Yes, Miss Rewse, that is the fact. Can you tell me anything that will help me?"

"No, no, Mr. Holmes, I fear not. But it is such a dreadful thing, and Mr. Bowyer is — I'm afraid he is so much prejudiced against Mr. Main that I felt I ought to do something — to say something at least to prevent you entering on the case with your mind made up that he has been guilty of such an awful thing. He is really quite incapable of it, I assure you."

"Pray, Miss Rewse," Holmes replied, "don't allow that apprehension to disturb you. If Mr. Main is, as you say, incapable of such an act as perhaps he is suspected of, you may rest assured no harm will come to him. So far as I am concerned at any rate I enter the case with a perfectly open mind. A man in my profession who accepted prejudices at the beginning of a case would have very poor results to show indeed. As yet I have no opinion, no theory, no prejudice, nothing indeed but a large outline of facts. I shall derive no opinion and no theory from anything but a consideration of the actual circumstances and evidences on the spot. I quite understand the relation in which Mr. Main stands in regard to yourself and your family. Have you heard from him lately?"

"Not since the letter informing us of my brother's death."

"Before then?"

Miss Rewse hesitated. "Yes," she said, "we corresponded. But — but there was really nothing — the letters were of a personal and private sort — they were."

"Yes, yes, of course," Holmes answered, with his eyes fixed keenly on the veil which Miss Rewse still kept down. "Of course I understand that. Then there is nothing else you can tell me?"

"No, I fear not. I can only implore you to remember that no matter what you may see and hear, no matter what the evidence may be, I am sure, sure, *sure* that poor Stanley could never do such a thing." And Miss Rewse buried her face in her hands.

Holmes kept his eyes on the lady, though he smiled slightly, and asked, "How long have you known Mr. Main?"

"For some five or six years now. My poor brother knew him at school, though of course they were in different forms, Mr. Main being the elder."

"Were they always on good terms?"

"They were always like brothers."

Little more was said. Holmes condoled with Miss Rewse as well as he might, and she presently took her departure. Even as she descended the stairs a messenger came with a short note for Mr. Bowyer enclosing a telegram just received from Cullanin. The telegram ran thus:

> *Body exhumed. Death from shot-wound. No trace of small-pox. Nothing yet heard of Main. Have communicated with coroner.*
>
> *O'Reilly*

II. Holmes and Mr. Bowyer traveled towards Mayo

together, Mr. Bowyer restless and loquacious on the subject of the business in hand, and Holmes rather bored thereby. He resolutely declined to offer an opinion on any single detail of the case till he had examined the available evidence, and his occasional remarks on matters of general interest, the scenery and so forth, struck his companion, unused to business of the sort which had occasioned the journey, as strangely cold-blooded and indifferent. Telegrams had been sent ordering that no disarrangement of the contents of the cottage was to be allowed pending their arrival, and Holmes well knew that nothing more was practicable till the site was reached. At Ballymaine, where the train was left at last, they stayed for the night, and left early the next morning for Cullanin, where a meeting with Dr. O'Reilly at the mortuary had been appointed. There the body lay stripped of its shroud, calm and gray, and beginning to grow ugly, with a scarcely noticeable breach in the flesh of the left breast.

"The wound has been thoroughly cleansed, closed and stopped with a carbolic plug before interment," Dr. O'Reilly said. He was a middle-aged, grizzled man, with a face whereon many recent sleepless nights had left their traces. "I have not thought it necessary to do anything in the way of dissection. The bullet is not present, it has passed clean through the body, between the ribs both back and front, piercing the heart on its way. The death must have been instantaneous."

Holmes quickly examined the two wounds, back and front, as the doctor turned the body over, and then asked: "Perhaps, Dr. O'Reilly, you have some experience of a gunshot wound before this?"

The doctor smiled grimly. "I think so," he answered, with just enough of brogue in his words to hint his nationality and no more. "I was an army surgeon for a good many years before I came to Cullanin, and saw service in Ashanti and in India."

"Come then," Holmes said, "you're an expert. Would it have been possible for the shot to have been fired from behind?"

"Oh, no. See! the bullet entering makes a wound of quite a different character from that of the bullet leaving."

"Have you any idea of the weapon used?"

"A large revolver, I should think; perhaps of the regulation size; that is, I should judge the bullet to have been a conical one of about the size fitted to such a weapon — smaller than that from a rifle."

"Can you form an idea of from what distance the shot was fired?"

Dr. O'Reilly shook his head. "The clothes have all been burned," he said, "and the wound has been washed, otherwise one might have looked for powder blackening."

"Did you know either the dead man or Dr. Main personally?"

"Only very slightly. I may say I saw just such a pistol as might cause that sort of wound in his hands the day before he gave out that Rewse had been attacked by small-pox. I drove past the cottage as he stood in the doorway with it in his hand. He had the breach opened, and seemed to be either loading or unloading it — which it was I couldn't say."

"Very good, doctor, that may be important. Now is there any single circumstance, incident or conjecture that you can tell me of in regard to this case that you have not already mentioned?"

Doctor O'Reilly thought for a moment, and replied in the negative. "I heard of course," he said, "of the reported new case of smallpox, and that Main had taken the case in hand himself. I was indeed relieved to hear it, for I had already more on my hands than one man can safely be expected to attend to. The cottage was fairly isolated, and there could have been nothing gained by removal to an asylum — indeed there was practically no accommodation. So far as I can make out nobody seems to have seen young Rewse, alive or dead, after Main had announced that he had the small-pox. He seems to have done everything himself, laying out the body and all, and you may be pretty sure that none of the strangers about was particularly anxious to have anything to do with it. The undertaker (there is only one here, and he is down with the small-pox himself now) was as much overworked as I was myself, and was glad enough to send off a coffin by a market cart and leave the laying out and screwing down to Main, since he had got those orders. Main made out the death certificate himself, and, since he was trebly qualified, everything seemed in order."

"The certificate merely attributed the death to small-pox, I take it, with no qualifying remarks?"

"Small-pox, simply."

Holmes and Mr. Bowyer bade Dr. O'Reilly good morning, and their cart was turned in the direction of the cottage where Algernon Rewse had met his death. At the Town Hall in the market place, however, Holmes stopped the cart and set his watch by the public clock. "This is more than half an hour before London time," he said, "and we mustn't be at odds with the natives about the time."

As he spoke, Dr. O'Reilly came running up breathlessly. "I've just heard something," he said. "Three men heard a shot in the cottage as they were passing, last Tuesday week."

"Where are the men?"

"I don't know at the moment; but they can be found. Shall I set about it?"

"If you possibly can," Holmes said, "you will help us enormously. Can you send them messages to be at the cottage as soon as they can get there today? Tell them they shall have a half-a-sovereign apiece."

"Right, I will. Good day."

"Tuesday week," said Mr. Bowyer as they drove off; "that was the date of Main's first letter, and the day on which, by his account, Rewse was taken ill. Then if that was the shot that killed Rewse he must have been lying dead in the place while Main was writing those letters reporting his sickness to his mother. The cold-blooded scoundrel!"

"Yes," Holmes replied, "I think it probable in any case that Tuesday was the day that Rewse was shot. It wouldn't have been safe for Main to write the mother lying letters about the small-pox before. Rewse might have written home in the meantime, or something might have occurred to postpone Main's plans, and then there would be impossible explanations required."

Over a very bad road they jolted on and in the end arrived where the road, now become a mere path, passed a tumble-down old farmhouse.

"This is where the woman lives who cooked and cleaned house for Rewse and Main," Mr. Bowyer said. "There is the cottage, scarce a hundred yards off, a little to the right of the track."

"Well," replied Holmes, "suppose we stop here and ask her a few questions? I like to get the evidence of all the witnesses as soon as possible. It simplifies subsequent work wonderfully."

They alighted, and Mr. Bowyer roared through the open door and knocked with his stick. In reply to his summons a decent-looking woman of perhaps fifty, but wrinkled beyond her age, and better dressed than any woman Holmes had seen since leaving Cullanin, appeared from the hinder buildings and curtsied pleasantly.

"Good morning, Mrs. Hurley, good morning," Mr. Bowyer said, "this is Mr. Sherlock Holmes, a gentleman from London, who is going to look into this shocking murder of our young friend Mr. Rewse and sift it to the bottom. He would like you to tell him something, Mrs. Hurley."

The woman curtsied again. "An' it's the jintleman is welcome, sor, and doin's as ut is." She had a low, pleasing voice, much in contrast with her unattractive appearance, and characterized by the softest and broadest brogue imaginable. "Will ye not come in? Mother av Hiven! An' thim two livin' together, an' fishin' an' readin' an' all, like brothers! An' trut' ut is he was a foine young jintleman indade, indade!"

"I suppose, Mrs. Hurley," Holmes said, "you've seen as much of the life of those two gentlemen here as anybody?"

"Treu ut is, sor; none more — nor as much."

"Did you ever hear of anybody being on bad terms with Mr. Rewse — anybody at all, Mr. Main or another?"

"Niver a soul in all Mayo. How could ye? Such a foine young jintleman, an' fair-spoken an' all."

"Tell me all that happened on the day that you heard that Mr. Rewse was ill — Tuesday week."

"In the mornin', sor, 'twas much as ord'nary. I was over there at half afther sivin, an' 'twas half an hour afther that I cud hear the jintlemen dhressin'. They tuk their breakfast — though Mr. Rewse's was a small wan. It was half afther nine that Mr. Main wint off walkin' to Cullanin, Mr. Rewse stayin' in, havin' letthers to write. Half an hour later I came away mesilf. Later than that (it was nigh elivin) I wint across for a pail from the yard, an' then, through the windy as I passed I saw the dear young jintleman sittin' writin' at the table calm an' peaceful — an' saw him no more in this warrl'."

"And after that?"

"Afther that, sor, I came back wid the pail, an' saw nor heard no more till two o'clock, whin Mr. Main came back from Cullanin."

"Did you see him as he came back?"

"That I did, sor, as I stud there nailin' the fence where the pig bruk ut. I'd been there an' had me oi down the road lookin' for him an hour past, expectin' he might be bringin' somethin' for me to cook for their dinner. An' more by token he gave me the toime from his watch, set by the Town Hall clock."

"And was it two o'clock?"

174

"It was that to the sthroke, an' me own ould clock, as right too whin I wint to set ut. An'"

"One moment; may I see your clock?"

Mrs. Hurley turned and shut an open door which had concealed an old hanging clock. Holmes produced his watch and compared the time. "Still right I see, Mrs. Hurley," he said; "your clock keeps excellent time."

"It does that, sor, an' nivir more than claned twice by Rafferty since me own father (rest his soul!) lift ut here. 'Tis no bad clock, as Mr. Rewse himsilf said oft an' again; an' I always kape ut by the Town Hall toime. But as I was sayin', Mr. Main came back an' gave me the toime; thin he wint sthraight to his house, an' no more av him I saw till may be half afther three."

"And then?"

"An' thin, sor, he came across, in a sad takin', wid a letther. 'Take ut,' sez he, 'an' have ut posted at Cullanin by the first that can get there. Mr. Rewse has the sickness on him awful bad,' he sez, 'an' ye must not be near the place or ye'll take ut. I have him to bed, an' his clothes I shall burn behin' the cottage,' sez he, 'so if ye see smoke ye'll know what ut is. There'll be no docthor wanted. I'm wan mesilf, an' I'll do all for 'um.' An' sure I knew him for a docthor ivir since he come. 'The cottage ye shall not come near,' he sez, 'till ut's over one way or another, an' yez can lave whativir av food an' dhrink we want midbetwixt the houses an' go back, an' I'll come and fetch ut. But have the letther posted,' he sez, 'at wanst. 'Tis not contagious,' he sez, 'bein' as I've dishinfected it mesilf. But kape yez away from the cottage.' An' I kept."

"And then did he go back to the cottage at once?"

"He did that, sor, an' a sore stew was he in to all seemin' — white as paper, and much need, too, the murtherin' scutt! An' him always so much the jintleman an' all. Well I saw no more av him that day. Next day he laves another letther wid the dirthy plates there mid-betwixt the houses, an' shouts for ut to be posted. 'Twas for the poor young jintleman's mother, sure, as was the other wan. An' the day afther there was another letther,

175

an' wan for the undhertaker, too, for he tells me it's all over, an' he's dead. An' they buried him next day followin'."

"So that from the time you went for the pail and saw Mr. Rewse writing, till after the funeral, you were never at the cottage at all?"

"Nivir, sor; an' can ye blame me? Wid children an' Terence himself sick wid bronchitis in this house?"

"Of course, of course, you did quite right — indeed you only obeyed orders. But now think; do you remember on any one of those three days; hearing a shot, or any other unusual noise in the cottage?"

"Nivir at all, sor. Tis that I've been thryin' to bring to mind these four days. Such may have been, but not that I heard."

"After you went for the pail, and before Mr. Main returned to the house, did Mr. Rewse leave the cottage at all, or might he have done so?"

"He did not lave at all, to my knowledge. Sure he *might* have gone an' he might have come back widout my knowin'. But see him I did not."

"Thank you, Mrs. Hurley. I think we'll go across to the cottage now. If any people come will you send them after us? I suppose a policeman is there?"

"He is, sor. An' the serjint is not far away. They've been in chyarge since Mr. Bowyer wint away last — but shlapin' here."

Holmes and Mr. Bowyer walked towards the cottage. "Did you notice," said Mr. Bowyer, "that the woman saw Rewse *writing letters?* Now what were those letters, and where are they? He has no correspondents that I know of but his mother and sister, and they heard nothing from him. Is this something else? — some other plot? There is something very deep here."

"Yes," Holmes replied thoughtfully, "I think our inquiries may take us deeper than we have expected; and in the matter of those letters — yes, I think they may lie near the kernel of the mystery."

Here they arrived at the cottage — an uncommonly substantial structure for the district. It was square, of plain, solid brick, with a slated roof. On the patch of ground behind it there

176

were still signs of the fires, wherein Main had burnt Rewse's clothes and other belongings. And sitting on the window-sill in front was a big member of the R.I.C., soldierly and broad, who rose as they came and saluted Mr. Bowyer.

"Good day constable," Mr. Bowyer said. "I hope nothing has been disturbed?"

"Not a shtick, sor. Nobody's as much as gone in. "

"Have any of the windows been opened or shut?" Holmes asked.

"This wan was, sor," the policeman said, indicating the one behind him, "when they took away the corrpse, an' so was the next round the corrner. Tis the bedroom windies they are, an' they opened thim to give ut a bit av air. The other windy behin' — sittin-room windy — has not been opened."

"Very well," Holmes answered, "we'll take a look at that unopened window from the inside."

The door was opened and they passed inside. There was a small lobby, and on the left of this was the bedroom with two single beds. The only other room of consequence was the sitting-room, the cottage consisting merely of these, a small scullery and a narrow closet used as a bath-room, wedged between the bedroom and the sitting room.

They made for the single window of the sitting-room at the back. It was an ordinary sash window, and was shut, but the catch was not fastened. Holmes examined the catch, drawing Mr. Bowyer's attention to a bright scratch on the grimy brass. "See," he said, "that nick in the catch exactly corresponds with the narrow space between the two frames of the window. And look," — he lifted the bottom sash a little as he spoke — "there is the mark of a knife on the frame of the top sash. Somebody has come in by that window, forcing the catch with a knife."

"Yes, yes!" cried Mr. Bowyer, greatly excited, "and he has gone out that way too, else why is the window shut and the catch not fastened? Why should he do that? What in the world does *this* thing mean?"

177

Before Holmes could reply the constable put his head into the room and announced that one Larry Shanahan was at the door, and had been promised half-a-sovereign.

"One of the men who heard a shot," Holmes said to Mr. Bowyer.

"Bring him in , constable."

The constable brought in Larry Shanahan, and Larry Shanahan brought in a strong smell of whisky. He was an extremely ragged person, with only one eye, which caused him to hold his head aside as he regarded Holmes, much as a parrot does. On his face sun-scorched brown and fiery red struggled for mastery, and his voice was none of the clearest. He held his hat against his stomach with one hand and with the other pulled his forelock.

"An' which is the honorable jintleman,"he said, "as do be burrnin' to prisint me wid a bit o' goold?"

"Here I am," said Holmes, jingling money in his pocket, "and here is the half-sovereign. It's only waiting where it is till you have answered a few questions. They say you heard a shot fired hereabout?"

"Faith, an' that I did, sor. 'Twas a shot in this house, indade, no other."

"And when was it?"

"Sure, 'twas in the afthernoon."

"But on what day?"

"Last Tuesday sivin-noight, sor, as I know by rayson av Ballyshiel fair that I wint to."

"Tell me all about it."

"I will, sor. 'Twas pigs I was dhrivin' that day, sor, to Ballyshiel fair from just beyond Cullanin. At Cullanin, sor, I dhropped in wid Danny Mulcahy, that intintioned thravellin' the same way, an' while we tuk a thrifle av a dhrink in comes Dennis Grady, that was to go to Ballyshiel similiarously. An' so we had another thrifle av a dhrin' or maybe a thrifle more, an' we wint togedther, passin' this way, as ye may not know, bein' likely a shtranger. Well, sor, ut was as we were just forninst this place that there came a divil av a bang that makes us shtop simultaneous. 'What's that?' sez Dan. 'Tis a gunshot,' sez I, 'an' 'tis in the brick house too.' 'That is so,' sez Dennis; 'nowhere else.' And we lukt at wan another. 'An' what'll we do?' sez I. 'What would yez?' sez Dan; ''tis non av our business.' 'That is so,' sez Dennis again, and we wint on. Ut was quare, maybe, but it might aisily be wan av the jintlemen emptyin' a barr'l out o' windy or what not. An' — an' so — an' so — " Mr. Shanahan scratched his ear, "an' so — we wint."

"And do you know at what time this was?"

Larry Shanahan ceased scratching, and seized his ear between thumb and forefinger, gazing severely at the floor with his one eye as he did so, plunged in computation. "Sure," he said, "'twould be — 'twould be — let's see — 'twould be — " he looked up, "'twould be half-past two maybe, or maybe a thrifle nearer three."

"And Main was in the place all the time after two," Mr. Bowyer said, bringing down his fist on his open hand. "That finishes it. We've nailed him to the minute."

"Had you a watch with you?" asked Holmes.

"Divil of a watch in the company, sor. I made an internal calculation. 'Tis foive mile from Cullanin, and we never lift till near half an hour after the Town Hall clock had struck twelve. 'Twould take us two hours and a thrifle more, considherin' the pigs an' the rough road, an' the distance, an' — an' the thrifle of dhrink." His eye rolled slyly as he said it. "That was my calculation, sor."

Here the constable appeared with two more men. Each had the usual number of eyes, but in other respects they were very good copies of Mr. Shanahan. They were both ragged, and neither bore any violent likeness to a teetotaler. "Dan Mulcahy and Dennis Grady," announced the constable.

Mr. Dan Mulcahy's tale was of a piece with Mr. Larry Shanahan's, and Mr. Dennis Grady's was the same. They had all hear the shot it was plain. What Dan had said to Dennis and what Dennis had said to Larry mattered little. Also they were all agreed that the day was Tuesday by token of the fair. But as to the time of day there arose a disagreement.

179

"'Twas nigh soon afther wan o'clock," said Dan Mulcahy.

"Soon afther wan!" exclaimed Larry Shanahan with scorn. "Soon afther your grandmother's pig! 'Twas half afther two at laste. Ut sthruck twelve nigh 'alf an hour before we lift Cullanin. Why, yez heard ut!"

"That I did not. Ut sthruck eleven, an' we wint in foive minutes."

"What fool-talk ye shpake Dan Mulcahy. 'Twas twelve sthruck; I counted ut."

"Thin ye counted wrong. I counted ut, an' 'twas elivin."

"Yez nayther av yez right," interposed Dennis Grady. "'Twas not elivin when we lift; 'twas not, be the mother av Moses!"

"I wondher at ye, Dennis Grady; ye must have been dhrunk as a Kerry cow," and both Mulcahy and Shanahan turned upon the obstinate Grady, and the dispute waxed clamorous till Holmes stopped it.

"Come, come," he said, "never mind the time then. Settle that between you after you've gone. Does either of you remember — not calculate, you know, but *remember* — the time you got to Ballyshiel? — the actual time by a clock — not a guess."

Not one of the three had looked at a clock at Ballyshiel.

"Do you remember anything about coming home again?"

They did not. They looked furtively at one another and presently broke into a grin.

"Ah! I see how *that* was," Holmes said good-humouredly. "That's all now, I think. Come, it's ten shillings each, I think." And he handed over the money. The men touched their forelocks again, stowed away the money and prepared to depart. As they went Larry Shanahan stepped mysteriously back again and said in a whisper, "Maybe the jintlemen wud like me to kiss the book on ut? An' as to the toime "

"Oh, no thank you, "Holmes laughed. "We take your word for it Mr. Shanahan." And Mr. Shanahan pulled his forelock again and vanished.

"There's nothing but confusion to be got from them," Mr. Bowyer remarked testily. "It's a mere waste of time."

"No, no, not a waste of time," Holmes replied, "nor a waste of money. One thing is made pretty plain. That is that the shot was fired on Tuesday. Mrs. Hurley never noticed the report, but these three men were close by, and there is no doubt that they heard it. It's the only single thing they agree about at all. They contradict one another over everything else, but they agree completely in that. Of course I wish we could have got the exact time; but that can't be helped. As it is it is rather fortunate that they disagreed so entirely. Two of them are certainly wrong, and perhaps all three. In any case it wouldn't have been safe to trust to mere computation of time by three men just beginning to get drunk, who had no particular reason for remembering. But if by any chance they had agreed on the time we might have been led into a wrong track altogether by taking the thing as fact. But a gunshot is not such a doubtful thing. When three independent witnesses hear a gunshot together there can be little doubt that a shot has been fired. Now I think you'd better sit down Perhaps you can find something to read. I'm about to make a very minute examination of this place, and it will probably bore you if you've nothing else to do."

But Mr. Bowyer would think of nothing but the business in hand. "I don't understand that window," he said, shaking his finger towards it as he spoke. "Not at all. Why should Main want to get in and out by a window? He wasn't a stranger."

Holmes began a most careful inspection of the whole surface of floor, ceiling, walls and furniture of the sitting-room. At the fireplace he stooped and lifted with great care a few sheets of charred paper from the grate. These he put on the window-ledge. "Will you just bring over that little screen," he asked, "to keep the draught from this burnt paper? Thank you. It looks like letter paper, and thick letter paper, since the ashes are very little broken. The weather has been fine, and there has been no fire in that grate for a long time. These papers have been carefully burned with a match or a candle."

"Ah! perhaps the letters poor young Rewse was writing in the morning. But what can they tell us?"

"Perhaps nothing — perhaps a great deal." Holmes was examining the cinders keenly, holding the surface sideways to the light.

"Come," he said, "see if I can guess Rewse's address in London. 17 Mountjoy Gardens, Hampstead. Is that it?"

"Yes. Is it there? Can you read it? Show me." Mr. Bowyer hurried across the room, eager and excited.

"You can sometimes read words on charred paper," Holmes replied, "as you may have noticed. This has curled and crinkled rather too much in the burning, but it is plainly notepaper with an embossed heading, which stands out rather clearly. He has evidently brought some notepaper with him from home in his trunk. See, you can just see the ink lines crossing out the address; but there's little else. At the beginning of the letter there is 'My d — ' then a gap, and then the last stroke of 'M' and the rest of the word 'mother.' 'My dear Mother,' or 'My dearest Mother' evidently. Something follows too in the same line, but that is unreadable. 'My dear Mother and Sister' perhaps. After that there is nothing recognizable. The first letter looks rather like 'W,' but even that is indistinct. It seems to be a longish letter — several sheets, but they are stuck together in the charring. Perhaps more than one letter."

"The thing is plain," Mr. Bowyer said. "The poor lad was writing home, and perhaps to other places, and Main, after his crime, burned the letters, because they would have stultified his own with the lying tale about small-pox."

Holmes said nothing, but resumed his general search. He passed his hand rapidly over every inch of the surface of everything in the room. Then he entered the bedroom and began an inspection of the same sort there. There were two beds, one at each end of the room, and each inch of each piece of bed linen passed rapidly under his sharp eye. After the bedroom he betook himself to the little bathroom, and then to the scullery. Finally he went outside and examined every board of a close fence that stood a few feet from the sitting-room window, and the brick-paved path lying between.

When it was all over he returned to Mr. Bowyer. "Here is a strange thing," he said. "The shot passed clean through Rewse's body, striking no bones, and meeting no solid resistance. It was a good-sized bullet, as Dr. O'Reilly testifies, and therefore must have had a large charge of powder behind it in the cartridge. After emerging from Rewse's back it *must* have struck something else in this confined place. Yet on nowhere — ceiling, floor, wall nor furniture, can I find the mark of a bullet nor the bullet itself."

"The bullet itself Main might easily have got rid of."

"Yes, but not the mark. Indeed, the bullet would scarcely be easy to get at if it had struck anything I have seen about here; it would have buried itself. Just look round now. Where could a bullet strike in this place without leaving its mark?"

Mr. Bowyer looked round. "Well, no," he said, "nowhere. Unless the window was open and it went out that way."

"Then it must have hit the fence or the brick paving between, and there is no sign of a bullet there," Holmes replied. "Push the sash, as high as you please, the shot couldn't have passed *over* the fence without hitting the window first. As to the bedroom windows, that's impossible. Mr. Shanahan and his friends would not only have heard the shot, they would have seen it — which they didn't."

"Then what's the meaning of it?"

"The meaning of it is simply this: either Rewse was shot somewhere else and his body brought here afterwards, or the article, whatever it was, that the bullet struck must have been taken away."

"Yes, of course. It's just another piece of evidence destroyed by Main, that's all. Every step we go we see the diabolical completeness of his plans. But now every piece of evidence missing only tells the more against him. The body alone condemns him past all redemption."

Holmes was gazing about the room thoughtfully. "I think we'll have Mrs. Hurley over here," he said; "she should tell us if anything is missing. Constable, will you ask Mrs. Hurley to step over here?"

Mrs. Hurley came at once and was brought into the sitting room. "Just look about you, Mrs. Hurley," Holmes said, "in this room and everywhere else, and tell me if anything is missing that you can remember was here on the morning of the day you last saw Mr. Rewse."

She looked thoughtfully up and down the room. "Sure, sor," she said, "'tis all there as ord'nary." Her eyes rested on the mantelpiece and she added at once, "Except the clock, indade."

"Except the clock?"

"The clock ut is, sure. Ut stud on that same mantelpiece on that mornin' as ut always did."

"What sort of clock was it?"

"Just a plain round wan wid a metal case — an American clock they said ut was. But ut kept nigh as good time as me own."

"It *did* keep good time, you say?"

"Faith an' ut did, sor. Mine an' this ran together for weeks wid nivir a minute betune thim."

"Thank you, Mrs. Hurley, thank you; that will do," Holmes exclaimed, with some excitement in his voice. He turned to Mr. Bowyer. "We must find that clock," he said. "And there's the pistol; nothing has been seen of that. Come, help me search. Look for a loose board."

"But he'll have taken them away with him probably."

"The pistol perhaps — although that isn't likely. The clock, no. It's evidence, man, evidence!" Holmes darted outside and walked hurriedly round the cottage, looking this way and that about the country adjacent.

Presently he returned. "No," he said, "I think it's more likely in the house." He stood for a moment and thought. Then he made for the fireplace and flung the fender across the floor. All round the hearthstone an open crack extended. "See there!" he exclaimed as he pointed to it. He took the tongs, and with one leg levered the stone up till he could seize it in his fingers. Then he dragged it out and pushed it across the linoleum that covered the floor. In the space beneath lay a large revolver and a common American round nickel-plated clock. "See here!" he cried, "see here!" and he rose and placed the articles on the mantelpiece. The glass before the clock-face was smashed to atoms, and there was a gaping rent in the face itself. For a few seconds Holmes regarded it as it stood, and then he turned to Mr. Bowyer. "Mr. Bowyer," he said, "we have done Mr. Stanley Main a sad injustice. Poor young Rewse committed suicide. There is proof undeniable," and he pointed to the clock.

"Proof? How? Where? Nonsense, man. Pooh! Ridiculous! If Rewse committed suicide why should Main go to all that trouble and tell all those lies to prove that he died of small-pox? More even that that, what has he run away for?"

"I'll tell you, Mr. Bowyer, in a moment. But first as to this clock. Remember, Main set his watch by the Cullanin Town Hall clock, and Mrs. Hurley's clock agreed exactly. That we have proved ourselves to-day by my own watch. Mrs. Hurley's clock still agrees. *This* clock was always kept in time with Mrs. Hurley's. Main returned at two exactly. Look at the time by that clock — the time when the bullet crashed into and stopped it."

The time was three minutes to one. Holmes took the clock, unscrewed the winder and quickly stripped off the back, exposing the works. "See," he said, "the bullet is lodged firmly among the wheels, and has been torn into snags and strips by the impact. The wheels themselves are ruined altogether. The central axle which carries the hands is bent. See there! Neither hand will move in the slightest. That bullet struck the axle and fixed those hands immovably at the moment of the time when Algernon Rewse died. Look at the mainspring. It is less than half run out. Proof that the clock was going when the shot struck it. Main left Rewse alive and well at half-past nine. He did not return till two — when Rewse had been dead more than an hour."

"But then, hang it all! How about the lies and the false certificate, and the bolting?"

"Let me tell you the whole tale, Mr. Bowyer, as I conjecture it to have been. Poor young Rewse was, as you told me, in a bad state of health — thoroughly run down, I think you said. You said something of his engagement and the death of the lady. This pointed clearly to a nervous — a mental upset. Very well. He broods, and so forth. He must go away and find change of scene and occupation. His intimate friend Main brings him here. The holiday has its good effect perhaps, at first, but after a while it gets monotonous, and brooding sets in again. I do not know whether or not you happen to know it, but it is a fact that four-fifths of all persons suffering from melancholia have suicidal tendencies. This may never have been suspected by Main, who otherwise might not have left him so long alone. At any rate he *is* left alone, and he takes the opportunity. He writes a note to Main and a long letter to his mother — an awful, heartbreaking letter, with a terrible picture of the mental agony wherein he was to die — perhaps with a tincture of religious mania in it, and prophesying merited hell for himself in the hereafter. This done, he simply stands up from the table, at which he has been writing, and with his back to the fireplace shoots himself. There he lies till Main returns an hour later. Main finds the door shut and nobody answers his knock. He goes round to the sitting-room window, looks through, and perhaps he sees the body. Anyway he pushes back the catch with his knife, opens the window and gets in, and *then* he sees. He is completely knocked out of time. The thing is terrible. What shall he — what can he do? Poor Rewse's mother and sister dote on him, and his mother is an invalid — heart disease. To let her see that awful letter would be to kill her. He burns the letter, also the note to himself. Then an idea strikes him. Even without the letter the news of her boy's suicide will probably kill the poor old lady. Can she be prevented hearing of it? Of his death she must know — that's inevitable. How as to the manner? Would it not be possible to concoct some kind lie? And then the opportunities of the situation occur to him. Nobody but himself knows of it. He is a medical man, fully qualified, and empowered to give certificates of death. More, there is an epidemic of small-pox in the neighborhood. What easier, with a little management, than to call the death one by small-pox? Nobody would be anxious to examine too closely the corpse of a small-pox patient. He decides that he will do it. He writes the letter to Mrs. Rewse announcing that her son has the disease, and he forbids Mrs. Hurley to come near the place for fear of infection. He cleans the floor — it is linoleum here, you see, and the stains were fresh — burns the clothes, cleans and stops the wound. At every turn his medical knowledge is of use. He puts the smashed clock and the pistol out of sight under the hearth. In a word he carries out the whole thing rather cleverly, and a terrible few days he must have passed. It never strikes him that he has dug a frightful pit for his own feet. You are suspicious, and you come across. In a perhaps rather peremptory manner you tell him how suspicious his conduct has been. And then a sense of his terrible position comes upon him like a thunderclap. He sees it all. He has deliberately of his own motion destroyed every evidence of the suicide. There is no evidence in the world that Rewse did not die a natural death, except the body, and that you are going to dig up. He sees now (you remind him of it in fact) that *he* is the one man alive who can profit by Rewse's death. And there is the shot body, and there is the false death certificate, and there are the lying letters, and the tales to the neighbors and everything. He has himself destroyed everything that proves suicide. All that remains points to a foul murder and to him as the murderer. Can you wonder at his complete breakdown and his flight? What else in the world could the poor fellow do?"

"Well, well — yes, yes," Mr. Bowyer replied thoughtfully, "it seems very plausible of course. But still, look at probabilities, my dear sir, look at probabilities."

"No, but look at *possibilities.* There is that clock. Get over it if you can. Was there ever a more insurmountable alibi? Could Main possibly be here shooting Rewse and half way between here and Cullanin at the same time? Remember, Mrs. Hurley saw him come back at two, and she had been watching for an hour, and could see more than half a mile up the road."

"Well, yes, I suppose you're right. And what must we do now?"

"Bring Main back. I think we should advertise to begin with. Say, 'Rewse is proved to have died over an hour before you came. All safe. Your evidence is wanted,' or something of that sort. And we must set the telegraph going. The police already looking for him, no doubt. Meanwhile I will look here for a clue myself."

The advertisement was successful in two days. Indeed Main afterwards said that he was at the time, once the first terror was over, in doubt whether or not it would be best to go back and face the thing out, trusting to his innocence. He could not venture home for money, nor to his bank, for fear of the police. He chanced upon the advertisement as he searched the paper for news of the case, and that decided him. His explanation of the matter was precisely as Holmes had expected. His only thought till Mr. Bowyer first arrived at the cottage had been to smother the real facts and to spare the feelings of Mrs. Rewse and her daughter, and it was not till that gentleman put them so plainly before him that he in the least realized the dangers of his position. That his fears for Mrs. Rewse were only too well grounded was proved by events, for the poor old lady only survived her son by a month.

These events took place some little while ago, as may be gathered from the fact that Miss Rewse has now been Mrs. Stanley Main for many years.

The Affair of Mrs. Seton's Child

It has struck me that many of my readers may wonder that, although I have set down in detail a number of interesting cases wherein Holmes figured with success, I have scarcely as much as alluded to his failures. For failures he had, and of a fair number. More than once he has found his search met, perhaps at the beginning, perhaps after some little while, by an impenetrable wall of darkness through which no clue led. At other times he has lost time on a false trail while his quarry escaped. At others still the stupidity or inaccuracy of some person upon whom he has depended for information has set his plans to naught. The reason why none of these cases have been embodied in the present papers is simply this: that a problem with no answer, a puzzle with no explanation, an incident with no satisfactory end, as a rule lends itself but poorly to purposes of popular narrative, and it is often difficult to make understood and appreciated any degree of skill and acumen unless it produces a clear and intelligible result. That such results attended Holmes's efforts in an extraordinary degree those who have followed my narratives so far will need no assurance; but withal impossibilities still remain impossibilities, for Holmes as for the dullest creature alive. On some other occasion I may perhaps set out at length a case in which Sherlock Holmes achieved nothing more than unqualified failure; for the present I shall content myself with a case which, although it was completely cleared up in the end, yet for some while baffled Holmes because of some of the reasons I have alluded to.

On the ground floor of a building near where Holmes resided were the offices of Messrs. Streatley & Raikes, an old-fashioned firm of family solicitors. Messrs. Streatley & Raikes's junior clerk appeared in Holmes's rooms one morning with the statement, "Mr. Raikes sends his compliments and will be obliged if you can step downstairs for a few minutes? It's a client of ours — a lady — and she's in a great state about losing her baby or something. Mr. Raikes would bring her up, only she seems too ill to get up the stairs."

This was the purport of the message, and in three minutes Holmes was in Streatley & Raikes's office.

"I thought the only useful thing possible would be to send for you, Mr. Holmes," Mr. Raikes explained; "indeed, if my client had been better acquainted with London, no doubt she would have come to you direct. She is in a bad state in the inner office. Her name is Mrs. Seton; her husband is a recent client of ours. Quite young, and rather wealthy people, so far as I know. Made a fortune early, I believe, in South Africa, and came here to live. Their child — their only child, a little toddler of two years or thereabout — disappeared yesterday in a most mysterious way, and all efforts to find it seem to have failed as yet. The police have been set going everywhere, but there is no news as yet. Mrs. Seton seems to have passed a dreadful night, and could think of nothing better to do this morning than to come to us. She has her maid with her, and looks to be breaking down entirely. I believe she's lying on the sofa in my private room now. Will you see her? I think you might hear what she has to say, whether you take the case in hand or not; something may strike you, and in any case it will comfort her to get your opinion. I told her all about you, you know, and she clutched at the chance eagerly. Shall I see if we may go in?"

Mr. Raikes knocked at the door of his inner sanctum and waited; then he knocked again and set the door ajar. There was a quiet "Come in," and pushing open the door the lawyer motioned Holmes to follow him.

On the sofa facing the door sat a lady, very pale, and exhibiting plain signs of grief and physical weariness. A heavy veil was thrown back over her bonnet, and her maid stood at her side holding a bottle of salts. As she saw Holmes she made as if to rise, but he stepped quickly forward and laid his hand on her shoulder.

"Pray don't disturb yourself, Mrs. Seton," he said; "Mr. Raikes has told me something of your trouble, and perhaps when

I know a little more I shall be able to offer you some advice. But remember that it will be very important for you to maintain your strength and spirits as much as possible."

"This is Mr. Sherlock Holmes, you know," Mr. Raikes here put in — "of whom I was speaking." Mrs. Seton inclined her head, and with a very obvious effort began. "It is my child, you know, Mr. Holmes — my little boy Charley; we can't find him."

"Mr. Raikes has told me so. When did you see the child last?"

"Yesterday morning. His nurse left him sitting on the floor in a room we call the small morning-room, where we sometimes allowed him to play when nurse was out, because the nursery was out of hearing, except from the bedrooms. I myself was in the large morning-room, and as he seemed to be very quiet. I went to look, and found he was not there."

"You looked elsewhere, of course?"

"Yes, but he was nowhere in the house, and none of the servants had seen him. At first I supposed that his nurse had gone back to the small morning-room and taken him with her — I had sent her on an errand — but when she returned I found that was not the case."

"Can he walk?"

"Oh, yes, he can walk quite well. But he could scarcely have come out from the room without my hearing him. The two rooms, the morning-room and the small sitting-room, are on opposite sides of the same passage."

"Do the doors face each other?"

"No; the door of the small room is farther up the passage than the other. But in any case he was nowhere in the house."

"But if he left the room he must have got out somehow. Is there no other door?"

"Yes, there is a French window, with the lower panels of wood, in the room; it gives on to a few steps leading down into the garden; but that was closed and bolted on the inside."

"You found no trace whatever of him, I take it, on the whole premises?"

191

"Not a trace of any sort, nor had anybody about the place seen him."

"Did you yourself actually see him in this room, or have you merely the nurse's word for it?"

"I saw her put him there. She left him playing with a box of toys. When I went to look for him the toys were there, scattered on the floor, but he had gone." Mrs. Seton sank on the arms of her maid and her breast heaved.

"I'm sure," Holmes said, "you'll keep your nerves as steady as you can, Mrs. Seton: much may depend on it. If you have nothing else to tell me now, I think I will come to your house at once, look at it, and question your servants myself. Meantime, what has been done?"

"The police have been notified everywhere, of course," Mr. Raikes said, handing Holmes a printed bill, damp from the press;" and here is a bill containing a description of the child and offering a reward, which is being circulated now."

Holmes glanced at the bill and nodded. "That is quite right," he said, "so far as I can tell at present. But I must see the place. Do you feel strong enough to come home now, Mrs. Seton?"

Holmes's business-like decision and confidence of manner gave the lady fresh strength. "The brougham is here," she said, "and we can drive home at once. We live at Cricklewood."

A fine pair of horses stood before the brougham, though they still bore signs of hard work; and indeed they had been kept at their best pace all that morning. All the way to Cricklewood Holmes kept Mrs. Seton in conversation, never for a moment leaving her attention disengaged. The missing child, he learned, was the only one, and the family had only been in England for something less than a year. Mr. Seton had become possessed of real property in South Africa, had sold it in London, and had determined to settle here.

A little way past Shoot-up Mill the coachman swung his pair off to the left, and presently entering a gate, pulled up before a large, old fashioned house.

Here Holmes immediately began a complete examination of the premises. The possible exits from the grounds, he found, were four in number: the two wide front gates giving on to the carriage-drive, the kitchen and stable entrance, and a side gate in a fence — always locked, however. Inside the house, from the central hall, a passage to the right led to another wherein was the door of the small morning-room. This was a very ordinary room, fifteen feet square or so, lighted by the glass in the French window, the bottom panes of which, however, had been filled in with wood. The contents of a box of toys lay scattered on the floor, and the box itself lay near.

"Have these toys been moved," Holmes asked, "since the child was missed?"

"No, we haven't allowed anything to be disturbed. The disappearance seemed so wholly unaccountable that we thought the police might wish to examine the place exactly as it was. They did not seem to think it necessary, however."

Holmes knelt and examined the toys without disturbing them. They were of very good quality, and represented a farmyard, with horses, carts, ducks, geese and cows complete. One of the carts had had a string attached so that it might be pulled along the floor.

"Now," Holmes said, rising, "you think, Mrs. Seton, that the child could not have toddled through the passage, and so into some other part of the house, without you hearing him?"

"Well," Mrs. Seton answered with indecision, "I thought so at first, but I begin to doubt. Because he *must* have done so, I suppose."

They went into the passage. The door of the large morning-room was four or five yards further toward the passage leading to the hall, and on the opposite side. "The floor in this passage," Holmes observed, "is rather thickly carpeted. See here, I can walk on it at a good pace without noise."

Mrs. Seton assented. "Of course," she said, "if he got past here he might have got anywhere about the house, and so into the grounds. There is a veranda outside the drawing-room, and doors in various places."

"Of course the grounds have been completely examined?"

"Oh, yes, every inch."

"The weather has been very dry, unfortunately," Holmes said, "and it would be useless for me to look for footprints on your hard gravel, especially of so small a child. Let us come back to the room. Is the French window fastened as you found it?"

"Yes; nothing has been changed."

The French window was, as is usual, one of two casements joining in the centre and fastened by bolts top and bottom. "It is not your habit, I see," Holmes observed, "to open both halves of the window."

"No; one side is always fastened, the other we secure by the bottom bolt because the catch of the handle doesn't always act properly."

"And you found that bolt fastened as I see it now?"

"Yes."

Holmes lifted the bolt and opened the door. Four or five steps led parallel with the face of the wall to a sort of path which ran the whole length of the house on this side, and was only separated from a quiet public lane by a low fence and a thin hedge. Almost opposite a small, light gate stood in the fence, firmly padlocked.

"I see," Holmes. remarked, "your house is placed close against one side of the grounds. Is that the side gate which you always keep locked?"

Mrs. Seton replied in the affirmative, and Holmes laid his hand on the gate in question. "Still," he said, "if security is the object I should recommend hinges a little less rural in pattern; see here," and he gave the gate a jerk upward, lifting the hinge-pins from their sockets and opening the gate from that side, the padlock acting as hinge. "Those hinges," he added, "were meant for a heavier gate than that;" and he replaced the gate.

"Yes," Mrs. Seton replied; "I am obliged to you; but that doesn't concern us now. The French window was bolted on the inside. Would you like to see the servants?" The servants were produced, and Holmes questioned each in turn, but not one would admit having seen anything of Master Charles Seton after he had been left in the small morning-room. A rather stupid groom fancied he had seen Master Charles on the side lawn, but then remembered that that must have been the day before. The cook, an uncommonly thin, sharp-featured woman for one of her trade, was especially positive that she had not seen him all that day. "And she would be sure to have remembered if she had seen him leaving the house" she said, "because she was the more particular since he was lost the last time."

This was news to Holmes. "Lost the last time?" he asked; "why, what is this, Mrs. Seton? Was he lost once before?"

"Oh, yes," Mrs. Seton answered, "six or seven weeks ago. But that was quite different. He strayed out at the front gate, and was brought back from the police station in the evening."

"But this may be most important," Holmes said. "You should certainly have told me. Tell me now exactly what happened on this first occasion."

"But it was really quite an ordinary sort of accident. He was left alone and got out through an open gate. Of course we were very anxious; but we had him back the same evening. Need we waste time in talking about that?"

"But it will be no waste of time, I assure you. What was it that happened, exactly?"

"Nurse was about to take him for a short walk just before lunch. On the front lawn he suddenly remembered a whip which had been left in the nursery, and insisted on taking it with him. She left him and went back for it, taking, however, some little time to find it. When she returned he was nowhere to be seen; but one of the gates was a couple of feet or more open — it had caught on a loose stone in swinging to — and no doubt he had wandered off that way. A lady found him some distance away, and, not knowing to whom he belonged, took him that evening to a police station, and as messages had been sent to the police stations, we had him back soon after he was left there."

"Do you know who the lady was?"

"Her name was Mrs. Clark. She left her name and address at the police station, and of course I wrote to thank her. But there was some mistake in taking it down, I suppose, for the letter was returned marked 'not known.' "

"Then you never saw this lady yourself?"

"No."

"I think I will make a note of the exact description of the child, and then visit the police station to which this lady took him six weeks ago. Fair, curly hair, I think, and blue eyes? Age two years and three months; walks and runs well, and speaks fairly plainly. Dress?"

"Pale blue llama frock with lace, white under-linen, linen overall, pale blue silk socks and tan shoes. Everything good as new except the shoes, which were badly worn at the backs, through a habit he has of kicking back and downward with his heels when sitting. They were rather old shoes, and only used indoors."

"If I remember aright nothing was said of those shoes in the printed bill?"

"Was that so? No, I believe not. I have been so worried."

"Yes, Mrs. Seton, of course. It is most creditable in you to have kept up so well while I have been making my inquiries. Go now and take a good rest while I do what is possible. By the way, where was Mr. Seton yesterday morning when you missed the boy?"

"In the City. He has some important business in hand just now."

"And today?"

"He has gone to the City again. Of course he is sadly worried; but he saw that everything possible was done, and, his business was very important."

"Just so. Mr. Seton was not married before, I presume — if I may?"

"No, certainly not; why do you ask?"

"I beg your pardon, but I have a habit of asking almost every question I can think of; I can't know too much of a case, you know, and most unlikely pieces of information sometimes turn out useful. Thank you for your patience; I will try another plan now."

Mrs. Seton had kept up remarkably well during Holmes's examination, but she was plainly by no means a strong woman, and her maid came again to her assistance as Holmes left.

Holmes himself made for the police station. Few inspectors indeed of the Metropolitan Police force did not know Holmes by sight, and the one here in charge knew him well. He remembered very well the occasion, six weeks or so before, when Mrs. Clark brought Mrs. Seton's child to the station. He was on duty himself at the time, and he turned up the book containing an entry on the subject. From this it appeared that the lady gave the address No. 89, Sedgby Road, Belsize Park.

"I suppose you didn't happen to know the lady," Holmes asked, "by sight or otherwise?"

"No, I didn't, and I'm not sure I could swear to her again," the inspector answered. "She wore a heavy veil, and I didn't see much of her face. One rum thing I noticed, though: she seemed rather taken with the baby, and as she stooped down to kiss him before she went away I could see an old scar on her throat. It was just the sort of scar I've seen on a man that's had his throat cut and got over it. She wore a high collar to hide it, but stooping shifted the collar, and so I saw it."

"Did she seem an educated woman?"

"Oh, yes; perfect lady; spoke very nice. I told her a baby had been inquired after by Mrs. Seton, and from the description I'd no doubt this was the one. And so it was."

"At what time was this?"

"7.10 p.m., exactly. Here it is, all entered property."

"Now as to Sedgby Road, Belsize Park. Do you happen to know it?"

"Oh, yes, very well. Very quiet, respectable road indeed. I only know it through walking through."

"I see a suburban directory on the shelf behind you. Do you mind pulling it down? Thanks. Let us find Sedgby Road. Here it is. See, there *is* no No. 89; the highest number is 67."

"No more there is," the inspector answered, running his finger down the column; "and there's no Clark in the road, that's more. False address, that's plain. And so they've lost him again, have they? We had notice yesterday, of course, and I've just got some bills. This last seems a queer sort of affair, don't it? Child sitting inside the house disappeared like a ghost, and all the doors and windows fastened inside."

Holmes agreed that the affair had very uncommon features, and presently left the station and sought a cab. All the way back to his rooms he considered the matter deeply. As a matter of fact he was at a loss. Certain evidence he had seen in the house, but it went a very little way, and beyond that there was merely no clue whatever. There were features of the child's first estrayal also that attracted him, though it might very easily be the case that nothing connected the two events. There was an unknown woman — apparently a lady — who had once had her throat cut, bringing the child back after several hours, and giving a false name and address, for since the address was false, the same was probably the case with the name. Why was this? This time the child was still absent, and nothing whatever was there to suggest in what direction he might be followed, neither was there anything to indicate why he should be detained anywhere, if detained he was. Holmes determined, while awaiting any result that the bills might bring, to cause certain inquiries to be made into the antecedents of the Setons. Moreover, other work was waiting, and the Seton business must be put aside for a few hours at least.

Holmes sat late in his rooms that evening, and at about nine o'clock Mrs. Seton returned. The poor woman seemed on the verge of serious illness. She had received two anonymous letters, which she brought with her, and with scarcely a word placed before Holmes's eyes. The first he opened and read as follows:

The writer observes that you are offering a reward for the recovery of your child. There is no necessity for this; Charley is quite safe, happy, and in good hands. Pray do not instruct detectives or take any such steps just yet. The child is well and shall be returned to you. This I swear solemnly. His errand is one of mercy; pray have patience.

Holmes turned the letter and envelope in his hand. "Good paper, of the same sort as the envelope," he remarked, "but only a half sheet, freshly torn off, probably because the other side bore an address heading; therefore most likely from a respectable sort of house. The writing is a woman's, and good, though the writer was agitated when she did it. Posted this afternoon, at Willesden."

"You see," Mrs. Seton said anxiously, "she knows his name. She calls him 'Charley.'"

"Yes, "Holmes answered; "there may be something in that, or there may not. The name Charles Seton is on the bills, isn't it? And they have been visible publicly all day today. So that the name may be more easily explained than some other parts of the letter. For instance, the writer says that the child's 'errand' is one of mercy. The little fellow may be very intelligent — no doubt is — but children of two years old as a rule do not practice errands of mercy — nor indeed errands of any sort. Can you think of anything whatever, Mrs. Seton, in connection with your family history, or indeed anything else, that may throw light on that phrase?"

He looked keenly at her as he asked, but her expression was one of blank doubt merely, as she shook her head slowly and answered in the negative. Holmes turned to the other letter and read this:

MADAM,

If you want your child you had better make an arrangement with me. You fancy he has strayed, but as a matter of fact he has been stolen, and you little know by whom. You will never get him back except through me, you may rest assured of that. Are you prepared to pay me one hundred pounds (£100) if I hand him to you, and no questions asked? Your present reward, £20, is paltry; and you may finally bid good-bye to your child if you will not accept my terms. If you do, say as much in an advertisement to the Standard, addressed to

VERITAS

"A man's handwriting," Holmes commented; "fairly well formed, but shaky. The writer is not in first-rate health — each line totters away in a downward slope at the end. I shouldn't be surprised to hear that the gentleman drank. Postmark, Hampstead; posted this afternoon also. But the striking thing is the paper and envelope. They are each of exactly the same kind and size as those of the other letter. The paper also is a half sheet, and torn off on the same side as the other; confirmation of my suspicion that the object is to get rid of the printed address. I shall be surprised if both these were not written in the same house. That looks like a traitor in the enemy's camp; the question is, which is the traitor?" Holmes regarded the letters intently for a few seconds and then proceeded. "Plainly," he said, "if these letters are written by people who know anything about the matter, one writer is lying. The woman promises that the child shall be returned without reward or search, and talks generally as if the taking away of the child, or the estrayal, or whatever it was, were a very virtuous sort of proceeding. The man says plainly that the child has been stolen, with no attempt to gloss the matter, and asserts that nothing will get the child back but heavy blackmail — a very different story. On the other hand, can there be any concerted design in these two letters? Arc they intended, each from its own side, to play up to a certain result?" Holmes paused and thought. Then he asked suddenly: "Do you recognize anything familiar either in the handwriting or the stationery of these letters?"

"No, nothing."

"Very well," Holmes said, "we will come to closer quarters with the blackmailer, I think. You needn't commit yourself to paying anything, of course."

"But, Mr. Holmes, I will gladly pay or do anything. The hundred pounds is nothing. I will pay it gladly if I can only get my child."

"Well, well, we shall see. The man may not be able to do what he offers, after all, but that we will test. It is too late now for an advertisement in tomorrow morning's *Standard,* but there is the *Evening Standard* — he may even mean that — and the next morning's. I will have an advertisement inserted in both, inviting this man to make an appointment, and prove the genuineness of his offer; that will fetch him if he wants the money, and can do anything for it. Have you nothing else to tell me?"

"Nothing. But have you ascertained nothing yourself? Don't say I've to pass another night in such dreadful suspense!"

"I'm afraid, Mrs. Seton, I must ask you to be patient a little longer. I have ascertained something, but it has not carried me far as yet. Remember that if there is anything at all in these anonymous letters (and I think there is) the child is at any rate safe, and to be found one way or another. Both agree in that." This he said mainly to comfort his client, for in fact he had learned very little. His news from the City as to Mr. Seton's early history had been but meager. He was known as a successful speculator, and that was almost all. There was an indefinite notion that he had been married once before, but nothing more.

All the next day Holmes did nothing in the case. Another affair, a previous engagement, kept him hard at work in his rooms all day, and indeed had this not been the case he could have done little. His City inquiries were still in progress, and he awaited, moreover, a reply to the advertisement. But at about half-past seven in the evening this telegram arrived — *Child returned. Come at once. — Seton.*

In five minutes Holmes was making north-west in a hansom, and in half an hour he was ringing the bell at the Setons' house. Within, Mrs. Seton was still semi-hysterical, clasping the child — an intelligent-looking little fellow — in her arms, and refusing to release her hold of him for a moment. Mr. Seton stood before the fire in the same room. He was a smart-looking, scrupulously dressed man of thirty-live or thereabouts, and he

201

began explaining his telegram as soon as he had wished Holmes good-evening.

"The child's back," he said, "and of course that's the great thing. But I'm not satisfied, Mr. Holmes. I want to know why it was taken away, and I want to punish somebody. It's really very extraordinary. My poor wife has been driving about all day — she called on you, by the bye, but you were out." (Holmes credited this to his landlady, who had been told he must not be disturbed), "and she has been all over the place uselessly, unable to rest, of course. Well, I have been at home since half-past four, and at about six I was smoking in the small morning-room — I often use it as a smoking-room — and looking out at the French window. I came away from there, and half an hour or more later, as it was getting dusk, I remembered I had left the French window open, and sent a servant to shut it. She went straight to the room, and there on the floor, where he was seen last, she found the child playing with his toys as though nothing had happened!"

"And how was he dressed — as he is now?"

"Yes, just as he was when we missed him."

Holmes stepped up to the child as he sat on his mother's lap, and rubbed his cheek, speaking pleasantly to him. The little fellow looked up and smiled, and Holmes observed: "One thing is noticeable: this linen overall is almost clean. Little boys like this don't keep one white overall clean for three days, do they? And see — those shoes — aren't they new? Those he had were old, I think you said, and tan-colored."

The shoes now on the child's feet were of white leather, with a noticeable sewn ornamentation in silk. His mother had not noticed them before, and as she looked he lifted his little foot higher and said, "Look, mummy, more new shoes!"

"Ask him, "suggested Holmes hurriedly, "who gave them to him."

His father asked him, and the little fellow looked puzzled. After a pause, he said, "Mummy."

"No," his mother answered, "*I* didn't."

He thought a moment, and then said, "No, no, not *vis* mummy — course not." And for some little while after that the only answer procurable from him was, "Course not," which seemed to be a favorite phrase of his.

"Have you asked him where he has been?"

"Yes," his mother answered, "but he only says, 'Ta-ta.' "

"Ask him again."

She did. This time, after a little reflection, he pointed his chubby arm toward the door, and said, "Been dere."

"Who took you?" asked Mrs. Seton.

Again Charley seemed puzzled. Then, looking doubtfully at his mother, he said, "Mummy."

"No, not mummy," she answered; and his reply was "Course not," after which he attempted to climb on her shoulder. Then, at Holmes's suggestion, he was asked whom he went to see. This time the reply was prompt.

"Poor daddy," he said.

"What, *this* daddy?"

"No, not *vis* daddy — course not." And that was all that could be got from him.

"He will probably say things in the next day or two which may be useful," Holmes said, "if you listen pretty sharply. Now I should like to go to the small morning-room."

In the room in question the door was still open. Outside the moon had risen and made the evening almost as clear as day. Holmes examined the steps and the path at their foot, but all was dry and hard, and showed no footmark. Then, as his eye rested on the small gate, "See here," he exclaimed suddenly, "somebody has been in, lifting the gate, as I showed Mrs. Seton when I was last here. The gate has been replaced in a hurry, and only the top hinge has dropped in its place; the bottom one is disjointed." He lifted the gate once more and set it back. The ground just along its foot was softer than in the parts surrounding, and here Holmes perceived the print of a heel. It was the heel-mark of a woman's boot, small and sharp, and of the usual curved D-shape. Nowhere else within or without was there the slightest mark. Holmes went some distance either way in the outer lane, but without discovering anything more.

"I think I will borrow those new shoes," Holmes said on his return. "I think I should be disposed to investigate further in any case, for my own satisfaction. The thing interests me. By the way, Mrs. Seton, tell me, would these shoes be more likely to have been bought at a regular shoemaker's or at a baby-linen shop?"

"Certainly I should say at a baby-linen shop," Mrs. Seton answered; "they are of excellent quality, and for babies' shoes of this fancy description one would never go to an ordinary shoemaker's."

"So much the better, because the baby-linen shops are fewer than the shoemakers'. I may take these, then? Perhaps before I go you had better make quite certain that there is nothing else about the child which is not your own." There was nothing, and with the shoes in his pocket Holmes regained his cab and traveled back to his rooms. The case, from its very bareness and simplicity, puzzled him. Why was the child taken? Plainly not to keep, for it had been returned almost as it went. Plainly also not for the sake of reward or blackmail, for here was the child safely back, before the anonymous blackmailer had had a chance of earning his money. More, the advertised reward had not been claimed. Also it could not be a matter of malice or revenge, for the child was quite unharmed, and indeed seemed to have been quite happy. No conceivable family complication, previous to the marriage of Mr. and Mrs. Seton, could induce anybody to take away and return the child, which was undoubtedly Mrs. Seton's. Then who could be the "poor daddy" and "mummy" — not "*vis* daddy" and not "*vis* mummy"— that the child had been with? The Setons knew nothing of them. It was difficult to see what it could all mean.

Arrived at his rooms, Holmes took a map, and setting the leg of a pair of compasses on the site of the Setons' house, described a circle, including in its radius all Willesden and Hampstead. Then, with the Suburban Directory to help him, he began searching out and noting all the baby-linen shops in the area. After all, there were not many — about a dozen. This done, Holmes stopped for the day.

In the morning he began his hunt. His design was to call at each of the shops until he had found in which a pair of shoes of that particular pattern had been sold on the day of little Charley Seton's disappearance. The first two shops he tried did not keep shoes of the pattern, and had never had them, and the young ladies behind the counter seemed vastly amused at Holmes's inquiries. Nothing perturbed, he tried the next shop on his list, in the Hampstead district. There they kept such shoes as a rule, but were "out of them at present." Holmes immediately sent his card to the proprietress, requesting a few minutes' interview.

The lady — a very dignified lady indeed — in black silk, grey corkscrew curls and spectacles, came out with Holmes's card between her fingers. He apologized for troubling her, and, stepping out of hearing from the counter, explained that his business was urgent. "A child has been taken away by some unauthorized person, whom I am endeavoring to trace. This person bought this pair of shoes on Monday. You keep such shoes, I find, though they are not in stock at present, and, as they appear to be of an uncommon sort, possibly they were bought here."

The lady looked at them. "Yes," she said, "this pattern of shoe is made especially for me. I do not think you can buy them at other places."

"Then may I ask you to inquire from your assistants if any were sold on Monday, and to whom?"

"Certainly." Then there were consultations behind counters and desks, and examinations of carbon-papered books. In the end the proprietress came to Holmes, followed by a young lady of rather pert and self-confident aspect. "We find," she said, "that two pairs of these shoes were sold on Monday. But one pair was afterwards brought back and exchanged for others less expensive. This young lady sold both."

"Ah, then possibly she may remember something of the person who bought the pair which was *not* exchanged."

"Yes," the assistant answered at once, addressing herself to the lady; "it was Mrs. Butcher's servant."

The proprietress frowned slightly. Oh, indeed," she said, "Mrs. Butcher's servant, was it? There have been inquiries about Mrs. Butcher before, I believe, though not *here.* Mrs. Butcher is a woman who takes babies to mind, and is said to make a trade of adopting them, or finding people anxious to adopt them. I know nothing of her, nor do I want to. She lives somewhere not far off, and you can get her address, I believe, from the greengrocer's round the corner."

"Does she keep more than one servant?"

"Oh, I think not; but no doubt the greengrocer can say." The lady seemed to feel it an affront that she should be supposed to know anything of Mrs. Butcher, and Holmes consequently started for the greengrocer's. Now this was just one of those cases in which dependence on information given by other people put Holmes on the wrong scent. He spent that day in a fatiguing pursuit of Mrs. Butcher's servant, with adventures rather amusing in themselves, but quite irrelevant to the Seton case. In the end, when he had captured her, and proceeded to open a cunning battery of inquiries, under plea of a bet with a friend that the shoes could not be matched, he soon found that *she* had been the purchaser who, after buying just such a pair of shoes, had returned and exchanged them for something cheaper. And the only outcome of his visit to the baby-linen shop was the waste of a day. It was indeed just one of those checks which, while they may hamper the progress of a narrative for popular reading, are nevertheless inseparable from the matter-of-fact experience of Holmes's profession.

With a very natural rage in his heart, but with as polite an exterior as possible, Holmes returned to the baby-linen shop in the evening. The whole case seemed barren of useful evidence, and at each turn as yet he had found himself helpless. At the shop the self-confident young lady calmly admitted that soon after he had left something had caused her to remember that it was the other customer who had kept the white shoes, and not Mrs. Butcher's servant.

"And do you know the other customer?" he asked.

"No; she was quite a stranger. She brought in a little boy from a cab and bought a lot of things for him — a suit of outdoor clothes as well as the shoes."

"Ah! now probably this is what I want. Can you remember anything of the child?"

"Yes; he was a pretty little fellow, about two years old or so, with curls. She called him Charley."

"Did she put the things on him in the shop?"

"Not the frock; but she put on the outer coat, the hat and the shoes. I can remember it all now quite well — now I have had time to think."

"Then what shoes did the child wear when he came in?"

"Rather old tan-colored ones."

"Then I think this is the person I am after. You say you never saw her at any other time before or since. Try to describe her."

"Well, she was a lady well dressed, in black. She had a very high collar to hide a scar on her neck, like the scars people have sometimes after abscesses, I think. I could see it from the side when she stooped down."

"And are you sure she had nothing sent home? Did she take everything with her?"

"Yes; nothing was sent, else we should know her address, you know."

"She didn't happen to pay with a bank-note, did she?"

"No; in cash." Holmes left with little more ceremony, and made the best of his way to his friend the inspector at the police station. Here was the woman with the scarred neck again — Charley's deliverer once, now his kidnapper. If only something else could be ascertained of her — some small clue that might bring her identity into view — the thing would be done.

At the station, however, there was something new. A man had just come in, very drunk, and had given himself into custody for kidnapping the child Charles Seton, whose description was set forth on the bill which still appeared on the notice-board outside the station. When Holmes arrived, the man was lolling, wretched and maudlin, against the rail, and, oblivious of most of the questions addressed to him, was ranting and sniveling by turns. His dress was good, though splashed with mud, and his bloated face, bleared eyes and loose, tremulous mouth proclaimed the habitual drunkard.

"I shay I'll gimmeself up," he proclaimed, with a desperate attempt at dignity; "I'll gimmeself up takin' away lil boy, I'll shacrifishe m'self. Solemn duty shacrifishe m'self f'elpless woman, ain't it? Ver' well then; gimmeself up takin' 'way lil boy, buyin' 'm pair shoes. No harm in that, issher? Hope not. Ver' well then." And he subsided into tears.

"What's your name?" asked the inspector.

"Whash name? Thash my bishnesh. Warrer wan' know name for? Grapertnence ask gellumshname. I'm gellum, thash wha' I am. Besht of shisters too, besht shis'ers" — sniveling again — "an' I'm ungra'ful beasht. But I shacrifishe 'self; she shan' get 'n trouble. D'y'ear? Gimmeself up shtealin' lil boy. Who says I ain' gellum?" Nothing more intelligible than this could be got out of him, and presently he was taken off to the cells. Then Holmes asked the inspector, "What will happen to him now?"

The inspector laughed. "Oh, he'll get very sober and sick and sorry by the morning," he said; "and then he'll have to send home for some money, that's all."

"And as to the child?"

"Oh, he'll forget all about that; that's only a drunken freak. The child has been recovered. You know that, I suppose?"

"Yes; but I am still after the person who took it away. It was a woman. Indeed, I've more than a suspicion that it was the woman who brought the child here when he was lost before — the one with the scar on the neck, you know."

"Is that so?" said the inspector. "Well, that's a rum go, ain't it? What did she bring him back here for if she wanted him again?"

"That I want to find out," Holmes answered. "And now I want you to do me a favor. You say you expect that man below will want to send home in the morning for money. Well, I want to be the messenger."

The inspector opened his eyes. "Want to be the messenger? Well, that's easily done; if you're here at the time I'll leave word. But why?"

"Well, I've a sort of notion I know something about his family, and I want to make sure. Shall I be here at eight in the morning, or shall we say nine?"

"Which you like; I expect he'll be shouting for bail before eight."

"Very well, we will say eight. Goodnight."

And so Holmes had to let yet another night go without an explanation of the mystery; but he felt that his hand was on the key at last, though it had only fallen there by chance. Prompt to his time at eight in the morning he was at the police station, where another inspector was now on duty, who, however, had been told of Holmes's wish.

"Ah," he said, "you're well to time, Mr. Holmes. That prisoner's as limp as rags now; he's begging of us to send to his sister."

"Does he say anything about that child?"

"Says he don't know anything about it; all a drunken freak. His name's Oliver Neale, and he lives at 10, Morton Terrace, Hampstead, with his sister. Her name's Mrs. Isitt; and you're to take this note and bring her back with you, or at any rate some money; and you're to say he's truly repentant," the inspector concluded with a grin.

The distance was short, and Holmes walked it. Morton Terrace was a short row of pleasant, old-fashioned villas, ivy-grown and neat, and No.10 was as neat as any. To the servant who answered his ring Holmes announced himself as a gentleman with a message from Mrs. Isitt's brother. This did not seem to prepossess the girl in Holmes's favor, and she backed to the end of the hall and communicated with somebody on the stairs before finally showing Holmes into a room, where he was quickly followed by Mrs. Isitt.

She was a rather tall woman of perhaps thirty-eight, and had probably been attractive, though now her face bore lines of sad grief. Holmes noticed that she wore a very high black collar.

"Good-morning, Mrs. Isitt," he said. "I'm afraid my errand is not altogether pleasant. The fact is, your brother, Mr Neale, was not altogether sober last night, and he is now at the police station, where he wrote this note."

Mrs. Isitt did not appear surprised, and took the note with no more than a sigh.

"Yes," she said, "it can't be concealed. This is not the first time by many, as you probably know, if you are a friend of his."

She read the note, and as she looked up Holmes said, "No, I have not known him long. I happened to be at the station last night, and he rather attracted my attention by insisting, in his intoxicated state, on giving himself up for kidnapping a child, Charles Seton."

Mrs. Isitt started as though shot. Pale of cheek, she glanced fearfully in Holmes's face, and there met a keen gaze that seemed to read her brain. She saw that her secret was known, but for a moment she struggled, and her lips worked convulsively.

"Charles Seton — Charles Seton?" she said.

"Yes, Mrs. Isitt, that is the name. The child, as a matter of fact, was stolen by the person who bought these shoes for it. Do you recognize them?"

He produced the shoes and held them before her. The woman sank on the sofa behind her, terrified, but unable to take her eyes from Holmes's.

"Come, Mrs. Isitt," he said, "you have been recognized. Here is my card. I am commissioned by the parents of the child to find who removed him, and I think I have succeeded."

She took the card and glanced at it dazedly; then she sank with a groaning sob with her face on the head of the sofa, and as she did so Holmes could see a scar on the side of her neck peeping above her high collar.

"Oh, my God!" the woman moaned. "Then it has come to this. He will die! he will die!"

The woman's anguish was piteous to see. Holmes had gained his point, and was willing to spare her. He placed his hand on her heaving shoulder and begged her not to distress herself.

"The matter is rather difficult to understand, Mrs. Isitt," he said. "If you will compose yourself, perhaps you can explain. I can assure you that there is no desire to be vindictive. I'm afraid my manner upset you. Pray reassure yourself. May I sit down?"

Nobody could by his manner more easily restore confidence and trust than Holmes when it pleased him. Mrs. Isitt lifted her head and gazed at him once more with a troubled though quieter expression.

"I think you wrote Mrs. Seton an anonymous letter," Holmes said, producing the first of those which Mrs. Seton had brought him. It was kind of you to reassure the poor woman."

"Oh, tell me," Mrs. Isitt asked, "was she much upset at missing the little boy? Did it make her ill?"

"She was upset, of course; but perhaps the joy of recovering him compensated for all."

"Yes; I took him back as soon as I possibly could, really I did, Mr. Holmes. And, oh! I was so tempted! My life has been so unhappy! If you only knew!" She buried her face in her hands.

"Will you tell me?" Holmes suggested gently. "You see, whatever happens, an explanation of some sort is the first thing."

"Yes, yes — of course. Oh, I am a wretched woman." She paused for some little while, and then went on: "Mr. Holmes, my husband is a lunatic." She paused again. "There was never a man, Mr. Holmes, so devoted to his wife and children as my husband. He bore even with the continual annoyance of my brother, whom you saw, *because* he was my brother. But a little more than a year ago, as the result of an accident, a tumor formed on his brain. The thing is incurable, except, as a remote possibility, by a most dangerous operation, which the doctors fear to attempt except under most favorable conditions. Without that he must die, sooner or later. Meantime he is insane, though with many and sometimes long intervals of perfect lucidity. When the disease attacked him there was little warning, except from pains in the head, till one dreadful night. Then he rose from bed a maniac and killed our child, a little girl of six, whom he was devotedly attached to. He also cut my own throat with his razor, but I recovered. I would rather say nothing more of that — it is too dreadful, though indeed I think about little else. There was another child, a baby boy, about a year old when his sister died, and he — he died of scarlet fever scarcely four months ago.

"My husband was taken to a private asylum at Willesden, where he now is. I visited him frequently, and took the baby, and it was almost terrible to see — a part of his insanity, no doubt — how his fondness for that child grew. When it died, I never dared to tell him. Indeed, the doctors forbade it. In his state he would have died raving. But he asked for it, sometimes earnestly, sometimes angrily, till I almost feared to visit him. Then he began to demand it of the doctors and attendants, and his excitement increased day by day. I was told to prepare for the worst. When I visited him he sometimes failed to recognize me, and at others demanded the child fiercely. I should tell you that it was only just about this time that it was found that the tumor existed, and the idea of the operation was suggested; but of course it was impossible in his disturbed condition. I scarcely dared to go to see him, and yet I did so long to! Dr. Bailey did indeed suggest that possibly we might find he would be quieted by being shown another child; but I myself felt that to be very unlikely.

"It was while things were in this state, and about six or seven weeks ago, that, walking toward Cricklewood one morning, I saw a little fellow trotting along all alone, who actually startled me — startled me very much — by his resemblance to our poor little one. The likeness was one of those extraordinary ones that one only finds among young children. This child was a little bigger and stronger than ours was when he died, but then it was older — probably very nearly the age and size our own would have been had it lived. Nobody else was in sight, and I fancied the child looked about to cry, so I went to it and spoke. Plainly it had strayed, and could not tell me where it lived, only that its name was Charley. I took it in my arms and it grew quite friendly. As I talked to it suddenly Dr. Bailey's suggestion came in my mind. If any child could deceive my poor husband, surely this was the one. Of course I should have to find its parents — probably through the police, but why not at any rate take it to Willesden in the meantime for an hour or so? I could not resist the temptation — I took the first available cab.

"The result of the experiment almost frightened me. My poor husband received the child with transports of delight, kissed it, and laughed and wept over it like a mother, rather than a father, and refused to give it up for hours. The child of course would not answer to its strange name at first, but he seemed an adaptable little thing, and presently began, calling my poor husband 'daddy.' I had not been so happy myself for months as I was as I watched them. I had told Dr. Bailey — what I fear was not strictly true — that I had borrowed the child from a friend. At length I felt I must go and take the boy to the police, and with great difficulty I managed to get it away, my poor husband crying like a child. Well, I took the little fellow to the station I judged nearest to where I found him, and gave him up to the care of the inspector. But I was a little frightened at having kept him so long, and gave a false name and address. Still, I learned from the inspector that the child had been inquired after, and by whom.

"My husband was quiet for some days after this, but then he began to ask for his boy with more vehemence than ever. He grew worse and worse, and soon his ravings were terrible. Dr. Bailey urged me to bring the child again, but what could I do? I formed a desperate idea of going to Mrs. Seton, telling her the whole thing, and imploring her to let me take the child again. But then would that be likely? Would she allow her child to be placed in the arms of a lunatic — one indeed who had already killed a child of his own? I felt that the thing was impossible. Still, I went to the house, and walked about it again and again, I scarcely knew why. And my poor husband, in his confinement screamed for his child till I dared not go near him. So it was when one morning — last Monday morning — I had passed the front of the Setons' house and turned up the lane at the side. I could see over the low fence and hedge, and as I came to the French window with the steps I saw that the window was open at one side and little Charley was standing on the top step. He recognized me, smiled and called just as my own child would have done; indeed, as I stood, there I almost fell into the delusion of my poor mad husband. I took the gate in my hands, shaking it impatiently, and in attempting to open it from the wrong end, found the hinges lift out. I could see that nobody else was in the room behind the French window. There was the temptation — the overwhelming temptation — and I was distracted. I took the little fellow hurriedly in my arms and pulled the window to, so that the bottom bolt fell into the floor socket; then I replaced the gate as I found it, and ran to where I knew there was a cab-stand. Oh! Mr. Holmes, was it so very sinful? And I meant to bring him back that same afternoon, I really did.

"The child was in indoor clothes, and had no hat. I called at a baby-linen shop and bought hat, cloak, frock, and a new pair of shoes. Then I hurried to Willesden. Again the effect was magical. My husband was happy once more; but when at last I attempted to take the child away he would not let it go. It was terrible. Oh, I can't describe the scene. Dr. Bailey told me that, come what might, I must stay that night in a room his wife would provide for me and keep the child, or perhaps I must sit up with my husband and let the child sleep on my knee, In the end it was the latter that I did.

"By the morning my senses were blunted, and I scarcely cared what happened. I determined that as I had gone so far I would keep the child that day at least; indeed, as I say, whether by the influence of my husband I know not, but I almost felt myself falling into his delusion that the child was ours. I went home for an hour at midday, taking the child, and then my wretched brother saw it and got the whole story from me. He told me that reward bills were out about the child, and then I dimly realized that its mother must be suffering pain, and I wrote the note you spoke of. Perhaps I had some little idea of delaying pursuit — I don't know. At any rate I wrote it, and posted it at Willesden as I went back. My husband had been asleep when I left, but now he was awake again and asking for the child once more. There is little more to say. I stayed that night and the next day, and by that time my husband had become tranquil and rational as he had not been for months. If only the improvement can be sustained, they think of operating tomorrow or the next day.

"I carried Charley back in the dusk, intending to put him inside one of the gates, ring, and watch him safely in from a little way off, but as I passed down the side lane I saw the French window open again and nobody near. I had been that way before and felt bolder there. I took his hat and cloak (I had already changed his frock, and, after kissing him, put him hastily through the window and came away. But I had forgotten the new shoes. I remembered them, however, when I got home, and immediately conceived a fear that the child's parents might trace me by their means. I mentioned this fear to my brother, and it appeared to frighten him. He borrowed some money of me yesterday, and, it seems, got intoxicated. In that state he is always anxious to do some noble action, though he is capable, I am grieved to say, of almost any meanness when sober. He lives here at my expense, indeed, and borrows money from his friends for drink. These may seem hard things for a sister to say, but everybody knows it. He has wearied me, and I have lost all shame of him. I suppose in his muddled state he got the notion that he would accuse himself of what I had done, and so shield me. I expect he repented of his self-sacrifice this morning, though."

Holmes knew that he had, but said nothing. Also he said nothing of the anonymous letter he had in his pocket, wherein Mr. Oliver Neale had covertly demanded a hundred pounds for the restoration of Charley Seton. He guessed, however, that that gentleman had feared making the appointment that the advertisement answering his letter had suggested.

To Mr. and Mrs. Seton, Holmes told the whole story, omitting at first names and addresses. "I saw plainly," he said in course of his talk, "that the child might easily have been taken from the French window. I did not say so, for Mrs. Seton was already sufficiently distressed, and the notion that the child was

215

kidnapped, and not simply lost, might have made her worse just then. The toys — the cart with the string on it in particular — had been dragged in the direction of the window, and then nothing would be easier than for the child to open the window itself. There was nothing but a drop bolt, working very easily, which the child must often have seen lifted, and you will remember that the catch did not act. Once the child had opened the window and got outside, the whole thing was simple. The gate could be lifted, the child taken, and the window pulled to, so that the bolt would fall into its place and leave all as before.

"As to the previous occasion, I thought it curious at first that the child should stray before lunch and yet not be heard of again till the evening, and then apparently not be over-fatigued. But beyond these little things, and what I inferred, from the letter, I had very little to help me indeed. Nothing, in fact, till I got the shoes, and they didn't carry me very far. The drunken rant of the man in the police station attracted me because he spoke not only of taking away the child, but of buying it shoes. Now nobody could know of the buying of the shoes who did not know something more. But I knew it was a woman who had taken Charley, as you know, from the heel-mark and the evidence of the shop people, so that when the bemused fool talked of his sister, and sacrificing himself for her, and keeping her out of trouble, and so on, I ranged the case up in my mind, and, so far as I ventured, I guessed it aright. The police inspector knew nothing of the matter of the shoes, nor of the fact of the person I was after being a woman, so thought the thing no more than a drunken freak.

"And now," Holmes said, "before I tell you this woman's name, don't you think the poor creature has suffered enough?"

Both Mrs. Seton and her husband agreed that she had, and that, so far as they were concerned, no further steps should be taken. And when she was told where to go, Mrs. Seton went once to offer Mrs. Isitt her forgiveness and sympathy.

But Mrs. Isitt's punishment came in twenty-four hours, when her husband died in the surgeon's hands.

The Case of the
Flitterbat Lancers

It was late on a summer evening that I drowsed in my armchair over a particularly solid and ponderous volume of essays on social economy. I was doing a good deal of reviewing at the time, and I remember that this particular volume had a property of such exceeding toughness that I had already made three successive attacks on it, on as many successive evenings, each attack having been defeated in the end by sleep. The weather was hot, my chair was very comfortable, and the book had somewhere about its strings of polysyllables an essence as of laudanum. Still something had been done on each evening, and now on the fourth I strenuously endeavored to finish the book. I was just beginning to feel that the words before me were sliding about and losing their meanings, when a sudden crash and a jingle of broken glass behind me woke me with a start, and I threw the book down. A pane of glass in my window was smashed, and I hurried across and threw up the sash to see, if I could, whence the damage had come.

The building in which my chambers (and Sherlock Holmes's rooms) were situated was accessible — or rather visible, for there was no entrance — from the rear. There was, in fact, a small courtyard, reached by a passage from the street behind, and into this courtyard, my sitting-room window looked.

"Hullo, there!" I shouted. But there came no reply. Nor could I distinguish anybody in the courtyard. Some men had been at work during the day on a drainpipe, and I reflected that probably their litter had provided the stone with which my window had been smashed. As I looked, however, two men came hurrying from the passage into the court, and going straight into the deep shadow of one corner, presently appeared again in a less obscure part, hauling forth a third man, who must have already been there in hiding. The third man struggled fiercely but without

217

avail, and was dragged across toward the passage leading to the street beyond. But the most remarkable feature of the whole thing was the silence of all three men. No cry, no exclamation, escaped any of them. In perfect silence the two hauled the third across the courtyard, and in perfect silence he swung and struggled to resist and escape. The matter astonished me not a little, and the men were entering the passage before I found voice to shout at them. But they took no notice, and disappeared. Soon after I heard cab wheels in the street beyond, and had no doubt that the two men had carried off their prisoner.

I turned back into my room a little perplexed. It seemed probable that the man who had been borne off had broken my window. But why? I looked about on the floor, and presently found the missile. It was, as I had expected, a piece of broken concrete, but it was wrapped up in a worn piece of paper, which had partly opened out as it lay on my carpet, thus indicating that it had just been crumpled round the stone.

I disengaged the paper and spread it out. Then I saw it to be a rather hastily written piece of manuscript music, whereof I append a reduced facsimile:

This gave me no help. I turned the paper this way and that, but could make nothing of it. There was not a mark on it that I could discover, except the music and the scrawled title, Flitterbat

Lancers, at the top. The paper was old, dirty, and cracked. What did it all mean? One might conceive of a person in certain circumstances sending a message — possibly an appeal for help — through a friend's window, wrapped round a stone, but this seemed to be nothing of that sort.

Once more I picked up the paper, and with an idea to hear what the Flitterbat Lancers sounded like, I turned to my little pianette and strummed over the notes, making my own time and changing it as seemed likely. But I could by no means extract from the notes anything resembling an air. I half thought of trying Sherlock Holmes's door, in case he might still be up and offer a guess at the meaning of my smashed window and the scrap of paper, when Holmes himself came in. He had been examining a bundle of papers in connection with a case just placed in his hands, and now, having finished, came to find if I were disposed for an evening stroll before turning in. I handed him the paper and the piece of concrete, observing, "There's a little job for you, Holmes, instead of the stroll." And I told him the complete history of my smashed window.

Holmes listened attentively, and examined both the paper and the fragment of paving. "You say these people made absolutely no sound whatever?" he asked.

"None but that of scuffling, and even that they seemed to do quietly."

"Could you see whether or not the two men gagged the other, or placed their hands over his mouth?"

"No, they certainly didn't do that. It was dark, of course, but not so dark as to prevent my seeing generally what they were doing."

Holmes stood for half a minute in thought, and then said, "There's something in this, Brett — what, I can't guess at the moment, but something deep, I fancy. Are you sure you won't come out now?"

I told Holmes that I was sure, and that I should stick to my work.

"Very well," he said; "then perhaps you will lend me these articles?" holding up the paper and the stone.

"Delighted," I said. "If you get no more melody out of the clinker than I did out of the paper, you won't have a musical evening. Goodnight!"

Holmes went away with the puzzle in his hand, and I turned once more to my social economy, and, thanks to the gentleman who smashed my window, conquered.

At this time my only regular daily work was on an evening paper so that I left home at a quarter to eight on the morning following the adventure of my broken window, in order, as usual, to be at the office at eight; consequently it was not until lunchtime that I had an opportunity of seeing Holmes. I went to my own rooms first, however, and on the landing by my door I found the housekeeper in conversation with a shortish, sun-browned man, whose accent at once convinced me that he hailed from across the Atlantic. He had called, it appeared, three or four times during the morning to see me, getting more impatient each time. As he did not seem even to know my name, the housekeeper had not considered it expedient to give him any information about me, and he was growing irascible under the treatment. When I at last appeared, however, he left her and approached me eagerly.

"See here, sir," he said, "I've been stumpin' these here durn stairs o' yours half through the mornin'. I'm anxious to apologize, and fix up some damage."

He had followed me into my sitting-room, and was now standing with his back to the fireplace, a dripping umbrella in one hand, and the forefinger of the other held up boulder-high and pointing, in the manner of a pistol, to my window, which, by the way, had been mended during the morning, in accordance with my instructions to the housekeeper.

"Sir," he continued, "last night I took the extreme liberty of smashin' your winder."

"Oh," I said, "that was you, was it?"

"It was, sir — me. For that I hev come humbly to apologize. I trust the draft has not discommoded you, sir. I regret the accident, and I wish to pay for the fixin' up and the general

220

inconvenience." He placed a sovereign on the table. "I 'low you'll call that square now, sir, and fix things friendly and comfortable as between gentlemen, an' no ill will. Shake."

And he formally extended his hand.

I took it at once. "Certainly," I said. "As a matter of fact, you haven't inconvenienced me at all; indeed, there were some circumstances about the affair that rather interested me." And I pushed the sovereign toward him.

"Say now," he said, looking a trifle disappointed at my unwillingness to accept his money, "didn't I startle your nerves?"

"Not a bit," I answered, laughing. "In fact, you did me a service by preventing me going to sleep just when I shouldn't; so we'll say no more of that."

"Well — there was one other little thing," he pursued, looking at me rather sharply as he pocketed the sovereign. "There was a bit o' paper round that pebble that came in here. Didn't happen to notice that, did you?"

"Yes, I did. It was an old piece of manuscript music."

"That was it — exactly. Might you happen to have it handy now?"

"Well," I said, "as a matter of fact a friend of mine has it now. I tried playing it over once or twice, as a matter of curiosity, but I couldn't make anything of it, and so I handed it to him."

"Ah!" said my visitor, watching me narrowly, "that's a puzzler, that Flitterbat Lancers — a real puzzler. It whips 'em all. Ha, ha'." He laughed suddenly — a laugh that seemed a little artificial. "There's music fellers as 'lows to set right down and play off anything right away that can't make anything of the Flitterbat Lancers. That was two of 'em that was monkeyin' with me last night. They never could make anythin' of it at all, and I was tantalizing them with it all along till they got real mad, and reckoned to get it out o' my pocket and learn it at home. Ha, ha! So I got away for a bit, and just rolled it round a stone and heaved it through your winder before they could come up, your winder being the nearest one with a light in it. Ha, ha! I'll be considerable obliged you'll get it from your friend right now. Is he stayin' hereabout?"

The story was so ridiculously lame that I determined to confront my visitor with Holmes, and observe the result. If he had succeeded in making any sense of the Flitterbat Lancers, the scene might be amusing. So I answered at once, "Yes; his rooms are on the floor below; he will probably be in at about this time. Come down with me."

We went down, and found that Holmes in. "This gentleman," I told him with a solemn intonation, "has come to ask for his piece of manuscript music, the Flitterbat Lancers. He is particularly proud of it, because nobody who tries to play it can make any sort of tune out of it, and it was entirely because two dear friends of his were anxious to drag it out of his pocket and practice it over on the quiet that he flung it through my windowpane last night, wrapped round a piece of concrete."

The stranger glanced sharply at me, and I could see that my manner and tone rather disconcerted him. Burt Holmes came forward at once. "Oh, yes," he said "just so — quite a natural sort of thing. As a matter of fact, I quite expected you. Your umbrella's wet — do you mind putting it in the stand? Thank you. Come in, come in."

We entered the room, and Holmes, turning to the stranger, went on: "Yes, that is a very extraordinary piece of music, that Flitterbat Lancers. I have been having a little bit of practice with it myself. I don't wonder you are anxious to keep it to yourself. Sit down."

The stranger, with a distrustful look at Holmes, complied. At this moment, the housekeeper entered from the hall with a slip of paper. Holmes glanced at it, and crumpled it in his hand. "I am engaged just now," was his remark, and the woman vanished.

"And now," Holmes said, as he sat down and suddenly turned to the stranger with an intent gaze, "and now, Mr Hooker, we'll talk of this music."

The stranger started and frowned. "You've the advantage of me, sir," he said; "you seem to know my name, but I don't know yours."

Holmes smiled pleasantly. "My name," he said, "is Holmes, Sherlock Holmes, and it is my business to know a great many things. For instance, I know that you are Mr Reuben B Hooker, of Robertsville, Ohio."

The visitor pushed his chair back, and stared. "Well — that gits me," he said. "You're a pretty smart chap, Mr Holmes. I've heard your name before, of course. And — and so you've been a-studyin' the Flitterbat Lancers, have you?" This with a keen glance at Holmes's face. "Well, s'pose you have. What's your idea?"

"Why," answered Holmes, still keeping his steadfast gaze on Hooker's eyes, "I think it's pretty late in the century to be fishing about for the Wedlake jewels."

These words astonished me almost as much as they did Mr Hooker. The great Wedlake jewel robbery is, as many will remember, a traditional story of the 'sixties. I remembered no more of it at the time than probably most men do who have at some time or another read the causes celebra of the century. Sir Francis Wedlake's country house had been robbed, and the whole of Lady Wedlake's magnificent collection of jewels stolen. A man named Shiels, a strolling musician, had been arrested and had been sentenced to a long term of penal servitude. Another man named Legg — one of the comparatively wealthy scoundrels who finance promising thefts or swindles and pocket the greater part of the proceeds — had also been punished, but only a very few of the trinkets, and those quite unimportant items, had been recovered. The great bulk of the booty was never brought to light. So much I remembered, and Holmes's sudden mention of the Wedlake jewels in connection with my broken window, Mr Reuben B. Hooker, and the Flitterbat Lancers, astonished me not a little.

As for Hooker, he did his best to hide his perturbation, but with little success. "Wedlake jewels, eh?" he said; "and — and what's that to do with it, anyway?"

"To do with it?" responded Holmes, with an air of carelessness. "Well, well, I had my idea, nothing more. If the Wedlake jewels have nothing to do with it, we'll say no more

223

about it, that's all. Here's your paper, Mr Hooker — only a little crumpled." He rose and placed the article in Mr Hooker's hand, with the manner of terminating the interview.

Hooker rose, with a bewildered look on his face, and turned toward the door. Then he stopped, looked at the floor, scratched his cheek, and finally sat down and put his hat on the ground. "Come," he said, "we'll play a square game. That paper has something to do with the Wedlake jewels, and, win or lose, I'll tell you all I know about it. You're a smart man and whatever I tell you, I guess it won't do me no harm; it ain't done me no good yet, anyway."

"Say what you please, of course," Holmes answered, "but think first. You might tell me something you'd be sorry for afterward."

"Say, will you listen to what I say, and tell me if you think I've been swindled or not? My two hundred and fifty dollars is gone now, and I guess I won't go skirmishing after it anymore if you think it's no good. Will you do that much?"

"As I said before," Holmes replied, "tell me what you please, and if I can help you I will. But remember, I don't ask for your secrets."

"That's all right, I guess, Mr Holmes. Well, now, it was all like this." And Mr Reuben B. Hooker plunged into a detailed account of his adventures since his arrival in London.

Relieved of repetitions, and put as directly as possible, it was as follows: Mr Hooker was a wagon-builder, had made a good business from very humble beginnings, and intended to go on and make it still a better. Meantime, he had come over to Europe for a short holiday — a thing he had promised himself for years. He was wandering about the London streets on the second night after his arrival in the city, when he managed to get into conversation with two men at a bar. They were not very prepossessing men, though flashily dressed. Very soon they suggested a game of cards. But Reuben B. Hooker was not to be had in that way, and after a while, they parted. The two were amusing enough fellows in their way, and when Hooker saw them again the next night in the same bar, he made no difficulty in talking with them freely. After a succession of drinks, they told him that they had a speculation on hand — a speculation that meant thousands if it succeeded — and to carry out which they were only waiting for a paltry sum of £50. There was a house, they said, in which was hidden a great number of jewels of immense value, which had been deposited there by a man who was now dead. Exactly in what part of the house the jewels were to be found they did not know. There was a paper, they said, which was supposed to contain some information, but as yet they hadn't been quite able to make it out. But that would really matter very little if once they could get possession of the house. Then they would simply set to work and search from the topmost chimney to the lowermost brick, if necessary. The only present difficulty was that the house was occupied, and that the landlord wanted a large deposit of rent down before he would consent to turn out his present tenants and give them possession at a higher rental. This deposit would come to £50, and they hadn't the money. However, if any friend of theirs who meant business would put the necessary sum it their disposal, and keep his mouth shut, they would make him an equal partner in the proceeds with themselves; and as the value of the whole haul would probably be something not very far off £20,000, the speculation would bring a tremendous return to the man who was smart enough to put down his £50.

Hooker, very distrustful, skeptically demanded more detailed particulars of the scheme. But these the two men (Luker and Birks were their names, he found, in course of talking) inflexibly refused to communicate.

"Is it likely," said Luker, "that we should give the 'ole thing away to anybody who might easily go with his fifty pounds and clear out the bloomin' show? Not much. We've told you what the game is, and if you'd like to take a flutter with your fifty, all right; you'll do as well as anybody, and we'll treat you square. If you don't — well, don't, that's all. We'll get the oof from somewhere — there's blokes as 'ud jump at the chance. Anyway, we ain't going to give the show away before you've done somethin' to prove you're on the job, straight. Put your money in, and you shall know as much as we do."

Then there were more drinks, and more discussion. Hooker was still reluctant, though tempted by the prospect, and growing more venturesome with each drink.

"Don't you see," said Birks, "that if we was a-tryin' to 'ave you we should out with a tale as long as yer arm, all complete, with the address of the 'ouse and all. Then I s'pose you'd lug out the pieces on the nail, without askin' a bloomin' question. As it is, the thing's so perfectly genuine that we'd rather lose the chance and wait for some other bloke to find the money than run a chance of givin' the thing away. It's a matter o' business, simple and plain, that's all. It's a question of either us trustin' you with a chance of collarin' twenty thousand pounds or you trustin' us with a paltry fifty. We don't lay out no 'igh moral sentiments, we only say the weight o' money is all on one side. Take it or leave it, that's all. 'Ave another Scotch?"

The talk went on and the drinks went on, and it all ended, at "chucking-out time," in Reuben B. Hooker handing over five £10 notes, with smiling, though slightly incoherent, assurances of his eternal friendship for Luker and Birks.

In the morning he awoke to the realization of a bad head, a bad tongue, and a bad opinion of his proceedings of the previous night. In his sober senses it seemed plain that he had been swindled. All day he cursed his fuddled foolishness, and at night he made for the bar that had been the scene if the transaction, with little hope of seeing either Luker or Birks, who had agreed to be there to meet him. There they were, however, and, rather to his surprise, they made no demand for more money. They asked him if he understood music, and showed him the worn old piece of paper containing the Flitterbat Lancers. The exact spot, they said, where the jewels were hidden was supposed to be indicated somehow on that piece of paper. Hooker did not understand music, and could find nothing on the paper that looked in the least like a direction to a hiding-place for jewels or anything else.

Luker and Birks then went into full particulars of their project. First, as to its history. The jewels were the famous

Wedlake jewels, which had been taken from Sir Francis Wedlake's house in 1866 and never heard of again. A certain Jerry Shiels had been arrested in connection with the robbery, had been given a long sentence of penal servitude, and had died in jail. This Jerry Shiels was an extraordinarily clever criminal, and traveled about the country as a street musician. Although an expert burglar, he very rarely perpetrated robberies himself, but acted as a sort of traveling fence, receiving stolen property and transmitting it to London or out of the country. He also acted as the agent of a man named Legg, who had money, and who financed any likely looking project of a criminal nature that Shiels might arrange.

Jerry Shiels traveled with a "pardner" — a man who played the harp and acted as his assistant and messenger in affairs wherein Jerry was reluctant to appear personally. When Shiels was arrested, he had in his possession a quantity of printed and manuscript music, and after his first remand his "pardner," Jimmy Snape, applied for the music to be given up to him, in order, as he explained, that he might earn his living. No objection was raised to this, and Shiels was quite willing that Snape should have it, and so it was handed over. Now among the music was a small slip, headed Flitterbat Lancers, which Shiels had shown to Snape before the arrest. In case of Shiels being taken, Snape was to take this slip to Legg as fast as he could.

But as chance would have it, on that very day Legg himself was arrested, and soon after was sentenced also to a term of years. Snape hung about in London for a little while, and then emigrated. Before leaving, however, he gave the slip of music to Luker's father, a rag-shop keeper, to whom he owed money. He explained its history, and Luker senior made all sorts of fruitless efforts to get at the information concealed in the paper. He had held it to the fire to bring out concealed writing, had washed it, had held it to the light till his eyes ached, had gone over it with a magnifying glass — all in vain. He had got musicians to strum out the notes on all sorts of instruments — backwards, forwards, alternately, and in every other way he could think of. If at any time he fancied a resemblance in the resulting sound to some

227

familiar song-tune, he got that song and studied all its words with loving care, upside-down, right-side up — every way. He took the words Flitterbat Lancers and transposed the letters in all directions, and did everything else he could think of. In the end he gave it up, and died. Now, lately, Luker junior had been impelled with a desire to see into the matter. He had repeated all the parental experiments, and more, with the same lack of success. He had taken his "pal" Birks into his confidence, and together they had tried other experiments till at last they began to believe that the message had probably been written in some sort of invisible ink which the subsequent washings had erased altogether. But he had done one other thing: he had found the house which Shiels had rented at the time of his arrest, and in which a good quantity of stolen property — not connected with the Wedlake case — was discovered. Here, he argued, if anywhere, Jerry Shiels had hidden the jewels. There was no other place where he could be found to have lived, or over which he had sufficient control to warrant his hiding valuables therein. Perhaps, once the house could be properly examined, something about it might give a clue as to what the message of the Flitterbat Lancers meant.

Hooker, of course, was anxious to know where the house in question stood, but this Luker and Birks would on no account inform him. "You've done your part," they said, "and now you leave us to do ours. There's a bit of a job about gettin' the tenants out. They won't go, and it'll take a bit of time before the landlord can make them. So you just hold your jaw and wait. When we're safe in the 'ouse, and there's no chance of anybody else pokin' in, then you can come and help find the stuff."

Hooker went home that night sober, but in much perplexity. The thing might be genuine, after all; indeed, there were many little things that made him think it was. But then, if it were, what guarantee had he that he would get his share, supposing the search turned out successful? None at all. But then it struck him for the first time that these jewels, though they may have lain untouched so long, were stolen property after all. The moral aspect of the affair began to trouble him a little, but the legal

228

aspect troubled him more. That consideration however, he decided to leave over for the present. He had no more than the word of Luker and Birks that the jewels (if they existed) were those of Lady Wedlake, and Luker and Birks themselves only professed to know from hearsay. At any rate, he made up his mind to have some guarantee for his money. In accordance with this resolve, he suggested, when he met the two men the next day, that he should take charge of the slip of music and make an independent study of it. This proposal, however, met with an instant veto.

Hooker resolved to make up a piece of paper, folded as like the slip of music as possible, and substitute one for the other at their next meeting. Then he would put the Flitterbat Lancers in some safe place, and face his fellow conspirators with a hand of cards equal to their own. He carried out his plan the next evening with perfect success, thanks to the contemptuous indifference with which Luker and Birks had begun to regard him. He got the slip in his pocket, and left the bar. He had not gone far, however, before Luker discovered the loss, and soon he became conscious of being followed. He looked for a cab, but he was in a dark street, and no cab was near. Luker and Birks turned the corner and began to run. He saw they must catch him. Everything now depended on his putting the Flitterbat Lancers out of their reach, but where he could himself recover it. He ran till he saw a narrow passageway on his right, and into this he darted. It led into a yard where stones were lying about, and in a large building before him he saw the window of a lighted room a couple of floors up. It was a desperate expedient, but there was no time for consideration. He wrapped a stone in the paper and flung it with all his force through the lighted window. Even as he did it he heard the feet of Luker and Birks as they hurried down the street. The rest of the adventure in the court I myself saw.

Luker and Birks kept Hooker in their lodgings all that night. They searched him unsuccessfully for the paper; they bullied, they swore, they cajoled, they entreated, they begged him to play the game square with his pals. Hooker merely replied that he had put the Flitterbat Lancers where they couldn't easily find it, and that he intended playing the game square as long as they did the same. In the end they released him, apparently with more respect than they had before entertained, advising him to get the paper into his possession as soon as he could.

"And now," said Mr Hooker, in conclusion of his narrative, "perhaps you'll give me a bit of advice. Am I playin' a fool-game running after these toughs, or ain't I?"

Holmes shrugged his shoulders. "It all depends," he said, "on your friends Luker and Birks. They may want to swindle you, or they may not. I'm afraid they'd like to, at any rate. But perhaps you've got some little security in this piece of paper. One thing is plain: they certainly believe in the deposit of the jewels themselves, else they wouldn't have taken so much trouble to get the paper back."

"Then I guess I'll go on with the thing, if that's it."

"That depends, of course, on whether you care to take trouble to get possession of what, after all, is somebody else's lawful property."

Hooker looked a little uneasy. "Well," he said, "there's that, of course. I didn't know nothin' of that at first, and when I did I'd parted with my money and felt entitled to get something back for it. Anyway, the stuff ain't found yet. When it is, why then, you know, I might make a deal with the owner. But, say, how did you find out my name, and about this here affair being jined up with the Wedlake jewels?"

Holmes smiled. "As to the name and address, you just think it over a little when you've gone away, and if you don't see how I did it. You're not so cute as I think you are. In regard to the jewels — well, I just read the message of the Flitterbat Lancers, that's all."

"You read it? Whew! And what does it say? How did you do it?" Hooker turned the paper over eagerly in his hands as he spoke.

"See, now," said Holmes, "I won't tell you all that, but I'll tell you something, and it may help you to test the real knowledge of Luker and Birks. Part of the message is in these words, which you had better write down: Over the coals the fifth dancer slides, says Jerry Shield the homey."

"What?" Hooker exclaimed, "fifth dancer slides over the coals? That's mighty odd. What's it all about?"

"About the Wedlake jewels, as I said. Now you can go and make a bargain with Luker and Birks. The only other part of the message is an address, and that they already know, if they have been telling the truth about the house they intend taking. You can offer to tell them what I have told you of the message, after they have told you where the house is, and proved to you that they are taking the steps they talked of. If they won't agree to that, I think you had best treat them as common rogues and charge them with obtaining your money under false pretenses."

Nothing more would Holmes say than that, despite Hooker's many questions; and when at last Hooker had gone, almost as troubled and perplexed as ever, my friend turned to me and said, "Now, Brett, if you haven't lunched and would like to see the end of this business, hurry!"

"The end of it?" I said. "Is it to end so soon? How?"

"Simply by a police raid on Jerry Shiels's old house with a search warrant. I communicated with the police this morning before I came here."

"Poor Hooker!" I said.

"Oh, I had told the police before I saw Hooker, or heard of him, of course. I just conveyed the message on the music slip — that was enough. But I'll tell you all about it when there's more time; I must be off now. With the information I have given him, Hooker and his friends may make an extra push and get into the house soon, but I couldn't resist the temptation to give the unfortunate Hooker some sort of sporting chance — though it's a poor one, I fear. Get your lunch as quickly as you can, and go at once to Colt Row, Bankside — Southwark way, you know. Probably we shall be there before you. If not, wait."

Colt Row was not difficult to find. It was one of those places that decay with an excess of respectability, like Drury Lane and Clare Market. Once, when Jacob's Island was still an island, a little farther down the river, Colt Row had evidently been an unsafe place for a person with valuables about him, and then it probably prospered, in its own way. Now it was quite respectable, but very dilapidated and dirty. Perhaps it was sixty yards long — perhaps a little more. It was certainly a very few yards wide, and the houses at each side had a patient and forlorn look of waiting for a metropolitan improvement to come along and carry them away to their rest.

I could see no sign of Holmes, nor of the police, so I walked up and down the narrow pavement for a little while. As I did so, I became conscious of a face at the window of the least ruinous house in the row, a face that I fancied expressed particular interest in my movements. The house was an old gabled structure, faced with plaster. What had apparently once been a shop window on the ground floor was now shuttered up, and the face that watched me — an old woman's — looked out from the window above. I had noted these particulars with some curiosity, when, arriving again at the street corner, I observed Holmes approaching, in company with a police inspector, and followed by two unmistakable plainclothesmen.

"Well," Holmes said, "you're first here after all. Have you seen any more of our friend Hooker?"

"No, nothing."

"Very well — probably he'll be here before long, though."

The party turned into Colt Row, and the inspector, walking up to the door of the house with the shuttered bottom window, knocked sharply. There was no response, so he knocked again, equally in vain.

"All out," said the inspector.

"No," I said; "I saw a woman watching me from the window above not three minutes ago."

"Ho, ho!" the inspector replied. "That's so, eh? One of you — you, Johnson — step round to the back, will you?"

One of the plainclothesmen started off, and after waiting another minute or two the inspector began a thundering cannonade of knocks that brought every available head out of the window of every inhabited room in the Row. At this the woman opened the window, and began abusing the inspector with a shrillness and fluency that added a street-corner audience to that already congregated at the windows.

"Go away, you blaggards!" the lady said, "you ought to be 'orse-w'ipped, every one of ye! A-comin' 'ere a-tryin' to turn decent people out o' 'ouse and 'ome! Wait till my 'usband comes 'ome — 'e'll show yer, ye mutton-cadgin' scoundrels! Payin' our rent reg'lar, and good tenants as is always been — and I'm a respectable married woman, that's what I am, ye dirty great cowards!" — this last word with a low, tragic emphasis.

Holmes remembered what Hooker had said about the present tenants refusing to quit the house on the landlord's notice. "She thinks we've come from the landlord to turn her out," he said to the inspector. "We're not here from the landlord, you old fool!" the inspector said. "We don't want to turn you out. We're the police, with a search warrant, and you'd better let us in or you'll get into trouble."

"'Ark at 'im!" the woman screamed, pointing at the inspector. "'Ark at 'im! Thinks I was born yesterday, that feller! Go 'ome, ye dirty pie-stealer, go 'ome!"

The audience showed signs of becoming a small crowd, and the inspector's patience gave out. "Here, Bradley," he said, addressing the remaining plainclothesman, "give a hand with these shutters," and the two — both powerful men — seized the iron bar which held the shutters and began to pull. But the garrison was undaunted, and, seizing a broom, the woman began to belabor the invaders about the shoulders and head from above. But just at this moment, the woman, emitting a terrific shriek, was suddenly lifted from behind and vanished. Then the head of the plainclothesman who had gone round to the back appeared, with the calm announcement, "There's a winder open behind, sir. But I'll open the front door if you like."

In a minute the bolts were shot, and the front door swung back. The placid Johnson stood in the passage, and as we passed in he said, "I've locked 'er in the back room upstairs."

"It's the bottom staircase, of course," the inspector said; and we tramped down into the basement. A little way from the stairfoot Holmes opened a cupboard door, which enclosed a receptacle for coals. "They still keep the coals here, you see," he said, striking a match and passing it to and fro near the sloping roof of the cupboard. It was of plaster, and covered the underside of the stairs.

"And now for the fifth dancer," he said, throwing the match away and making for the staircase again. "One, two, three, four, five," and he tapped the fifth stair from the bottom.

The stairs were uncarpeted, and Holmes and the inspector began a careful examination of the one he had indicated. They tapped it in different places, and Holmes passed his hands over the surfaces of both tread and riser. Presently, with his hand at the outer edge of the riser, Holmes spoke. "Here it is, I think," he said; "it is the riser that slides."

He took out his pocketknife and scraped away the grease and paint from the edge of the old stair. Then a joint was plainly visible. For a long time the plank, grimed and set with age, refused to shift; but at last, by dint of patience and firm fingers, it moved, and was drawn clean out from the end.

Within, nothing was visible but grime, fluff, and small rubbish. The inspector passed his hand along the bottom angle. "Here's something," he said. It was the gold hook of an old-fashioned earring, broken off short.

Holmes slapped his thigh. "Somebody's been here before us," he said "and a good time back too, judging from the dust. That hook's a plain indication that jewelry was here once. There's plainly nothing more, except — except this piece of paper." Holmes's eyes had detected — black with loose grime as it was — a small piece of paper lying at the bottom of the recess. He drew it out and shook off the dust. "Why, what's this?" he exclaimed. "More music!"

We went to the window, and there saw in Holmes's hand a piece of written musical notation, thus:

Holmes pulled out from his pocket a few pieces of paper. "Here is a copy I made this morning of the Flitterbat Lancers, and a note or two of my own as well," he said. He took a pencil, and, constantly referring to his own papers, marked a letter under each note on the last-found slip of music. When lie had done this, the letters read:

> *You are a clever cove whoever you are but there was a cleverer says Jim Snape the horney's mate.*

"You see." Holmes. said handing the inspector the paper. "Snape, the unconsidered messenger, finding Legg in prison, set to work and got the jewels for himself. The thing was a cryptogram, of course, of a very simple sort, though uncommon in design. Snape was a humorous soul, too, to leave this message here in the same cipher, on the chance of somebody else reading the Flitterbat Lancers."

"But," I asked, "why did he give that slip of music to Laker's father?"

"Well, he owed him money, and got out or it that way. Also, he avoided the appearance of 'flushness' that paying the debt might have given him, and got quietly out of the country with his spoils."

The shrieks upstairs had grown hoarser, but the broom continued vigorously. "Let that woman out," said the inspector, "and we'll go and report. Not much good looking for Snape now, I fancy. But there's some satisfaction in clearing up that old mystery."

We left the place pursued by the execrations of the broom wielder, who bolted the door behind us, and from the window defied us to come back, and vowed she would have us all searched before a magistrate for what we had probably stolen. In the very next street we hove in sight of Reuben B. Hooker in the company of two swell-mob-looking fellows, who sheered off down a side turning in sight of our group. Hooker, too, looked rather shy at the sight of the inspector.

"The meaning of the thing was so very plain," Holmes said to me afterwards, "that the duffers who had the Flitterbat Lancers in hand for so long never saw it at all. If Shiels had made an ordinary clumsy cryptogram, all letters and figures, they would have seen what it was at once, and at least would have tried to read it; but because it was put in the form of music, they tried everything else but the right way. It was a clever dodge of Shiels's, without a doubt. Very few people, police officers or not, turning over a heap of old music, would notice or feel suspicious of that little slip among the rest. But once one sees it is a cryptogram (and the absence of bar lines and of notes beyond the stave would suggest that) the reading is as easy as possible. For my part I tried it as a cryptogram at once. You know the plan — it has been described a hundred times. See here — look at this copy of the Flitterbat Lancers. Its only difficulty — and that is a small one — is that the words are not divided. Since there are positions for less than a dozen notes on the stave, and there are twenty-six letters to be indicated, it follows that crotchets, quavers, and semiquavers on the same line or space must mean different letters. The first step is obvious. We count the notes to ascertain which sign occurs most frequently, and we find that the crotchet in the top space is the sign required — it occurs no less than eleven times. Now the letter most frequently occurring in an ordinary sentence of English is *e*. Let us then suppose that this represents *e*. At once a coincidence strikes us. In ordinary musical notation in the treble clef the note occupying the top space would be *E*. Let us remember that presently.

"Now the most common word in the English language is *the*. We know the sign for *e*, the last letter of this word, so let us see if in more than one place that sign is preceded by two others identical in each case. If so, the probability is that the other two signs will represent *t* and *h*, and the whole word will be *the*. Now it happens in no less than four places the sign *e* is preceded by the same two other signs — once in the first line, twice in the second, and once in the fourth. No word of three letters ending in *e* would be in the least likely to occur four times in a short sentence except the. Then we will call it *the*, and note the signs preceding the *e*. They are a quaver under the bottom line for the *t*, and a crotchet on the first space for the *h*. We travel along the stave, and wherever these signs occur we mark them with *t* or *h*, as the case may be.

"But now we remember that *e*, the crotchet in the top space, is in its right place as a musical note, while the crotchet in the bottom space means *h*, which is no musical note at all. Considering this for a minute, we remember that among the notes which are expressed in ordinary music on the treble stave, without the use of ledger lines, *d*, *e* and *f* are repeated at the lower and at the upper part of the stave. Therefore, anybody making a cryptogram of musical notes would probably use one set of these duplicate positions to indicate other letters, and as *A* is in the lower part of the stave, that is where the variation comes in. Let us experiment by assuming that all the crotchets above *f* in ordinary musical notation have their usual values, and let us set the letters over their respective notes. Now things begin to shape. Look toward the end of the second line: there is the word *the* and the letters *f f t h*, with another note between the two *f*'s. Now that word can only possibly be *fifth*, so that now we have the sign for *i*. It is the crotchet on the bottom line. Let us go through and mark the *I*'s.

"And now observe. The first sign of the lot is *i*, and there is one other sign before the word the. The only words possible here beginning with *i*, and of two letters, are *it*, *if*, *is* and *in*. Now we have the signs for *t* and *f*, so we know that it isn't *it* or *if*. Is would be unlikely here, because there is a tendency, as you see, to regularity in these signs, and *t*, the next Idler alphabetically to s, is at the bottom of the stave. Let us try *n*. At once we get the word dance at the beginning of line three. And now we have got enough to see the system of the thing. Make a stave and put *G A B C* and the higher *D E F* in their proper musical places. Then fill in the blank places with the next letters of the alphabet downward, *h i j*, and we find that *h* and *i* fall in the places we have already discovered for them as crotchets. Now take quavers, and go on with *k l m n o*, and so on as before, beginning on the *A* space. When you have filled the quavers, do the same with semiquavers — there are only six alphabetical letters left for this — *u v w x y z*. Now you will find that this exactly agrees with all we have ascertained already, and if you will use the other letters to fill up over the signs still unmarked you will get the whole message:

> *In the Colt Row ken over the coals the fifth dancer slides says Jerry Shiels the homey.*

"'Dancer,' as perhaps you didn't know, is thieves' slang for a stair, and 'homey' is the strolling musician's name for cornet player. Of course the thing took a little time to work out, chiefly because the sentence was short, and gave one few opportunities. But anybody with the key, using the cipher as a means of communication, would read it easily.

"As soon as I had read it, of course I guessed the purport of the Flitterbat Lancers. Jerry Shiels's name is well-known to anybody with half my knowledge of the criminal records of the century, and his connection with the missing Wedlake jewels, and his death in prison, came to my mind at once. Certainly here was something hidden, and as the Wedlake jewels seemed most likely, I made the shot in talking to Hooker."

"But you terribly astonished him by telling him his name and address. How was that?" I asked curiously.

Holmes laughed aloud. "That," he said; "why, that was the thinnest trick of all. Why, the man had it engraved on the silver band of his umbrella handle. When he left his umbrella outside, the housekeeper (I had indicated the umbrella to her by a sign) just copied the lettering on one of the ordinary visitors' forms, and brought it in. You will remember I treated it as an ordinary visitor's announcement." And Holmes laughed again.

Editor's Note: The twenty-five Sherlock Holmes cases that were eventually rewritten as "Martin Hewitt" adventures by Holmes's neighbor and journalist friend, Brett, had numerous facts altered before publication. In addition to changing Holmes's name, description, and location of residence, Brett also altered a number of dates in these stories as well, making it appear that the narratives were spread out over a number of years, rather than over just one year.

This chronology for the "Martin Hewitt" stories shows when the adventures actually took place throughout 1876, during the time that Brett lived at upstairs from Holmes at 24 Montague Street:

1876

Jan 19-20	"The Case of the Dead Skipper"
Late Jan	"The Nicobar Bullion Case"
Feb 15-18	"The Affair of Mrs. Seton's Child"
Late Feb	"The Case of the Dixon Torpedo"
Early Mar	"The Stanway Cameo Mystery"
Mid-Mar	"The Case of the Late Mr. Rewse"
Early Apr	"The Case of the Lost Foreigner"
Mid-Apr	"The Case of Ward Lane Tabernacle"
Apr 17-18	"The Affair of the Tortoise"
Apr 24-25	"The Quinton Jewel Affair"
Apr 28	"The Ivy Cottage Mystery"
May 1	"The Case of Laker, Absconded"
June 21-23	"The Loss of Sammy Crockett"
Mid-July	"The Case of the 'Flitterbat Lancers' "
July 25-27	"The Case of Mr. Geldard's Elopement"
Early Sept	"The Lenton Croft Robberies"
Early Sept	"The Case of the Missing Hand"
Mid-Sept	"The Affair of Samuel's Diamonds"
Mid-Sept	"The Case of Mr. Jacob Mason"
Mid-Sept	"The Case of the Lever Key"
Sept 23	"The Case of the Burnt Barn"
Sept 25	"The Case of the Admiralty Code"
Sept 25-27	"The Adventure of Channel Marsh"
Early Oct	"The Case of Mr. Foggatt" Part I
Late Nov	"The Case of Mr. Foggatt" Part II
Nov 29-30	"The Holford Will Case"

About the Author

Arthur Morrison (1863-1945) was born and raised in the East End of London. He became a journalist and novelist, writing realistic stories telling of the lives of slum residents.

In 1894, Morrison created the character of Martin Hewitt, a London detective whose adventures were first published in *The Strand.* Morrison would go on to write twenty-five Hewitt tales.

Gradually, Morrison ceased writing fiction, and became a noted expert and collector of Japanese art.

About the Editor

David Marcum began his study of the lives of Sherlock Holmes and Dr. Watson as a boy in 1975 when, while trading with a friend to obtain Hardy Boys books, he received an abridged copy of *The Adventures of Sherlock Holmes*, thrown in as a last-minute and little-welcomed addition to the trade. Soon after, he saw *A Study in Terror* on television and began to search out other Holmes stories, both Canon and pastiche. He borrowed way ahead on his allowance and bought a copy of the Doubleday edition of *The Complete Sherlock Holmes* and started to discover the rest of the Canon that night. His parents gave him Baring-Gould's *Sherlock Holmes of Baker Street* for Christmas and his fate was sealed.

Since that time, he has been reading and collecting literally thousands of Holmes's cases in the form of short stories, novels, movies, radio and television episodes, scripts, comic books, unpublished manuscripts, and fan-fiction. In addition, he reads mysteries by numerous other authors, including those that he considers the classics, Nero Wolfe, Ellery Queen, Hercule Poirot, and Holmes's logical heir, Solar Pons.

When not immersed in the activities of his childhood heroes, David is employed as a licensed civil engineer, and lives in Tennessee with his wife and son. He has finally traveled to Baker Street in London, the location he most wanted to visit in the whole world, as well as other parts of England and Scotland on an incredible trip-of-a-lifetime Holmes Pilgrimage.

Questions and comments may be addressed to:

thepapersofsherlockholmes@gmail.com

Also from MX Publishing

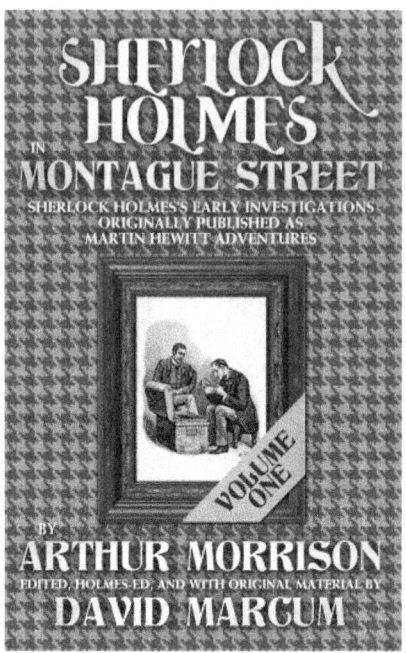

Sherlock Holmes in Montague Street - Volume I

"It's been suggested that Hewitt was the young Mycroft Holmes, but David Marcum has a more plausible and attractive theory – that he was Sherlock, early in his career as an investigator . . . these are remarkably convincing in their new guise."
– Roger Johnson, Editor, "The District Messenger" and *The Sherlock Holmes Journal,* The Sherlock Holmes Society of London

MX Publishing is the world's leading Sherlock Holmes books publisher with over 150 titles.

www.mxpublishing.com

Also from MX Publishing

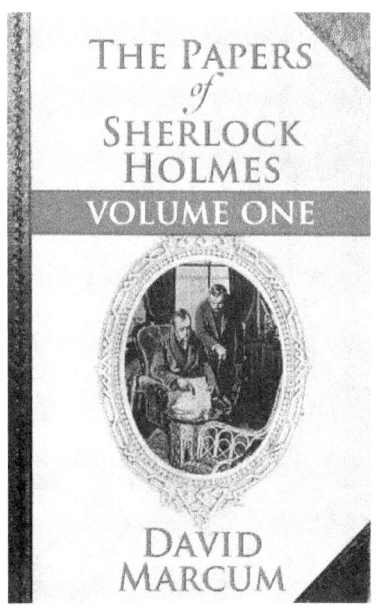

The Papers of Sherlock Holmes - Volume I

Traditional Sherlock Holmes stories from David Marcum

"The Papers of Sherlock Holmes [Volume I] *by David Marcum contains [six] intriguing mysteries . . . very much in the classic tradition . . . He writes well, too.*"
– Roger Johnson, Editor, "The District Messenger" and *The Sherlock Holmes Journal,* The Sherlock Holmes Society of London

MX Publishing is the world's leading Sherlock Holmes books publisher with over 150 titles.

www.mxpublishing.com

Also from MX Publishing

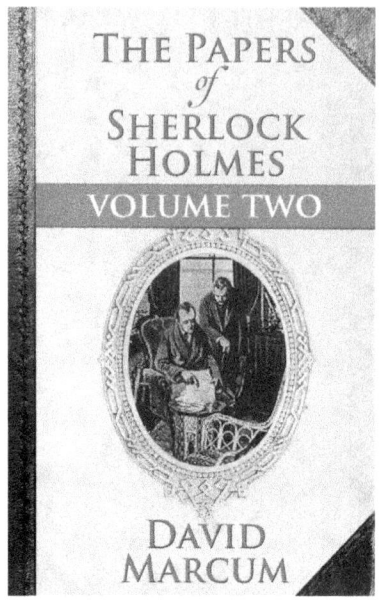

The Papers of Sherlock Holmes - Volume II

More traditional Sherlock Holmes stories from David Marcum

"Marcum offers [three more] clever pastiches."
– Steven Rothman, Editor, *The Baker Street Journal*

MX Publishing is the world's leading Sherlock Holmes books
publisher with over 150 titles.

www.mxpublishing.com

Also from MX Publishing

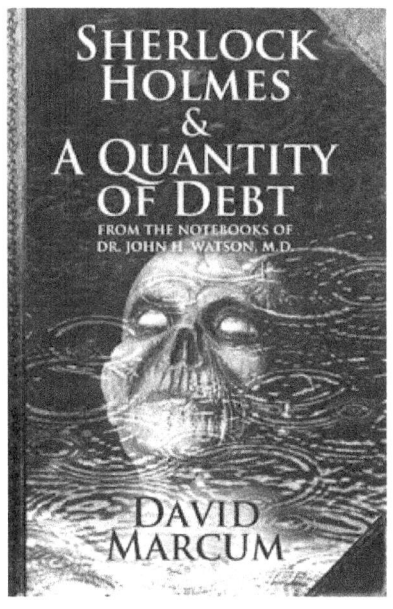

**Sherlock Holmes and
A Quantity of Debt**

Another traditional Sherlock Holmes story from David Marcum

"This is a welcome addendum to Sherlock lore that respectfully
fleshes out Doyle's legendary crime-solving couple in the
context of new escapades . . . ."
– Peter Roche, Examiner.com

MX Publishing is the world's leading Sherlock Holmes books
publisher with over 150 titles.

www.mxpublishing.com

Coming Soon from MX Publishing

SHERLOCK HOLMES
in
MONTAGUE STREET

Volume III

More Early Investigations
of Sherlock Holmes
Originally Published as
Martin Hewitt Adventures

MX Publishing is the world's leading Sherlock Holmes books
publisher with over 150 titles.

www.mxpublishing.com

Also from MX Publishing

Sherlock Holmes Travel Guides

In ebook an interactive guide to London

400 locations linked to Google Street View.

Also from MX Publishing

Cross over fiction featuring great villains from history

 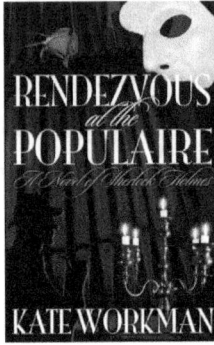 

Fantasy Sherlock Holmes

Also from MX Publishing

Carrying the seal of the Conan Doyle Estate.....

On the most secret and dangerous assignment of their lives, Sherlock Holmes and Dr. Watson are sent into the newborn Soviet Union to rescue The Romanovs: Nicholas and Alexandra and their innocent children. Will Holmes and Watson be able to change history? Will they even be able to survive?

..and in 2014 the sequel 'The Revenge of Sherlock Holmes'

www.mxpublishing.com